Courage on Little Round Top

A HISTORICAL NOVEL

THOMAS M. EISHEN

First print edition published by Skyward Publishing

Copyright 2005. All publishing and copyrights were return to the author.

Courage on Little Round Top is the first in the Courage at Gettysburg series. It is followed by *Courage on Cemetery Ridge*.

Visit Thomas Eishen on Facebook for photo albums on the ground covered by the 15th Alabama and the 20th Maine

Also on Facebook, visit Battle of Gettysburg for the largest collection of photos of the Gettysburg National Military Park on the Internet

High Quality Gettysburg photographs are available for purchase at tommyeishen.com

Cover Image by Edwin Forbes, a witness to the battle courtesy the Library of Congress.

Book layout and cover design by Marie Stirk

Acknowledgments

Thanks to Juilia Oehmig, Susan Ravdin, Robert Krick, Kathleen Harrison, Robert Prosperi, Melvin Johnson, John Slonaker, Richard Sommers, Gene Geiger, James Hanson, James Huston, Jennie Rathbun, Michael Knapp, and Ed Wenschof. Larry R. Nottingham and Dr. Thomas A.Desjardin also spent several hours with me on the slopes of Little Round Top.

A special thanks to Robert Wicker's granddaughter Anne Magorian, R.F. Wicker, Virginia Wicker Austin, Zelda Main, Ruth Brown, Martha Hixon, Ollie Joyce Eaton, Florence Davis, June Walton, George Nightingale, Robert Vaughan, Jim and Charlotte Harris, Robin Weaver, Joyce Martin, Lynn Linhart, Leah Gary, Morris Penny, and Ron and Heda Christ.

Also, I would like to thank Gettysburg NMP, University of Maine, U.S. Army Military History Institute, Auburn University, The Library of Congress, Harvard University, National Archives, the U.S. Department of the Interior, Bowdoin College Library, the Pejepscot Historical Society, Schlesinger Library of Radcliff College, Rice University, University of Houston, University of Texas, Texas A&M University, Clayton Clayton Library Center for Genealogical Research, The Alabama Department of Archives and History, Bullock County Courthouse, and The Fort Delaware Society.

For Brenda

A Note to the Reader

This is the story of two men and the events that brought them to the rocky slope of Vincent's Spur on the eastside of Little Round Top during Longstreet's Charge on the second day of the Battle of Gettysburg. I have strived to be faithful to the historical record, including the personal histories of each man. The fiction is contained in the interpersonal relationships, gaps in the historical record, and the dialog.

Chain of Command

Army of Northern Virginia
General Robert E. Lee
Lieutenant General James Longstreet
Major General John B. Hood
Brigadier General Evander McIvor Law
Colonel William C. Oates
First Lieutenant J.J. Hatcher
Second Lieutenant Robert Horne Wicker

Army of the Potomac
Major General George G. Meade
Major General George Sykes
Brigadier General James Barnes
Colonel Strong Vincent
Colonel Joshua Lawrence Chamberlain

Prologue

An angry cloud of gray smoke assaulted the bright afternoon summer sky as another shell exploded overhead. Private Robert Horne Wicker wanted to duck as fragments showered the company, but he held his head high and kept his eyes to the front. *What the hell are you doing? Run man run like the wind* came a voice from the deep recesses of his mind, but his legs ignored the Voice, and he kept in step to the beats of the regiment's drums.

A shell hit the hard, sun-baked ground in front of the company, throwing fragments in all directions. Jimmy McLaney, directly in front of Robert, doubled over and fell on his face. Stepping over McLaney, Robert glanced down. Their eyes met. Robert was grateful that his bullet catcher was still alive.

The war's cruel fact was that a company's front rank bore the brunt of the enemy's fire, serving as bullet catchers for those in the second rank.

Robert watched as F. M. Emmerson moved over to fill McLaney's place, taking over as Robert's shield.

This time to his left, another explosion was answered by a haunting, agonizing scream, followed by the muffled sound of a body hitting the ground. Another man, another friend, was down. *Who?* He wanted to look, but that was

forbidden. The orders were eyes front. With his rifle carried at right shoulder arms, he gently swung his elbow. It
found his friend Bill Sellers. Robert took comfort that he
was where he was supposed to be, six inches to Bill's left.

Robert then felt something brush against his left elbow.
It was Bill's cousin Elisha, checking his position in line. So
it went up and down the ranks of Company L as the men
quickly and discreetly checked with their elbows to make
sure they were still in line with the man to their right.

On the right of the front rank, the captain served as
Guide for the company keeping his eyes on the company
to his right and the regimental battle flag, six paces in
front of the center of the line. Where the flag went, the
captain followed, and the company followed him.

From the corner of his eye, Robert caught sight of the
Louisiana regiment approaching the hill's crest. He still
could not hear musket fire. Where is the Yankee infantry? Another artillery shell exploded in front of them.

"Steady boys," the captain shouted.

A cloud of dark smoke billowed from beyond the hill's
crest, decimating the front rank of the Louisiana regiment. The second rank let go a volley of their own, and
the hill's crest belched smoke and flame.

The Yankees were on the backside of the hill. Clever.
The position protected them from artillery but still gave
them a clear field of fire. With his heart pounding, he took
another step. God, help me. Give me strength, so I don't run
away, he said to himself. A few seconds later, the Fifteenth
Alabama Volunteer Regiment reached the crest of the hill.
Forty yards down its backside kneeled the angry blue line.

"Ready!" The command radiated down the battle line.
Robert snapped his rifle butt to his right shoulder and
raised his right elbow as high as he could, allowing him
to aim over the top of Emmerson's musket.

"Aim!" He picked out a target in the Yankees' front rank. "Fire!" He held his breath as he slowly squeezed the trigger. Both ranks exploded. The smoke burned his eyes and obscured his target as the blast pounded against the wax he'd stuffed into his ears.

Robert jerked down his rifle and reached into his cartridge box for another round. He bit off its end, poured the black powder down the barrel before stuffing the paper wrapper and Minie Ball into the end of the barrel. He grabbed the rammer from under the barrel in one fluid motion, shoved the bullet home, and slid it back in place.

As Robert raised his musket back to eye level, he noticed Emmerson was kneeling. Damn.

With his right hand, he half-cocked the hammer and then flipped off the old percussion cap. As he reached into his pouch for a new one, something slammed into his right side, doubling him over.

He dropped to his knees, and his rifle fell to the ground. Just then, his eyes caught sight of the neat hole punched in his dark gray uniform coat. He was surprised. There was no pain.

He slid his left hand inside his coat, and shivers went down his spine when he touched the warm wetness of his blood. He found the wound and pressed his palm against it. Weakened, he fell over on his side. Still, there was no pain.

A few seconds later, the pain came crashing in on his brain. He locked his jaw, fighting back the scream building in his gut. He wasn't going to share his pain with anyone else, but there was nothing he could do to control the tears rapidly filling his eyes. The regiment kept moving. He looked up to see Elisha step to the right, filling his place in line. They're leaving me behind.

Chapter 1

July 1, 1863

Private Bill Sellers scratched his crotch. "Well, dang it all, I can't believe I let you talk me into comin' up here."

Second Lieutenant Robert Wicker ran his hand over the patch in his gray wool coat. It'd been over a year, and yet, along its edges, he could still see the dark brown stain of his blood.

They'd left him behind. He didn't blame them. They were doing their duty. They couldn't stop for the wounded.

"You listenin' to me?" Bill asked, stepping back under the sweeping branches of the oak tree.

"Of course I was," answered Robert.

"You're a piss poor liar," Bill said as he unbuttoned his uniform coat. "You look bothered up about somethin' . . . so you gonna tell me what it is?"

Robert pulled a loose thread from the patch. "It's nothing."

Along with the large scar on his abdomen's right side, the patch was a constant reminder of his brush with death.

"That's bullshit, Bobby. I can see it on your face. You got somethin' on your mind."

As Robert glanced up, his lips parted, his mouth started to move. He wanted to say it, tried to shout it: *You damn it! You bother me. You son-of-a-bitch; you left me behind.*

Instead, he replied in a calm, steady voice, "I said nothing."

Glancing back at his coat, Robert gently brushed dirt away from around the patch. When he touched the stiffness of the dark brown stain, all the doubts, fears, and self-pity came rushing back to him. Suddenly, his father's words brought his confidence and a smile back.

"What ya grinnin' about?" Bill asked.

"Just something my father told me last summer when I was home on sick leave."

"And?"

"And none of your business," Robert said, laughing. His face kept a grin as he recalled the conversation.

"Pop, I'm scared. I can't go back. I just can't," Robert finally admitted after moping around the house for a couple of weeks.

George Washington Wicker, a veteran of the Alabama Indian Wars, put an arm around his oldest son's shoulder. "Only an idiot has no fears."

"Good to know I'm not an idiot," Robert blurted out. The older man laughed, and after getting over his embarrassment, Robert did too.

Robert then flipped his coat around so he could brush the dirt off the back of it. The coat was like an old friend. They'd been through so much together.

Bill hung his cap in the tree. He then took off his coat and shook it a few times. "You know, you really need a new uniform."

"I like this one just fine."

"But it's a private's, and it's lookin' pretty ratty."

"It's fine. Anyway, with the Union blockade, the gray dye is getting hard to come by."

"There's nothin' wrong with havin' a brown uniform. In fact, it's even patriotic, seein' as they is colored with good, old southern birch dye and all."

"So, why don't you have one?" Robert asked.

"'Cause I like my gray uniform just as much as you like yours. But a private can get away with lookin' ratty."

Is it the uniform? Robert chased the thought away. Even if the uniform was part of the reason, it was too late to do anything about it.

He spit on a mud stain and rubbed it with his thumb. It didn't come off. The coat had indeed seen better days.

Taking a step back from his uniform, Robert felt a muscle cramp as it sent a sharp pain down his right leg. He lost his balance, dropped down on one knee, and braced himself against the tree's trunk.

"You all right?"

"I'm fine," Robert mumbled. "Just another leg cramp. It'll pass."

"You was right smart eatin' all that fruit. You should'a listened to me," Bill said.

Rubbing his thigh, Robert felt the pain ease. "I don't want to hear it."

"Oh, of course not. If I was you, I wouldn't wanna hear it either, but I'm not you, and I just can't help myself. I told you—"

"I said I don't want to hear it!" Robert snapped. He wasn't in the mood to listen to Bill's badgering. He'd been stupid, and he didn't need anyone to remind him of it. He should have known better than to gorge himself on the cherries that weren't ripe.

"You're lucky it's only muscle cramps. You could've come down with heatstroke and died."

"Aren't you ever going to shut up?"

Bill smiled, saying, "Not until you admit you should've listened to me."

Robert felt his face flush red as he glared up at Bill. He was about to shout a few obscenities, but he hesitated. Bill's broad grin told the story. The angrier he got, the more Bill enjoyed it.

"Hand me my canteen," he finally said.

"Noooo . . . not until you admit I was right."

As Robert jerked his head, his eyes narrowed, and his nostrils flared.

Bill laughed. "You know, you look like a damn bull in heat."

"It's not funny."

"Yeah, it is," Bill said, reaching for the canteen. He took it off the branch and handed it down to Robert.

"Thanks," said Robert before he took a long drink.

"You still think walkin' up here was such a good idea?" Bill asked.

"Yes, I do." Robert slid over to the tree, resting his back against its trunk. "The breeze makes it feel much cooler."

Bill then looked up into the still leaves of the oak tree. "I see what you mean. It's like a big blow comin' off the Gulf of Mexico."

"Just wait a few minutes," Robert said as he poured water into the cup of his hand and splashed his face. He rubbed the excess from his light brown, full beard. Only twenty-five, Robert was younger than most of the men in the company. Being of average height, five-foot, and seven inches, with baby blue eyes and a face to match, he liked that the beard made him look older. The oldest of nine children, he wasn't used to being one of the youngest. The beard helped give him confidence when dealing with his unfamiliar role.

A familiar doubt flashed through his mind. Maybe they thought I was too young? He wanted to kick himself for feeling that way again.

"You just can't stand to admit you're wrong," Bill said, looking down at his friend.

"Sure I can, but just not to you," Robert said, laughing.

"You're a pain in the ass."

"Now, is that any way to talk to a superior officer?"

"Superior officer? Hell, you're only a junior . . ."

The words hung in the air. Robert could tell Bill regretted it before he'd even been able to finish junior second lieutenant. Robert grimaced as he looked up at the bare collar on his uniform. Robert hadn't always felt that way. He was proud of being promoted to Second Lieutenant. After Cold Harbor, Emmerson, Robert's one-time bullet catcher, replaced Hooks, who had died of disease at Stanardsville, Virginia, as Second Lieutenant. After his recovery, Robert kidded Emmerson about being lucky he knelt when he did at Cold Harbor. It was good-natured, and they'd both laughed about it.

At Second Manassas, a fragment from an artillery shell had wounded Emmerson. Thirteen days later, he died, and after his promotion to Second Lieutenant, Robert realized he was the lucky one.

Bill lowered his head as his smile faded. "Bobby, I'm sorry."

"Don't be."

"It's not right! You should be —"

Robert's temper flared again. "I don't want to talk about it."

"But—"

"Damn it, Bill, shut up about it!" Robert yelled. He could tell he'd hurt Bill's feelings, but he didn't care. Two times he'd been elected captain of Company L, and two times the promotion board had found him unfit for command. Talking about it wasn't going to change anything.

Just before they'd crossed the Potomac into Pennsylvania, Colonel William C. Oates, commanding the Fifteenth Alabama Regiment, had transferred another officer into Company L, Second Lieutenant J. J. Hatcher from Company D.

Almost ten years older than Robert, Hatcher was the original first sergeant of Company D and then promoted to junior second lieutenant. He was promoted to senior second lieutenant two months later. A married man with a couple of kids knew how to keep discipline in the company and didn't care what they thought of him.

Robert wondered if maybe he cared too much. Perhaps that was why the board had turned him down. While Hatcher outranked him, his promotion to company commander was still not official. The men hadn't elected him yet. Of course, these days, as Robert had learned the hard way, elections were becoming increasingly meaningless. Promotion decisions were now up to a board of officers, a board that had twice turned him down.

Taking a deep breath, Robert felt it was his right to protest the board's decision—something several of his men had wanted him to do—but he hadn't decided what to do, and until he did, it wasn't doing the men any good to keep talking about it.

Just then, a stiff breeze rustled the leaves and branches of the stately oak tree. "Look out!" Bill yelled.

As Robert ducked, his belt, with sword and pistol attached, fell from the tree and barely missed his head.

"Thanks," Robert said.

"You're welcome. The branch broke."

Robert nodded as he reached over and picked up his belt.

Bill pulled his canteen over his head and took a drink.

"Hey, when you gonna get yourself a new buckle?"

"I'm not; this one's just fine."

"Wouldn't you rather have a CSA buckle instead of wearing that Yankee one turned upside down? You could easily pick one up after the next fight."

Robert stared at the tarnished and scratched brass buckle for a few seconds, trying to remember what it had looked like the first time he'd worn it. The smooth, golden brass surface had gleamed brightly under the soft winter sun.

He ran his fingertips across its front, feeling the pits and scratches in the brass, remembering how it felt the first time he had touched it, right after the Battle of Fredericksburg. It hadn't been smooth than either. He remembered the stickiness caused by the dark red stain covering the front of it, a stain that only hours before had been the breath of life of a young Yankee major. But there was no sorrow in Robert's soul for the young officer. He was the enemy.

"So, you gonna pick up a new one?" Bill asked.

"No. I don't mind wearing a dead Yankee's belt buckle, but I don't want to wear one belonging to one of our own."

"But Bobby, it's an SN buckle. Now wearin' a Southern Nation buckle might be fittin' for a private but not an officer. As I said, you need a buckle and a new uniform. I'm tellin' ya; you gotta start lookin' like an officer."

Robert wondered if Bill was right. *Did they turn me down because I don't look like an officer?* No, that wasn't it. While his uniform was looking a bit ratty, it wasn't any worse than most of the regiment's company commanders. He knew it was more than just the uniform. It was him.

"I don't care. I'm not wearing anything that comes from one of our dead. When the army issues me a CSA buckle, then I'll wear it with pride. Until then, this one will do just fine."

"Bobby, there ain't any -"

"My point exactly, now make yourself useful, and get my letter out of my right coat pocket."

Bill pulled the envelope out and handed it to Robert. Bill walked a few feet away and stretched out on the grass.

Taking a deep breath, Robert unfolded the letter that had arrived in the morning's mail call. He used his index finger to slit the envelope before pulling out the sheet of paper. Carefully, he opened it and smiled when he noticed his mother's handwriting.

Dear Bobby,

The house is quiet. Your younger brothers and sisters are in bed. Your father is on his way back from Mobile, and all the relatives have gone home. For the first time in my life, I feel truly alone.

I hope you don't mind, but your father told me all about Cold Harbor. Now, I think I understand how you felt. I'm glad the family is coming back in the morning, so I won't be alone, just like you're not alone with Bill and Elisha being with you. I want you to remember that. You're not alone.

Back in April, Jane and Martha came down sick with Typhoid. Bobby, they're both gone. Martha went first; then we buried Jane this morning.

Your Aunt Helen is going to stay with us for a while. Don't worry; we'll be fine. You just better

*be mind'en your mother and be taken good care
of yourself.*

> *Much love,*
>
> *Mother*

As he reread it, then again, he closed his eyes and shook his head. *It can't be right.* Not Martha. Not Jane. He'd left them home, safe. It wasn't supposed to be like this. He remembered the way he had felt for his mother when his brother William died. She could understand babies dying; babies were weak and defenseless, but William was ten, and now Martha and Jane, grown women.

Moistness filled his eyelids as pain settled in his soul. It was strangely comforting, though, to think that death could still inflict pain after the last two years.

The feeling of hurt passed quickly and was replaced by regret. Robert decided he should've been there. He was the oldest, and he'd always looked after his baby sisters. If he'd been home, maybe he could have helped his mother nurse them back to health. The thought passed quickly. Robert was there when William was sick, and he hadn't made any difference. But *I'm older now, and* he thought as he rubbed his hands through his matted hair. Robert knew it didn't make any difference. He'd also been there when Martin got sick. He then whispered, "God bless my sisters, bless William and Martin."

In his mind, he saw Martin reach up his hand.

"Help me, Bobby, boy, please help me. I'm burning up."

Robert poured water on his handkerchief and wiped Martin's face with one hand as he took hold of Martin's hand with the other. Martin smiled and then closed his eyes.

As his smile slowly faded, his breaths became shallow and slower. Then finally, they stopped. Robert sat there waiting for Martin to take another breath, a breath that never came.

Bill sat up. "Bobby, you say somethin'?"

Robert's shoulders shook as tears rolled down his cheeks.

"Bobby, you, all right? What's wrong?"

Robert started to speak, but he stopped himself. He couldn't bring himself to say it — he didn't want to say it — so he reached out his hand that held the letter.

Bill crawled over, took it, and scan it. "Bobby, I'm so sorry. Is there anything I can do?"

Robert sat quietly and shook his head.

"Would you like to be left alone?"

"Please, but don't go far."

Bill nodded and walked back to his spot in the grass and slowly lowered his body to the ground once more.

Wiping his eyes, Robert closed them again. He didn't want to think about his pain. Not now. It was too much. He needed to escape.

He took several deep breaths, developing a slow, methodical rhythm to his breathing. His mind soon found a place of safety, somewhere between consciousness and unconsciousness. Not awake. Not asleep. No thoughts. No dreams.

After a time, a noise invaded his brain. What is it? No, don't do this, he thought as he tried to ignore it, but it seemed to hover around him like a swarm of gnats.

The sound buzzed in his ear. No matter how hard he concentrated, it wouldn't leave him alone. He tried to place the sound. *Was it waves beating against a beach? No.* They weren't near a large body of water. *Distant thunder? Maybe.* But he didn't think so. When it dawned on him what it was, it took his breath away.

When he opened his eyes, the bright light blinded him. Putting his hand in front of his eyes, he glanced toward the left and saw that Bill was lying in the grass, sound asleep.

"Bill, wake up!"

Trying to stand, Robert felt his right calf muscle tightened. He stumbled, knocking over his canteen. The water gurgled as it poured onto the ground.

Slowly he bent and picked it up. As he corked the canteen, he looked toward the Fifteenth Alabama camp, just to the west of a small pond. Nothing seemed unusual, except men, some gathered around a few little pigs. He wondered where they had found the pigs. Since the area had already played host to several brigades, he tried to figure out how the others had missed them.

He'd heard somewhere that Dutch farmers were very resourceful in hiding their food and livestock. One farmer had hidden three cows in the basement of his house. The cows disagreed with the farmer that the cellar was the right place to hide. They showed their displeasure by bellowing loudly, eventually giving themselves away. Robert thought it would be funny if the men had found the pigs in some farmer's cellar. Focusing harder on the scene, he laughed as one of the pigs broke free and started running. As if chasing a prize, three gray-clad figures scurried close behind. Robert chuckled when two of the men collided and fell on their faces.

With only one pursuer, it looked like the pig might have a chance for freedom when suddenly the remaining man launched himself at the pig's rear legs. The two of them rolled over each other a few times. The man jumped, raising his arms above his head. Robert didn't understand what was happening, but he could hear others in the group as they applauded and yelled.

Robert then noticed the pig wasn't moving. It was on its side, its head at an odd angle. Looking closer, Robert saw that the man held a blood-covered knife.

Robert couldn't help but feel sympathy for the pig, so close to freedom right before it instantly faced death. At least the poor animal didn't suffer.

His mind then all too quickly turned to his sisters. Did they suffer? A vision of them lying in bed flashed through his mind. He tried to force the image away, turning his attention back to the rest of the pigs who were now meeting the same fate as the near escapee. Death came quickly for them too.

Robert turned slightly to glance back toward Bill. "Sellers, get your ass up now; that's an order!"

Bill sat up and yawned, "What's got you riled?"

"Artillery."

"I don't hear nothin'."

"I hear it," Robert said.

"Well, I don't. Maybe you're just imagin' it. I mean gettin' that letter and all maybe—"

"If you'd shut up and listen, maybe you could hear it."

Bill frowned but, in a few seconds, smiled. "Well, what do you know? You're right. I can hear it."

"Fine. Now, go find Hatcher. They might not be able to hear the artillery fire above the camp noises. Tell him I'll check the pickets west of camp."

"Yes, sir."

Robert watched Bill trot down the hill and past the church. He then went back to retrieve his equipment. He was still buckling his belt and straightening his uniform when he came out from under the tree.

He listened to the sound of the artillery for a few seconds as he turned his head from side to side. It was coming from the east. Standing on the summit of his small hill, he looked past the small town of New Guilford, Pennsylvania, all the way to the base of the South Mountain, almost seven miles away. There was no smoke. The artillery fight must be on the other side. The South Mountain range rose like a wall, ascending above the low rolling farmland. It ran from almost due north, in what looked like a crescent shape, to the southeast.

Robert shifted his eyes northeast. He could see the gap the Army of Northern Virginia was using to cross the mountain. The Second and Third Corps were already on the other side. Two divisions of the First Corps were supposed to cross this afternoon.

He shook his head. It was the cavalry's fault. If they'd gotten back from their ride around the Union army, the Fifteenth Alabama and the rest of Law's Brigade would be marching to the sound of the guns instead of being stuck guarding crossroads.

Robert turned toward the west and tried to trot down the hillside, but his leg refused. He settled for an amble. Halfway down, he glanced toward the south, and looked over the spread-out tents of the five Alabama regiments of Brigadier General Law's Brigade. It was the largest brigade in Hood's Division of Longstreet's First Corps.

Once Robert got to the road, he was able to pick up his pace. The walking was much more comfortable on the smooth, hard-packed road, and the pain in his leg lessened.

As he came around a curve into a wooded area, he heard, "Halt! Who goes there?"

It took Robert a moment to see the picket guard peeking from behind a large tree on the right side of the road. "Lieutenant Wicker, Company L, Fifteenth Alabama."

"Advance to be recognized," the guard responded jovially. As Robert approached, Joe Henderson stepped out from behind the tree, holding his rifle at the order arms position across his body. Joe straightened up and turned slightly to the right so Robert couldn't help but see the new corporal stripes. Joe did a present arms rifle salute.

"Corporal Henderson commanding the picket guard. At your service, sir." Robert gritted his teeth to keep from laughing and returned the salute. Joe looked like a schoolboy with a new toy.

"Report," Robert barked in a very military fashion.

"It's been real quiet, sir. We ain't seen no signs of any Yankees. Hell, there ain't even been any traffic on the road, not even any civilians."

"What about the artillery?"

"Sir?"

Robert tightened the muscles in his face and narrowed his pale blue eyes. He straightened his back, stretching his five-foot, seven-inch frame closer to the taller Henderson's eye level.

"Corporal, picket duty is a serious business. I expect you to be alert to all possible dangers. If you had been, you wouldn't be asking me what I'm talking about!"

Joe lowered his eyes to the ground and turned his head from one side to the other. After a few seconds, his expression changed. "Dang it if you ain't right, sir. It sure is artillery. On this side of the mountains?"

"I don't think so, but–"

"I know. It don't matter none. We still should've heard it. I won't let nothin' like this here happen again."

Relaxing a little, Robert said, "I know you won't." He noticed Joe's stripes.

"At ease, Corporal. Now tell me, how in the hell did you get those sewed on so quickly? Hatcher just promoted you this morning."

"I did it myself, sir. What d'ya think?"

"Nice job."

"Thanks."

"You out here alone?"

"No, sir. Kelly, Gillmore, and Lloyd, they're right behind you."

Robert twisted around as they stepped out from the bushes about five yards back. They all did a rifle salute, and Robert returned it.

"Where's the rest of the squad?" Company L's two platoons were composed of two squads of eight men each.

"I've got George, and his comrades posted up the road a ways. He's supposed to let any approaching traffic pass. We'll stop'em here."

"Very good. How does George like having his older brother as squad leader?" Robert asked.

"He said it didn't make no difference to him. Hell, ain't like it's nothin' new. I've been bossing him around ever since we was kids." Joe smiled.

"Aren't you missing somebody, Joe?" Robert asked, wondering where Bill's cousin Elisha was.

From the woods, a booming voice said, "Where the hell did everybody go? Where in the hell is the road? Lordy, please don't let me be lost in Yankee country!"

"Private Sellers, shut up and get over here!" Joe yelled.

"If I knew where you were, Corporal, I sure in the hell wouldn't be bellowing."

"What's the matter with Elisha?" Robert asked. It wasn't like him to behave like this.

"Cherries, sir. They got him all out of kilter."

Elisha stumbled out of the woods holding his stomach, his thin face pale and sweaty.

God, did I look that bad yesterday? Robert wondered, remembering he'd spent the morning hanging his backside over the company's latrine pit and the afternoon rolled up in a ball under a shade tree.

"Joe, can you spare him for a few minutes?"

"Sure, Lieutenant, he ain't good for nothin' anyway."

"Joe, I resent that remark. I might be feelin' poorly, but I wouldn't say I'm good for nothin'."

"Private Sellers, that will be Corporal Henderson to you, and today you are a shit-for-brains, do-nothing-but-squat-behind-a-tree-private."

"Come on, shit-for-brains," Robert said, heading back down the road.

Elisha stood there for a few seconds with a blank look on his face. The longer he stood, the more they laughed. Finally, he shook his head and trotted after Robert.

When he caught up to him, Elisha whispered, "Come on, Bob, don't egg him on. You'ns keep this up, and everybody in camp is gonna be callin' me shit-for-brains."

Smiling at him, Robert looked over his shoulder at Henderson's squad. "Corporal, you are guarding the western flank of the brigade. Keep a sharp eye out and send for help at the first sign of trouble. By the way, Joe, the general will probably send out other officers to check on you. I expect you to make Company L proud."

"That we will, sir," Joe answered him.

"Thanks, Joe."

After twenty yards, Robert stared down at the ground.

"I got a letter from my mother today. Typhoid fever hit the family. Martha and Jane are dead."

"I'm so sorry. I know how it feels," Elisha said.

Robert faced his friend. "I know you do. It isn't easy, is it?"

"No, Bobby. I'm afraid not."

Patting Robert on the back, Elisha asked, "Can I do anythin' for ya?"

"Not really, but thanks for asking."

"If you think of somethin'—"

"You'll be the first to know. Now, you better get back."

"All right," Elisha said.

"Just remember to stay away from the fruit," Robert said, smiling.

"You can count on that."

As Robert kept on walking, he drew a deep breath. Just knowing that Elisha knew what it was like made him feel better. He wondered how long it had been. It seemed like a long time, yet it had been only a little short of two years. He remembered how excited the two Sellers brothers were when the company reached Virginia. They were going to see action together and shoot Yankees. Within a few weeks, they were both very sick. Elisha recovered. Evander didn't. Yes, Elisha knew.

Walking faster on the way back to camp, Robert noticed that his leg was finally loose and free of the pain.

As expected, he found Hatcher with the rest of the company commanders gathered around the colonel's tent. A concerned Hatcher met him as he approached the front of the tent. "Everything good with the pickets?"

"Yes, sir."

"Good," Hatcher said before he paused a second and leaned closer to Robert. "Bill told me about your sisters. I'm sorry."

Robert doubted Hatcher's concern. "Thank you, sir."

"I discussed it with the colonel, and I'm afraid we can't let you take leave."

Leave? The colonel? What the hell?

"I'm sorry."

"I understand, sir." Of course, he understood. Hell, they were within earshot of the enemy; why even suggest it to the colonel. *Does he want to get rid of me?*

First Lieutenant John Oates of Company G, the colonel's younger brother, walked up to them.

"Hey, Bobby, did you hear about Alex Baugh?"

Robert shook his head, thankful not everyone knew about his sisters yet. He wasn't in the mood for a long line of thoughtful men telling him how sorry they were his sisters were dead. He was already sorry enough for all of them.

"I heard he was home visiting his parents. Once word got out, he was back in town, and he left in the middle of the night. It looks like the yeller dog was just too embarrassed to see anyone." Robert could understand that. Baugh was a coward. During the battle at Cold Harbor, he shot himself to get out of the army.

"Attention," one of the officers called as Colonel Oates approached.

Before anyone could move, Oates called, "As you were." William C. Oates, the thirty-year-old colonel commanding the Fifteenth Alabama Regiment, surveyed his junior officers.

Oates spoke in a clear, firm voice. "General Law and I know about as much as you do. Hill's and Ewell's corps are across South Mountain. They were supposed to concentrate near Cashtown or Gettysburg.

"General Law feels we will be staying here tonight."

There were several moans.

"Quiet down," Oates ordered. "I don't like it any more than you do, but orders are orders. General Law expects to get orders to move early in the morning. I want you to get your companies ready. I checked the map. Gettysburg is about twenty miles away.

"Have each man issued rations for three days. Have the excess baggage packed in the wagons. Tomorrow I want us traveling light and fast. I'm hoping we can get most of the miles done before the sun gets too high in the sky."

Oates took off his forage cap and beat it against his leg a few times. "I don't have to tell you the importance of defeating the enemy on his own ground. If we drive them away from here, the major cities of the North, including Washington, will be ours for the taking. I expect all your men to do their duty for God and country. Lieutenant Wicker, I need to speak with you. The rest of you, dismissed." After the other officers left, the colonel walked over to him.

"J.J. told me about your sisters. I'm sorry. I wish I could let you go home, but I can't. I need you here."

"I understand, sir."

The colonel patted Robert on the back and then walked away.

Robert looked up at the hazy, blue sky. It would be nice to go home, he thought, taking a deep breath. He was sure his mother could use his help.

Suddenly, he heard laughter behind him and jerked his head around, but no one was there. He shrugged his shoulder before turning to follow Hatcher back to the company's tents.

As he walked, he listened for the distant sound. He could just barely hear its low rumble. Somewhere on the other side of the mountain, the artillery continued to sing its song of death.

Chapter 2

George Meade, commanding General of the Army of the Potomac, stepped away from his staff, hoping it would be quiet enough so he could hear the distant artillery. For a few moments, he stood perfectly still, not breathing. He couldn't hear it, but he knew it was there.

The endless days of marching and playing catch up, with the Army of Northern Virginia, were over. He'd finally brought the Rebel army into battle.

He almost laughed. Twelve miles north across the Maryland state line, near the town of Gettysburg, Pennsylvania, his army was fighting without him, and yet he felt relieved. Of course, if anyone besides John Reynolds had been leading the fight, he would be apprehensive.

Meade still didn't know why President Lincoln had picked him instead of Reynolds to command the army a few days ago. Like many others, he felt John Reynolds was the finest officer he had ever met. This morning, Reynolds brought the left flank of the army into battle against the Rebels. For the time being, Meade had decided to remain at headquarters to coordinate the rest of the army's advance. He had every confidence that John could handle things until he got there.

Again, he held his breath for the sound of artillery. He still couldn't hear the sounds of battle that stirred such fear in him.

"Father."

The voice of his son and aide, Captain George Meade Jr., startled the general.

"What is it, George?" he snapped.

"Sorry, sir. You just received an urgent message from General Howard."

Message *from Howard? Why would Howard send a message? Unless, Reynolds is -.* "What happened to Reynolds?"

"How did you know?"

"It's the only reason for Howard to send a dispatch directly to me. What happened?"

"General Reynolds was shot down while positioning his men. General Howard says he was killed instantly by a bullet to the head."

The older Meade closed his eyes and said a silent prayer for his dead friend. Unfortunately, now was not the time to grieve. He was facing a severe command problem.

Major General Oliver Howard was now in command at Gettysburg. Meade didn't know Howard very well. But after what had happened at Chancellorsville, where Stonewall Jackson had overrun Howard's Eleventh Corps, he knew Howard wasn't up to commanding the left flank of the Army of the Potomac. There was no way he could leave the battle in Howard's hands.

"Do you have any orders, sir?"

"No, George, not yet. I need to think. Reynolds will be a hard man to replace." Young George walked away.

"What do I do now?" he whispered. He wanted to immediately ride for the sound of the guns. He shook his head. If he did, who would coordinate the advance of the rest of the army? And what if Lee drove back the left flank of the army? Who would redirect the army to the planned defensive position, between the Rebels and Washington, along the banks of Pipe Creek?

Meade kicked his foot in the dirt. He'd have to send someone to take command at Gettysburg. *But who?* Slocum was the obvious choice. He was senior to Howard, but from his last dispatch, it would be extremely late in the day before his Twelfth Corps could get there.

The sound of riders caught his attention. He looked up to see the Second Corps commander riding with his staff. Meade's indecision vanished. He would send his friend, Major General Winfield Hancock.

"Good afternoon, sir." Hancock saluted.

Meade gave a quick salute in return. "Good to see you, Win."

"I hear John has encountered the Rebs at Gettysburg."

"I have some bad news. John is dead."

Hancock slouched over. "Damn."

"Win, I have a serious problem, and I need your help. I don't trust Howard. I have to stay here at Headquarters, so I want you to ride to Gettysburg and take command until Slocum arrives."

"George, I can't do that. Howard outranks me."

"I don't care if Howard outranks you! I have the authority to place whoever I want in command, and I'll have an order written up saying so. I want you to turn over your command and get to Gettysburg. Who is your senior division commander?"

"John Gibbon. George, I don't think this is a good idea. Is there any way I can talk you out of this?"

"No, you can't. Now come on; let's get that order written so you can get up to Gettysburg."

❦

Through his field glasses, General Robert E. Lee watched as one of his brigades came marching down the hill to the north. The red and blue Southern Cross Battle Flags waved majestically above the four regiments as they marched in two perfectly aligned ranks across the wheat fields west of Gettysburg. A wave of smoke obscured his view for a few minutes, but then it slowly cleared, and he continued to follow their progress. *Whose brigade is it?* From reports he'd received, he knew it must be one belonging to Robert Rodes' Division of Ewell's Corps.

Lee looked at a stone wall blocking the brigade's path to the town. There seemed to be movement, almost like the bobbing of heads. *Yankees?*

He turned back to the brigade. They were advancing without skirmishers. "They're blind," he whispered under his breath. "If Yankees are behind that wall . . ."

He pulled down his field glasses and stared across the fields that separated him from the advancing brigade. He felt helpless as the men drew closer to the stone wall. "Maybe I'm just seeing things," he whispered.

An instant later, a wave of smoke rose from behind the wall. The brigade's front rank was gone, the remainder of the second line was diving for cover. Lee's heart went out to the men. Poor leadership had just wasted their lives.

The firing spread and grew up and down the battle line. Lee closed his eyes and prayed he'd made the right decision to push ahead with the attack. He prayed that those men, who'd just been cut down in the prime of their lives, had not died in vain.

He hadn't planned for this attack. He hadn't had time to concentrate the entire army. Longstreet's Corps was still on the other side of the mountains, and only God knew where Jeb Stuart and his cavalry were.

Lee turned his back to the fighting as he wiped away the sweat from his forehead. The heat would be hard on his men. He prayed it would be harder on the northern boys.

He paced and waited. When the fighting intensified, he turned back in time to see gray troops pouring around a white barn, a mile to the east, at the crest of the next ridge. They were driving the Yankees back. "Yes, we have done it again," he barely whispered as if his breath would break the glorious spell. "Victory is ours."

"They're running, sir." Ambrose Hill walked up to Lee.

"That they are, General Hill. It looks like we're going to be lucky today."

"General Heth and I deeply regret we let this morning's action get so out of hand. We didn't mean to violate your orders to avoid a general engagement."

"There's no reason to go over it again, General. It was not my intention to bring on a battle before we had concentrated the army, but I will not run from this victory."

There was no need to rehash the morning's activities. Lee had approved the attack on what seemed to be only a detachment of state militia—while unfortunate, mistaking dismounted cavalry for the militia was understandable. It was bad luck the First Corps of the Army of the Potomac had reinforced the cavalry before it was driven away.

No matter. What was done was done. If General Stuart had come back on time, none of this would have happened. General Heth would have known what he was facing instead of guessing.

He turned to face Hill. "How is General Heth feeling?"

"The head wound is not serious, but I'm afraid that he will be off his feet for a few days."

Lee nodded. He would have to find someone to take over Heth's Division. "Any word from General Stuart?"

"No, sir, not that I know of."

"Could you send a messenger to General Ewell and see if he has heard from Stuart?"

"Yes, sir."

When Hill walked away, Lee turned his field glasses to the northeast. From the smoke, he could tell that Ewell's men were also driving the Yankees back toward town. This was turning into a great victory.

He searched to the north for any signs of a large column of men on horseback. Hopefully, Stuart would hear the battle and rush to rejoin the army. Lee lowered the glasses, disappointed there was no sign of Stuart.

Stuart had assured him that if the Yankees crossed to the Potomac River's north bank, he would rush back to the army. One of Lee's conditions before he approved Stuart's plan to take his cavalry on a ride around the Union army, disrupting its communications and supply lines.

That was seven days ago. It seemed like an eternity, being in enemy territory for seven days without the army's eyes and ears. He took a deep breath and thanked God for Longstreet's spy, Henry Harrison, whose information had saved the army from inevitable disaster.

If he hadn't been for Harrison's warning two nights before, the Army of Northern Virginia would still be spread out over a forty-mile stretch of southern Pennsylvania. The Yankee army would have picked them apart piece by piece.

Lee looked through the glasses again. He smiled. He couldn't have created a better battle plan. Hill attacked from the west as Ewell moved down from the north. The Union troops, west of town, were attacked from two sides. They fought bravely, but now they were running.

He strained his field glasses toward the large, bald hill southeast of town. Yankee troops were streaming up its northern sloops. Near the hill's summit stood alone, towering tree, which seemed to be a rallying point for the Union troops. The Yankees were getting reorganized; he could see their artillery batteries moving into a defensive position. The smile faded from his lips. He couldn't allow the Yankees to hold that hill.

Lee turned to Colonel Armistead Long, his military secretary. "Armistead, we need to send an order to General Ewell encouraging him to take that hill."

"Yes, sir."

Win Hancock rode up the Emmitsburg Road with his staff streaming behind him. To the west and north, smoke hung low across the landscape.

As they got closer to town, he saw the blue troops moving up the hill to his right. He followed them, and within a few minutes, he found Howard near the gate to the Evergreen Cemetery.

"Win, I'm surprised to see you. I didn't think your corps would be able to get here until tomorrow."

"My corps isn't with me," Hancock said as he dismounted his horse. "I stopped by George's headquarters, and he asked me to ride on ahead. Oliver, this is a little difficult. George asked me to take command until either he or Slocum arrives."

"Why?"

Hancock didn't know what to say, so he said nothing.

Howard slumped over and turned his back on Hancock. He bowed his head for a few seconds; he then straightened up and turned back to Hancock. "Does he want my resignation?"

"No."

A shell exploded above the summit of the hill. "I don't like this," Howard said.

"Oliver, I can understand—"

"Have you ever been relieved from command?"

"Can't say that I have."

"Then you can't understand how I feel." Howard took off his hat and ran his fingers through his matted hair. "I don't like it, but orders are orders. What do you want me to do?"

"Can you fill me in on what happened this morning?" Win asked as another shell flew overhead. The enemy was testing the range. Once they had it down, things were going to be rough.

Before Howard could answer, John Buford, rode up to join them.

"John, good to see you," Hancock said.

"Good to see you too, sir."

"Could you update Win on the morning's fight?" Howard asked.

"Glad to, sir. This morning I posted my cavalry on the ridge west of town." Buford handed Hancock his field glasses and pointed out the white barn located on the crest of the ridge west of town past a large brick building topped by a copula.

"The barn was roughly the center of my line. The First Corps reinforced me, and the Eleventh Corps extended the line north of town."

Howard interrupted. "As we came through town, I noticed this hill was a natural defensive position. I left one of my divisions here to start preparing a fall-back position."

Hancock nodded and looked back at Buford to continue. "We fought them all day, sir, but they just kept coming. We were up against the Second and Third Corps. That's almost two-thirds of the Army of Northern Virginia."

Hancock scanned the area north of town. He wondered why Howard had moved two divisions forward to a weak and ill-defined defensive position instead of fortifying this hill. When things got rough, why hadn't he ordered a tactical retreat, instead of waiting for the line to collapse?

Hancock then looked at Howard. He wanted to ask why but thought better of it. One thing was for sure: Howard was right—this hill would make a strong defensive position. If they could hang on until dark, tomorrow the Rebs would have hell to pay trying to take it away from them.

"What is the name of this hill?" Hancock asked.

Howard pointed to the white marble headstones of the town cemetery on the east slope of the hill.

"Cemetery Hill?" Hancock asked.

Howard nodded.

Hancock shook his head and looked away. He could already see the newspaper headlines: "Hancock Makes His Last Stand on Cemetery Hill."

"Gentleman, let's see if we can keep the Rebels from taking this hill away from us."

Chapter 3

Colonel Joshua Lawrence Chamberlain dismounted. He pulled the reins over his horse's head and then began leading him. The Twentieth Maine Volunteer Regiment commanding officer was hot and tired, and so were his men. He didn't feel right that he got to ride while they had to walk. He rubbed his hand along the top of his long mustache and then through his wet, matted hair. He squirmed to keep his shirt from sticking to his chest, but his efforts were in vain. Though the heat was bearing down, he continued, each long stride making his dark blue wool pants rub on the inside of his thighs. As he walked, he wondered how many of his men would sell their souls for a blast of chilly weather from home. Pondering this question, he heard the pounding of horses' hoofs. As he glanced over his shoulder, he saw his brothers John and Tom as they rode forward to join him at the front of the regiment.

"Why are you walking?" John demanded as he jumped from his saddle.

Lawrence looked over at him and smiled. John didn't smile back. Neither did Tom, who stayed on his horse. "Because the horse needed a rest," he said as he chuckled.

John's eyes narrowed. "That's not funny. You are still recovering from heatstroke. You have no business walking."

"John's right. Get back up on your horse!" Tom ordered.

Lawrence looked up at him. "Lieutenant," he said, raising his voice, "you don't give me orders. Is that clear?"

"John did."

"He's a civilian. I can't control what he says."

"That's not fair."

Lawrence's cheeks reddened. "Tom, I warned you when you joined the regiment that you weren't going to get any special treatment. I wouldn't put up with that kind of disrespect from any of the other officers, and I'm not going to put up with it from you just because we're brothers."

"Oh, I see, Brother John can talk to you any way he wants, but I can't."

"Unfortunately for both of us, yes. That's the way it is. And you better start calling me, sir."

"Yes, sir."

"When was the last time you checked the flankers?"

With the Twentieth Maine marching at the head of the column, it was their job to supply the flankers to protect the rest of the brigade during the march.

"Just got back," Tom replied. "There are still signs of Rebel cavalry, but they don't seem interested in tangling with massed infantry. Sir, I respectfully request that the colonel please get back up on his horse."

"You two going to keep this up until I do?"

"Yes," replied both the younger brothers in unison.

John put his hand on Lawrence's shoulder. "I don't want to lose another brother."

Lawrence hung his head. "This is war. On any day, at any time, the Lord could call me to join him."

John spun Lawrence around to face him. "Joshua."
Lawrence glanced up with a confused look on his
face. No one in the family ever called him Joshua. To
them, he would always be Lawrence—Lawrence Joshua
Chamberlain. They couldn't bring themselves to call him
Joshua, and they didn't care that he liked the sound
of Joshua Lawrence better. His father was Joshua
Lawrence, as was his father, and he wished he'd been
named for both of them.

His eyes met John's. *Damn.* He knew John could tell
that the use of the name had had the desired effect.

John's eyes narrowed. "If you die of heatstroke, what
am I going to tell Fannie—he's dead because he was too
stupid to ride his horse?"

Neither John nor Tom had ever talked to him like that.
Only Horace had dared to be so blunt with the oldest
brother. Lawrence looked away; it'd only been a year.
He swallowed hard. Lawrance believed Horace was better off passing over to God's loving hands, but how he
missed him. Lawrence stopped and let his horse walk
up to him. In one fluid motion, he flung himself into the
saddle. John also mounted his horse. From Company G,
marching directly behind them, Lawrence heard a scattering of applause. It looked like his brothers weren't the
only ones who thought he should be riding.

Lawrence looked over at John. "It's good having you here."

"I am glad you still think so." John smiled. "Too bad
sister Sarah decided not to come."

"It would be nice to see her, but I'm not sure she
would have appreciated twenty miles a day in the saddle." Lawrence turned to Tom. "Do you know how far it
is to Hanover?"

"We passed a farmhouse a ways back. The old farmer
said it was only about three more miles."

"Since we are leading the corps through town, I think it would be a good idea if we tighten up the formation. Pass the word to the company commanders."

"Yes, sir." Tom wheeled his horse to the right and dropped behind his brothers.

"You sorry you came?" Lawrence asked John.

"No, why?"

"This isn't the kind of visit I'd hoped for when I invited you and sis to join us. I thought we'd be spending the summer near Fredericksburg, but old Bobby Lee had a different idea."

"Do you think we will catch up with them soon?"

"I hope so. All this forced marching is hard on the men. Twenty miles a day is hard in any weather, but in this heat."

John took off his wide-brimmed hat and shook some dirt out of it. He ran fingers through his wavy brown hair. "I'll tell you something; I'm sure glad I don't have to wear my wool coat on a day like this."

Lawrence looked over at John, who had his white shirt open at the collar and his coat tied to his saddle. Lawrence wanted to do the same, but it wouldn't be good for discipline for the colonel to go riding around out of uniform. So instead, every brass button on his double-breasted coat remained buttoned in proper military fashion.

"Lawrence, why do you have six men under arrest?"

"It's a long story, John. They were part of the Second Maine regiment. Last month, the enlistment for the original members of the Second Maine ran out, and they got sent home."

"Sent home? Why?"

"Do you remember when the war started how everyone thought it was only going to last a couple of months?"

John nodded.

"Well, just to be safe, the government enlisted some of the first regiments, like the Second Maine, for two years in case the war ran a little longer than they expected."

"So, you are telling me the Second Maine's enlistment ran out last month?"

"Fortunately, or unfortunately," Lawrence said, "depending on how you want to look at it, the government learned from their error and changed the enlistments to three years or the end of the war. Over the last two years, the Second Maine received one hundred twenty replacements. They weren't real happy when the rest of the regiment was sent home."

"They had the new enlistment papers?" John asked.

Lawrence nodded.

"So, what was their problem?"

"They all claimed they were promised they would only serve with the Second," Lawrence answered him.

"Oh . . . so what did they do?"

Lawrence chuckled. "They mutinied."

"Doesn't the army shoot mutineers?"

"Our corps commander sent them to his only other Maine regiment with orders that if I couldn't get them to join the Twentieth, I was to shoot them."

"He did not."

"Oh, yes, he did. So far, one hundred fourteen have joined. I'm still working on the remaining six."

"You're going to have to shoot them?"

"No . . . I'm not. I've talked to Colonel Vincent, and he understands I can't order Maine men to be shot. I'd never be able to go home, but if we can't get them to change their minds soon, I'm going to have to turn them over to someone else who can."

"Do they have to fight? I mean, what if I could talk them into being litter bearers? I might be able to persuade them to help their fellow man despite their feelings toward the army. Would that be good enough?"

"I don't know. Maybe. I'll have to check with Colonel Vincent."

"Do I have your permission to broach the subject with them?"

"Don't make any promises."

"I understand. No promises." John smiled as he pulled his horse off to the side and dismounted.

As Lawrence rode, his eyes grew heavy. As he closed them, it took only a few minutes for him to fall asleep.

Lawrence took her in his arms. Then he kissed her in a way he had never dared before, in a way Lawrence had wanted to since the first time he'd seen her. He picked her up in his arms and took her to the bed, laying her softly, ever so gently, in the middle of it. He moved his hands across her body, exploring parts that before this afternoon wouldn't have been proper.

"I love you, Fannie," he whispered in her ear.

"I love you too," replied Frances Caroline Adams Chamberlain, his bride of just a few hours. A loud burst of children's laughter invaded their bedchamber, followed by a sudden chill. Lawrence shivered as he saw himself dragging a sled through the heavy, wet snow.

"Faster, Daddy, faster," the young voices called out to him. He glanced over his shoulder to see the smiling faces of the other two loves of his life, Daisy and Wyllys.

"Daddy, please pull the sled faster," Daisy called out to him. He took long strides to comply with her request. The children's laughter warmed his heart. Suddenly, the sound of a baby crying replaced the laughter.

The horse stumbled, jerking Lawrence awake. He patted his new horse on the neck to thank him for waking him. That's one dream he didn't want to finish.

It felt good to be out front. Yesterday's rain had helped beat down the dust, but Lawrence was sure the men in the back of the corps were suffering. The dust kicked up from the thousands of men and horses, combined with the heat and humidity, made breathing at the back of the column difficult.

Lawrence heard horses galloping up from behind. He looked back to see his commanding officer riding up to join him. Colonel Strong Vincent looked the part of a military leader. He was tall with dark hair, a strong chin, and wide sideburns. From Erie, Pennsylvania, he'd studied at Harvard and practiced law before the war.

Beside him rode Private Oliver Norton, carrying the brigade's triangular red and white headquarters flag with the Fifth Corps Maltese cross in its center.

"You decided riding is better than walking, Colonel Chamberlain?"

"Yes, sir, after my brothers convinced me it was a shame to let this excellent horse go to waste."

"I agree with them. I can't afford to have you sick again."

"Yes, sir."

"I've gotten word there was a cavalry fight up ahead in Hanover. What have you heard from your flankers?"

"They've been watching us, but they haven't caused any trouble. Do we know where the Rebel army is?"

"North, but I haven't heard where."

"I wonder what Stuart's cavalry is doing screening us from the east. It doesn't make any sense," Lawrence said.

"Could be Stuart is cut off from Lee. If so, Lee's blind. Maybe we can catch them unprepared like they did Howard at Chancellorsville. Any more of the Second Maine men decide to join you?"

"No, sir."

"When are you going to get around to shooting them?" Vincent chuckled.

"When hell freezes over." Lawrence grinned. It had become their running joke. "John did come up with an idea. What if they volunteered to be litter bearers? Do you think it would satisfy General Meade's orders?"

"Would it satisfy you?" Vincent asked.

Lawrence nodded.

"I think General Meade now has more important things to worry about, and if it is fine with you, then it is fine with me."

"Thank you, sir. I'll let you know what happens."

"One more thing, I've got a feeling we are going to catch the Rebels soon, and I need all my officers fit for combat." Vincent leaned closer. He lowered his voice as if he didn't want anyone else to hear. "I think it would be a good idea if you refrained from walking. I can't afford you to get sick again. Ashby's Gap was a small fight, and Jim Rice did a fine job filling in for you, but I want you in command of the Twentieth in the coming battle.

"I know you think Ames was a fine regular army officer, but I think the regiment will respond better to your methods than his. That will only happen, though if you are fit for duty. Am I making myself clear?"

"Yes, sir. I'll stay on my horse."

Vincent nodded and gave his horse a couple of quick kicks; he guided his horse to the column's front; Norton followed close behind.

Will I do as well as Ames? Lawrence wondered.

The growing crowds on the outskirts of Hanover distracted him. A group of girls and women dressed in red, white, and blue sang "The Star-Spangled Banner" as a band played. Lawrence thought the band sounded funny, almost like one of the drummers was out of beat.

He took out his sword and gave a salute to what looked like a delegation of town officials. As he rode away from the band, the music seemed to fade away, but the out-offbeat drummer was still there.

Just past town, they came to the site of the morning's cavalry fight. The drummer was still with them. This time he seemed to beat out a march for those lying dead along the road. Lawrence bowed his head in a silent tribute.

A little further down the road, an officer from General Skyes' staff directed the regiment to a field on the road's east side. The men stacked arms and fanned out for water and fence rails—the two most essential items to an army on the march. Lawrence felt sorry for the farmers in the area, but everyone had to do his part to support the national army. The farmers' fence rails would be fuel for the evening campfires.

As Lawrence got off his horse, he noticed the drumming had stopped. He stretched his back. Sergeant Ruel Thomas, his orderly, rushed up to him. "Colonel, how ya feelin'?"

"I'm fine. Why do you ask?"

"Just wonderin', sir, you walked apiece—"

"Ruel, I heard enough from my brothers and Colonel Vincent. I'm not going to put up with it from you too." Lawrence was surprised when Ruel smiled at him.

"Sorry, sir. I didn't mean no offense."

"Here, take my horse and treat him well. He isn't going to get a break tomorrow." Ruel led the horse away with what seemed to Lawrence like a strange look of satisfaction on his face.

Several of the company commanders started gathering around. Lawrence exchanged greetings with each of them, and he learned that the day's march had gone well with very few stragglers. They excitedly discussed the strange beating sound they had heard as they came through Hanover. Several believed the sound was massed artillery.

Lawrence's stomach started making funny noises, and he realized how hungry he was. Turning to Tom, he said, "Could you go check the quartermaster's wagons and see if they have anything for the regiment to eat besides hardtack and salt pork?"

"Yes, sir." Tom hurried away.

Lawrence knew some of the officers didn't like the idea that he had picked his brother to be his adjutant. He didn't care. He wanted someone he could trust.

Tom listened well and carried out his wishes without having to be asked twice. He could depend on Tom, and that was more important than pleasing the other junior officers.

John rode up. "Any luck with the prisoners?" Lawrence asked.

"They didn't seem interested in the idea. What did Vincent say?" John climbed down from his horse.

"He said it was up to me. Would you mind trying again?"

"Sure, Lawrence. How are you feeling?"

"I feel fine."

"You don't look fine. You need to take better care of yourself. Did you drink enough water today?"

"I'm fully recovered from the heatstroke."

John shook his head.

"Well, almost. And I feel much better than I did last week."

"I would hope so. You almost died last week."

"I wasn't that sick. It was more embarrassing than anything else."

"Oh, you weren't that sick? They had to carry you to the field hospital. I'd hate to see it when you think you are sick. If you don't start taking care of yourself pretty soon, I'm afraid I'm going to get a chance to see it."

Lawrence glanced at the other officers. They were all nodding.

"John, I'm fine. You don't have to worry about me."

John laughed. "Yeah, I don't have to worry about you. You take good care of yourself. Just like the other day when you refused to ride in the wagon. You could barely stay in the saddle; then it started raining."

"I was suffering from heatstroke—I figured it might do me some good to ride in the rain."

"Lawrence!"

"All right, John. I'll try to do a better job of looking after myself."

Tom walked up to his brothers. "I don't know about you two," he said softly, "but I'm kind of hungry." He opened a small cloth revealing three freshly butchered pieces of beef.

"Is there enough for the entire regiment?" Lawrence asked.

"Yes," Tom said.

"You two go ahead," Lawrence said. "I'll wait until the men get theirs."

"Sir . . . go eat. I'll make sure the regiment gets their ration of beef," Captain Ellis Spear said.

Lawrence spun around, "Ellis, I'll wait for the men— it's the proper thing to do."

"Sir, you've been sick and—"

"Ellis, not you too?"

"Sir, when you appointed Arthur and me to share the duties of your second in command, you encouraged us to speak freely with you. And that is what I'm doing now.

You need to keep up your strength. You're not going to do us any good if you get sick again. Go eat with your brothers. I'll take care of the men this evening."

Lawrence started to protest, but he saw the look in Ellis's eyes. He'd seen it before, back when Ellis was his student at Bowdoin College.

"I suppose you've got Ruel making a fire for us."

Tom shook his head. "Didn't he tell you? Ruel isn't feeling well, and Sergeant . . . I mean Private Buck" — Tom made the same mistake many in the regiment had made in the last month—"is filling in for him this evening."

"I just saw Ruel. He looked fine."

Tom shrugged his shoulders.

Lawrence spied the top of his tent going up. "George taking care of my tent too?"

"Yes, sir. He got a few of the other privates to help him with it."

"Thank you, Ellis. Let me know if you have any problems."

"I will, sir."

John and Tom followed Lawrence over to his tent. They found Private George Buck warming a skillet over the fire. George started to stand, but Lawrence waved him down.

"Good afternoon, George. How did you get stuck with me this evening?" Lawrence asked as he noticed a piece of meat in the middle of the skillet, he glanced at George, and their eyes met.

Shrugging his shoulders, George replied, "Sir, just doin' a friend a favor. I hope you don't mind."

"George?"

"Well, truth is we had a little wager and I lost."

"What was the wager about?"

"Sir, you don't want to know."

"Yes, I do."

"I bet Ruel he didn't have guts enough to say something to you about not riding your horse."

John and Tom broke out laughing, and Lawrence's face flushed red as he jerked his head toward his brothers. When they saw his face, they howled even louder.

Lawrence started to tell them to shut up but stopped himself. *What's the point? It will just encourage them.* "Tom, you going to hold on to the meat all night, or are you going to give it to the private to cook?"

George heard the emphasis placed on the word private; he ignored it. He knew it was meant as a rebuke and deservingly so. Tom walked over and handed him the three other steaks. George placed them in the skillet and then used his fork to flip over his steak.

George felt guilty. He hadn't meant to embarrass the colonel. As the regiment marched through Hanover, he had recognized the odd sound as the firing of massed artillery. It came to him that maybe the day's march wasn't going to be as short as everyone thought.

He was surprised when they'd been directed off the side of the road. His instincts told him this wasn't going to be their camp for the night. Then he had seen the cattle. As the butchers efficiently started doing their work, turning the cattle into fresh meat for the corps, his stomach growled. He wanted, no, he had to have a fresh steak. His gut told him there wouldn't be time. He quickly found Ruel and dared him to say something to the colonel. Then he found Lieutenant Chamberlain and directed him to the butchers.

George glanced up. The colonel was looking at him.

"George, did you go to Ruel with this dare before or after you knew about the steaks?"

"Sir—" the blare of bugles cut him off. George stabbed his steak and flopped it on a tin plate. A few seconds later came the familiar bugle call of *Dan, Dan, Dan, Butterfield, Butterfield.*

That's what it sounded like to George. The former brigade commander, Dan Butterfield, wrote the special bugle call so the Third Brigade would always know that the next burgle call was for them. Within seconds, the Third Brigade buglers blew assembly.

George stood up and held out the plate to Lawrence. "Here, sir, switch steaks with me. Mine's done."

"Thanks, George," Lawrence said as he took the plate. Private Joe Tyler came running toward him. Lawrence nodded at Joe, and the Twentieth Maine's bugler sounded assembly. The regiment's drummer boys jumped to their feet, and within seconds they joined Joe in repeating the call.

"What's going on, Lawrence?" John asked.

"I don't know, but I suspect it has something to do with that drumming sound we heard."

An officer came running toward them. "Colonel Chamberlain! Colonel Chamberlain!"

It was one of Colonel Vincent's aides. "Over here, Captain." Lawrence waved.

"Sir, Colonel Vincent sends his regards." The captain didn't bother saluting. George noticed the colonel didn't seem to mind the slight. "Sir, there was a fight at Gettysburg. I'm afraid things didn't go well. General Reynolds is dead; the First and Eleventh Corps were driven from the field of battle. They regrouped on the hills east of town and are in desperate need of support. Orders are to march to Gettysburg immediately."

"Captain, how far is it to Gettysburg?"

"I heard someone say it was about seven miles, but I can't speak as to the accuracy of that estimate."

"Thank you for the report."

The captain saluted and hurried off.

Sad news about Reynolds, George thought to himself. He had met him once when he was on picket duty. George knew he would be hard to replace.

"Sir, you better eat up," George said.

Lawrence picked up the steak and took a bite.

"How is it, sir?"

"Good, George. Thanks."

"You're welcome."

As the last chords of assembly died away, the regiment's company commanders rushed toward the colonel.

Just then, Sergeant Major Sam Miller blocked their path. "Gentlemen, let's give the colonel a few minutes so he can finish eatin'."

George chuckled when some of the officers protested the sergeant major's interference. They should know better. As the ranking enlisted man in the regiment, George knew Sam saw the colonel's health and well-being as his responsibility. Sam would make sure he had time to finish eating.

The Colonel stuffed the last of the meat into his mouth and wiped his hands on his pant leg as he looked over at his brother John. "It will be at least a half-hour before we will be ready to resume the march, so take your time and get some rest."

"Thanks, Lawrence. I could use it."

George dug into his streak as the colonel laid his plate next to him.

"George, you never answered my question."

"Sir, the officers, are waiting for you," George said without looking up.

"Ruel's going to be very upset with you."

"Ayuh," George replied as he took another bite of the steak.

Lawrence shook his head and turned in the direction of the regiment's officers. He could see the excitement and anticipation on their faces. He walked quickly over to them, and with each footstep, his excitement grew. The army had suffered another in a long series of defeats, but this was different. They were on northern soil, and instead of pulling back, the rest of the army was rushing to join the fight.

Captain Charles Billings called the officers to attention as Lawrence walked up.

"As you were," Lawrence said immediately. "Gentlemen, there was a battle in Gettysburg today. We have orders to move forward. In fifteen minutes, I will call the regiment into formation. Please have your companies ready."

"Sir." Young Lieutenant Holman Melcher spoke up. "You think we might get into this fight?"

Lawrence could see the question was on the minds of all his officers. After what had happened at Chancellorsville, he didn't blame them.

"All I can tell you is that this time the Twentieth Maine isn't going to be stuck behind the lines guarding telegraph lines."

All the officers cheered.

Chapter 4

Another cannon fired from General Lee's left. He looked to see if there were any others ready for firing, but the cannon's smoke blocked his view. No matter. Hill's men were just sighting in their guns. They were too beaten up by the mornings' action to get involved in any more heavy fighting today.

Taking out his field glasses to get a better look of the bald hill, Lee saw the Union troops and his first thought was that they looked like blue ants scurrying about. His attention immediately turned to the reality of the situation. He realized that his men had to take the hill today. Tomorrow would be much more difficult. Lee then wondered what was keeping Ewell. He'd sent him word over an hour ago to press the attack.

He wished Thomas were here, for he knew if his friend Thomas "Stonewall" Jackson were leading those troops, he wouldn't even have to suggest continuing the attack. Thomas would have already done it. Lee drew a deep breath. No sense thinking about it. Thomas was dead and nothing could bring him back.

As Lee looked around, he noticed that his staff was busy getting the headquarters set up. He had picked a stone house on the Chambersburg Road, close to the Lutheran Theological Seminary, as his personal headquarters. He'd made it clear to his men that the headquarters tents were to be set up across the street to minimize the inconvenience to Mrs. Thompson, the home's owner.

Everything looked in order; his staff was getting the headquarters organized, yet for some strange reason he felt helpless. They'd beaten the Yankees again, but the work wasn't done. He wondered why Ewell hadn't followed up his attack.

At that moment, Lee saw the riders coming up the Chambersburg Pike. The men followed Lieutenant General James Longstreet who was in the lead. Lee let out a deep sigh. It was good to see a strong leader like Longstreet. Lee had always felt Longstreet was his "Old War Horse," a strong and determined fighter.

Patiently, Lee waited as Longstreet dismounted and turned his horse over to an aide. As Longstreet walked up, Lee noticed for the first time the gray hairs in Longstreet's long flowing beard. With a soft chuckle, Lee decided that both of them were indeed getting old. Another thought then struck Lee as he remembered that Longstreet was only forty-two years old. At fifty-seven, Lee wondered how old he must look to his men.

"General." Longstreet saluted.

"We beat them again," Lee said, feeling like a schoolboy telling his father that he had just whipped up on the town bully. "They're trying to reassemble up on that bald hill." He pointed to Cemetery Hill. "I've ordered General Ewell to press the attack. I'm hopeful he'll be able to drive them from those heights."

"Congratulations, sir. You've done it. You've got them out in the open. We can now move the army to the right, between Meade and Washington, and make them come to us on the ground of our choosing."

Lee turned toward the heights southeast of town. "General Longstreet, the enemy is here; we have driven them from the field. I can't ask the army to leave the battlefield in the hands of the enemy."

"Respectfully, sir," Longstreet raised his voice, "We agreed that this invasion would be a defensive campaign. The plan was to force the enemy into the open. We have done that. I repeat—we must get behind them . . . get between them and Washington and force Meade to come to us and attack us at the location of our choosing."

Lee exhaled, "But we have beaten them here. I didn't plan on this fight. I didn't want to get into a battle before the army was concentrated, but it has happened, and we beat them. Once again, we've driven the enemy from the field of battle. How can I tell the men that we're going to retreat?"

"Sir, the Union army has the high ground. Wouldn't it be better for us to make a tactical maneuver and get around behind them? We can find ground of our choosing. They'll have to attack us. We'll be between them and their capital city."

"General, I understand your position. I'll take it under advisement." There was an awkward silence. Lee took a couple of steps towards the distant bald hill. "What's the status of your corps?"

"The lead elements of McLaws' Division should be up soon. It will be close to morning before Hood's Division arrives. Picket's Division will leave Chambersburg in the morning. Also, Law's Brigade from Hood's Division has picket duty at New Guilford. I've issue orders for them to be on the road by three AM."

"I'm going up to the cupola," Lee said, pointing to the top of the large brick building that served as the main building of the Lutheran Seminary. "I want to get a better view of Ewell's progress. Would you like to join me?"

"Sir, thank you for asking, but I'd better check on McLaws' men."

"Very well. I'm sure I'll see you later this evening."

"Yes, sir."

Lee walked to the seminary building. He was truthful with Longstreet when he said he'd take his plan under advisement. The plan had some merit, but it would be difficult to maneuver in the face of the enemy without cavalry to screen the infantry's movements and scout the way. Maybe Stuart would make it back before he would be forced to make a decision.

He paused for a moment at the building's entryway so litter bearers could bring out the bodies of two dead Yankees. The Union troops had turned the ground floor of the Lutheran Seminary into a makeshift field hospital. When their line collapsed, the most seriously wounded were left behind. Lee knew that his surgeons would do what they could for the injured, no matter the color of the uniform. Unfortunately, for many of these brave men, all the doctors could do was make dying a little more comfortable.

As Lee waited, he noticed a small pile of arms and legs. His chest tightened as he drew a deep breath. "Rooney. I wonder if he lost his leg," he whispered. He felt weak and grabbed the door frame to steady himself as he looked around, but no one seemed to notice.

As he entered the crowded, noisy room, it suddenly became very still. A young private lying on the bare wooden floor reached up to him. Lee took the man's hand and squeezed as he gave him the warm smile of a father proud of his son. There was nothing more he could do. A large blood-soaked bandage covered the man's chest and his skin was already a ghostly white. Lee knew death would soon come.

"God bless you," the man whispered.

"And may He have mercy on you."

Other hands reached out to him as he slowly worked his way through the room—smiling, touching, and giving the wounded words of encouragement, yet he felt guilty. As he felt the cold, clammy hands of injured or dying men, he thought of Rooney. *Where was he? Did they have to amputate his leg? Was he going to be all right?*

Brigadier General William Henry Fitzhugh Lee, Rooney to his friends and family, was Lee's second son. He'd been wounded and captured at Brandy Station and there hadn't been any word on his condition.

Like any father, Lee was very worried about his son, but he wasn't just any father. He was the General of the Army. The hopes and dreams of all the men around him rested squarely on his shoulders. He couldn't afford to show any signs of being worried about a merely personal concern.

A private guided him up the stairs to the second floor then into a bare large room with an unfinished floor and a staircase in the middle of the room. The two elegant half circle windows in the bare brick walls seemed so out of balance in the unfinished space.

He dismissed the private then climbed up the stairs, as he turned at the end of the first flight, he looked up through the large *rectangular opening and to the arch way (formed by two of the columns supporting the roof) silhouetted by the pale blue sky and clouds.*

As he came up to the white railing surrounding the copula, he heard a cannon roar behind him. He turned and tracked the explosive shell's lighted fuse as it traced a path across the early evening sky, exploding about fifty- feet above the bald hill. He followed along the rail to the other side of the copula looking east in the direction of the Yankees.

He looked through his field glasses as a Yankee cannon fired an answering volley. He could tell the shell was going to be wide and to the right of the main seminary building. It could be that the gunners knew Yankee wounded were inside.

Lee tested the white wooden railing to make sure it could support his weight before he leaned on it. He then zeroed in on the bald hill where he saw the Union troops digging in. The longer it took Ewell to make his attack, the more dead and wounded men would cover the ground.

Lee's gaze did not waver as he scanned the area for the gray-clad troops. He found them on a small hill to the north. He couldn't see any organized activity that suggested an attack would be starting soon. They just seemed to be standing around watching the Yankees build up their defenses.

Why aren't they attacking? When he lowered his field glasses and examined the panoramic view of the area, the first thing he noticed was the town. Gettysburg was not a large town, but its narrow streets would make attacking through it exceedingly difficult. Battle plans would be hard to prepare, for the town separated the centers of the two armies.

If Ewell doesn't carry that hill today and I attack tomorrow, the advance will have to start from one of the flanks, not the center, he thought.

Lee shook his head as he pondered his dilemma. A.P. Hill had gotten him into a battle he wasn't ready to fight. Dick Ewell showed up at the right place and right time and helped Hill drive the enemy from the field.

Raising his field glasses, he again focused in on the bald hill. *I don't understand,* he thought. With an opportunity to finish the job, Ewell delays, and Longstreet feels we should leave the town to the Union army and retreat to ground more to his liking.

Lee then scanned the landscape to the north. There was still no sign of Stuart. "Where is he?" he muttered.

There were footsteps on the wooden stairs. "General, do you mind if I join you?" Colonel Armistead Long called up through the opening.

"Glad to have the company, Armistead," Lee answered his secretary. "Have we gotten any messages from General Ewell?"

"None since Lieutenant Smith delivered Ewell's request that Hill provide support for the attack," Armistead said as he worked his way around the copula to join Lee.

"Armistead, have you heard from your wife lately?"

"No, sir. I haven't."

"Looking at the Yankees got me to wondering how your mother-in-law was doing. She's a fine woman, and I feel sadness for her loss."

"Last I heard, sir, she's doing well, all things considered. I wasn't aware that you knew her, sir."

"I don't know her well, but before the war, I came across her and Edwin at various social functions. She impressed me as a fine woman. When you have the opportunity to write your wife, could you ask her to convey my condolences to her mother?"

"I would be happy to, sir."

Those were happier times. They were one country, one army. The war had split the country, the army, and even families.

Armistead gave Lee a funny look. Lee could tell what he was thinking. It'd been two months since they'd gotten word that Union Major General Edwin Sumner had died of an illness. Before the war, Armistead had served on his father-in-law's staff. They were almost like father and son. When Virginia seceded, he made the very difficult decision to follow his conscience and resign from the Union army to join Lee's staff.

After a few moments, Lee broke the silence. "I've been thinking a lot about family lately."

"Ah, I understand, sir. I'm worried about him too."

Lee nodded and then turned back to the east, facing the Union line. "Armistead, I'm blind, and I don't like it one bit. Stuart has never let me down before, but now I fear he has let us all down. I think it's time for him to come home. I need you to find some men who are familiar with the area. We are going to send them out to find Stuart and bring him back to us."

"Yes, sir."

"After we get that taken care of, I would like you to ride with me to see General Ewell. I'm sure he's not going to continue the battle this evening. I need to find out why and the condition of his corps."

"Yes sir, but General, I think you need to get something to eat before we go over to see General Ewell. You haven't eaten since early today. You need to keep up your strength."

"You're right. Would you mind asking Mrs. Thompson if she would mind fixing me a little something? I am feeling hungry."

"No, sir. I will do it right away."

Lee turned back to his men on the small hill. They were still standing around. He wondered why they didn't attack. Tomorrow would be much more challenging.

Near the entrance to the cemetery, Win Hancock got off his horse. The sun had already set behind South Mountain. He hoped for a quick twilight. He would only feel comfortable once total darkness had set in over the hills southeast of Gettysburg. He was surprised the Rebels hadn't followed up their victory by storming Cemetery Hill. It would have been an easy position to take a few hours ago. Now, old Bobby Lee would have to work hard if he wanted it.

Shortly after five, the Twelfth Corps arrived with Major General Henry Slocum in the lead. Slocum decided to let Hancock temporarily retain command, since he was in the midst of placing troops and preparing a defense for the sure-to-come Rebel attack.

After a short conference, Hancock and Slocum agreed to split the Twelfth Corps, placing each division on a flank of the quickly assembling defensive line. The First Division took a position on the right, near a hill owned by the Culp family. The Second Division extended the line on the left, running down Cemetery Ridge towards a bare-faced hill the locals called Little Round Top.

Hancock removed his hat. The weight of overall command was finally off his shoulders. Slocum had finally agreed to take control of the army. For the first time in over a month, Hancock found himself with nothing to do. It would be morning before his own corps would make it to Gettysburg.

Loosely holding his horse's reins, he looked up into the ever-blackening sky. For a moment he felt almost like a school kid again, looking up at the twinkling stars. He let the weight and pressure of command slip from his shoulders, and, for a few minutes, he breathed deeply and relaxed.

A group of soldiers came riding by Hancock, headed for General Slocum's headquarters. In the flickering light from surrounding campfires, Hancock recognized Major General Dan Sickles, the Third Corps commander, riding in the lead. He was pleased when they passed without recognizing him. He didn't want Sickles to spoil his evening.

Hancock was not surprised to see him. Sickles had earlier sent word that he was rushing one of his two divisions to Gettysburg with all possible speed and the other division would be up after dark.

Although his corps was much farther away when the fighting started, Sickles had almost beaten Slocum's corps to Gettysburg. While Slocum had waited for orders, Sickles had rushed to the sounds of the guns without waiting for word from the commanding general. It was typical Sickles.

Sickles had the heart of a soldier. He always rushed to the sound of the fighting. Too bad he didn't have the brains for it. Having the heart of a soldier, but not the brains, gets good men killed.

Hancock knew it really wasn't Sickles' fault. After all, he was a lawyer, not a soldier. Sickles knew all about law and politics, being a United States Congressman from New York, but he just didn't have the head for being a soldier.

Hancock knew it was Sickles' political pull that had propelled him from colonel to major general in one year. It certainly wasn't his actions on the field of battle.

Sickles was rash and inexperienced—a costly combination. At Chancellorsville, while a signal Rebel brigade tied down Sickles' entire corps, Stonewall Jackson was able to get the rest of his corps behind the Eleventh Corps. Crashing through the woods into Howard's Corps while they were setting up camp for the night, Jackson quickly routed them. It spelled the end of the Union army's advance at Chancellorsville.

While Howard got the blame, Hancock knew it was Sickles' fault. An experienced officer would have seen that he was only facing a rear-guard unit and pressed the attack. Instead, Sickles let his corps get bogged down and Howard's Eleventh paid the price. Still, Hancock couldn't deny Sickles was a very sharp lawyer. Any other man would be in jail for murder, but Sickles had gotten away with it.

A few years back, he'd caught his wife having an affair, as rash as ever, Sickles up and shot the man dead. It didn't matter to Sickles that his wife was carrying on with the son of an American legend. So, what if Phillip Key's father had written "The Star-Spangled Banner"? He shouldn't have been messing with his wife.

During the trial, Sickles thought up a new type of defense. His attorneys argued that the rage in his heart had overcome his sense of reason. Obviously, he couldn't be held accountable for an act he had committed during this period of temporary insanity.

Hancock almost laughed. Sickles got away with murder because he was temporarily insane.

Hancock felt sorry for Andrew Humphreys, the only experienced officer in Sickles' corps. David Birney, the Third's other division commander, was also a lawyer. Poor Andrew—stuck between two lawyers. Lord, have mercy on him.

Hancock looked back at the stars and chased the thoughts about the Third Corps from his mind. Fortunately, they were Meade's problem, not his. Hancock took a deep breath and turned to the east as the moon slowly rose above the trees. He took comfort in the heavenly guardian of the night, bringing peace to the fields around Gettysburg. He knew things would be much different in the morning.

Chapter 5

Bill Sellers rested his right index finger on his black queen. Carefully, he scanned the board, making sure he hadn't missed a move. Slowly, he pulled his hand away and said triumphantly, "Checkmate." He'd beaten Robert for the third game in a row.

Bill looked across the board into his friend's eyes. Even in the dim light of the campfire, he noticed that Robert was a thousand miles away. It didn't matter. Chess was like war. You played to win and there were no excuses or rewards for coming in second place.

"You wanna lose another?"

"No, I think three games is enough."

"Bobby, play another. It'll do you good. Keep your mind off things."

"Lieutenant Wicker, I don't think it's proper for you to allow a private to call you by your Christian name," Colonel Oates announced as he and acting Captain J.J. Hatcher stepped out of the darkness into the light of the fire. Bill and Robert jumped to their feet and saluted. The colonel returned it. Robert glanced at Hatcher. It was apparent he disapproved of Robert's socializing with an enlisted man. "I meant no disrespect to the Lieutenant, Colonel William, cousin, sir," Bill spoke up.

Even in the low light of the fire, Robert saw Hatcher's face flash red, "Private Sellers—"

Oates cut him off with a fatherly tone, "I wish you wouldn't call me that."

"But, Colonel, before you took your long vacation, I used to call you Billyboy. I just reckoned Colonel William sounded more military-like."

"It's hard commanding a regiment filled with relatives," Oates said, glancing to Robert.

"I'm glad he's your relative and not mine," Robert chuckled.

"Bobby, I mean Lieutenant, that wasn't called for," Bill protested.

"Maybe not, but it's true." Robert laughed. "It's bad enough that we grew up together. If we were related, you would be unbearable."

"You'ns keep talkin' like that, I'm gonna get all bothered up. I just might even start thinkin' of transferrin' over to the Fifty-first Mounted Infantry. Matthew would appreciate havin' me around."

"Maybe he would, but I already wrote the colonel commanding the Fifty-first. He doesn't want you either," Oates quipped. Even Hatcher chuckled at that remark. "By the way, Lieutenant, how's your little brother doing?"

"I haven't heard from him in a while, sir. The last time he wrote they were in Tennessee."

Oates shook his head. "War is no place for children."

"I agree, sir, but Matthew is fifteen and we have drummer boys who aren't that old," Robert said.

"I know, I know. Still, war is a hard place for a boy to grow up."

"At least Matthew gets to ride around the countryside. It's got to be better than marching. I sure could have used a horse today," Robert chuckled.

"Your old wound bothering you?"

Bill roared with laughter. "No, cousin, it wasn't the war wound that had him all out of kilter today."

"Fruit?" Oates asked.

Bill nodded.

"Lieutenant, you should have known better," the colonel said firmly.

"Yes, sir. I should have."

Elisha stepped out from the darkness. "What all y'all talkin' about?"

"Oh God, another cousin!" the colonel moaned.

Elisha frowned. "What's botherin' you, sir? Cousin Bill makin' trouble again?"

"Me? I don't—"

Cutting Bill off in mid-sentence, Oates raised his voice, "Gentlemen." Bill noticed the change in the colonel's voice from cousin to commanding officer. Obviously so did Robert and Elisa as all of them quieted down.

Colonel Oates nodded approvingly. "I'd like to continue this family reunion, but there is work to be done. We received word from General Hood this evening we march at three in the morning. Lieutenant Hatcher, make sure your men get some rest tonight and keep them away from the fruit."

"Yes, sir. I'll have the men ready."

"Very well. Goodnight, Lieutenants . . . cousins."

Robert, Hatcher, and the Sellers boys came to attention and saluted. Oates returned their salutes, took a step back, and walked away from the firelight, shaking his head again as his jaw tightened. He didn't know what he was going to do with his Sellers cousins.

William Oates really didn't mind having family in the regiment. In fact, he was extremely happy to have his brother John with him, but the Sellers were a different matter. They were much younger, and they had never really been close to him, yet they treated him like he was an intimate member of the family. Maybe it was their way of making up for lost time.

"Your long vacation," that's what the family liked to call it. Oates rubbed his forehead. *No regrets*, he told himself. Yes, he'd missed his family, but it'd been an exciting adventure, or at least, it seemed that way, looking back on it.

Yes, he'd been hot-tempered. *What was her first name?* He couldn't remember. It didn't matter. It really had nothing to do with her. *Or did it?* Miss Post, the spiritual medium. If he hadn't discovered she was a fake, her father wouldn't have had a reason to come after him. There wouldn't have been a fight, and he wouldn't have had to run from the law for cracking open the old man's skull.

No. It wasn't Miss Post or her father. It was him. If he hadn't had that fight, it would have been something else, maybe something worse.

No regrets? Maybe some. He knew he was angry, hot-tempered, easy to provoke, his father's son. He shuddered at the thought, yet he knew full well that he would never beat a son the way his father had hit him.

He realized more and more that the war had somehow changed him. He no longer looked for an excuse to fight. He'd seen enough fighting to last a lifetime.

He knew it was the reason he really hadn't gotten angry with the Sellers boys. Before the war, he would have taken their lack of strict military courtesy as an insult and punished them severely. Now, he saw it as their way of just trying to be like family.

"Could you two excuse me and the lieutenant?" From Hatcher's sharp tone, they all knew the question was in reality an order. The Sellers boys saluted and left.

Robert knew what Hatcher was angry about, and he didn't care. He and Bill Sellers had been friends for as long as Robert could remember. He wasn't going to stop being Bill's friend just because he outranked him.

"When you going to start acting like an officer?" Hatcher snapped.

"They're my friends."

"It breaks down discipline in the ranks."

"Bullshit." He never meant to say it out loud, but before he could stop himself, it was over and done with. Before Hatcher could say anything, Robert added "sir."

"What did you say?"

"You heard me," Robert snapped back.

"That's insubordination!"

"It's the truth. Elisha and Bill have been my friends since we were kids. Me being an officer doesn't change that."

"The other men see—"

"That my friendship doesn't gain either of them any special treatment," Robert snapped this time purposely leaving off the sir.

"I can see why the board passed you over for promotion."

"Why? Cause I don't act like an asshole around my friends?"

"You're out of line," Hatcher said, his eyes narrowing as he stood there silently fuming.

Robert made a gurgling sound in his throat. He knew he had Hatcher boxed in a corner. He'd only been with the company a week, not even enough time to learn all the names of the thirty-eight men in the company, let alone gain their trust.

"Have the first sergeant pass the marching orders to the company," Hatcher finally said.

Robert stood at attention and saluted. "Yes, sir."

Hatcher walked away into the night. Robert knew he was pushing things, but he didn't care. Right now, Hatcher needed him and they both knew it. After the coming battle, things would be different, but until then Robert wasn't going to let Hatcher push him around.

As Robert walked into the darkness, the light from hundreds of campfires cast strange shapes into the night. From fifty feet away, Robert saw First Sergeant Dixon Bonner and Sergeant Leven Vison sitting in front of their fire. Dixon let out a belly laugh that seemed to carry all across the camp. Robert smiled. It was good to hear laughter.

"All right, what's so funny?" Robert asked as he waved for them to keep their seats.

"Leven says he don't snore."

"Well golly. Can't say I ever heard myself."

"I wish I could say the same," Robert quipped as he sat down next to Dixon.

"Tarnation, Lieutenant, why'd you go and say somethin' like that? You've never heard me snore."

"Me and half the regiment hear you every night."

"Dang it all anyway; it wasn't me you heard. It was Martin."

Robert turned away from the light. With quivering lips, tears welled in his eyes, "Damn it, Leven, that wasn't funny," he snapped.

Dixon grimaced, knowing it was one of Leven's sick jokes—blaming the dead for his own snoring. Most nights, they'd all laugh about it, but tonight wasn't most nights.

Leven looked at Dixon and shrugged his shoulders.

Dixon mouthed, "Sisters."

Leven slapped his forehead with the palm of his hand. "Sorry, Lieutenant. I shouldn't have disrespected old Martin like that."

Robert nodded as he wiped his eyes.

Dixon broke the silence. "Bobby, I bet you haven't et nothin' all day. How would ya like some boar head soup? I made it myself."

Robert looked back to the fire and cleared his throat. "Soup sounds good . . . did we pay for the hogs?"

"Chester pigs," Dixon said as he reached for a bowl.

"What?"

Dixon crouched near the fire and used a spoon to stir the pot a couple of times before dishing the soup into the bowl. "The old farmer said they was Chester pigs, not hogs."

"What's the difference?"

"Well, he said them Chester pigs were worth twice as much as common old hogs," Dixon said, handing the bowl and spoon to Robert.

Robert took a taste. "It doesn't taste any different to me then soup made with hogs, so what did we pay him?"

"The same as we paid the farmer last week for the hogs we bought." Dixon laughed. Robert grinned and dug into the soup.

Dixon hunched over to put another stick on the fire. "I did as you said and double-checked the rifles. They looked right smart the second time."

Robert nodded.

Dixon hated to admit that Hatcher's decision to do weapons inspection had been a good one. It'd been a couple of weeks since anyone in the company had fired a weapon, so he had given them an hours' warning before doing the inspection.

He also could tell that Hatcher was surprised when Robert pulled his blanket in front of his tent and disassembled, cleaned, and reassembled his Colt .36 caliber pistol in full view of the men. Hatcher did like most officers and retired to his tent.

Dixon agreed with Robert, a good leader never asked his men to do something he wasn't willing to do. Robert always made it a point to sit down right in front of the men so they could see how serious he was about keeping his own weapon clean. With its seven-and-a half-inch long octagonal barrel with seven grooves and a left-hand twist, the Colt had excellent accuracy at close range.

During the inspection, Hatcher was surprised over how few problems he found. Dixon knew there shouldn't have been any. The men had followed Robert's example and had taken the inspection seriously.

"Thanks for doing the follow-up, Robert said. "Hatcher and the colonel came by. We march at three in the morning. Is there anything else we need to take care of?" Robert asked Dixon.

"Right before we march, we better send out a canteen detail," Dixon quickly replied. With the rest of the army in contact with the enemy, he guessed General Law was going to set a fast pass with few stops; they better make sure everyone at least started with a full canteen.

Robert made a slight nod. After about a minute, Robert finished the soup and handed the bowl back to Dixon.

"Thanks. It was very good."

"Want some more?"

"No. I'm full."

"You know. I'm going to miss this," said Leven.

"Miss what?" Dixon asked, turning his eyes toward Leven.

"Sittin' around the campfire with the two of you."

"I ain't as confident as you," Dixon said. He could see the confused expression on Robert's face.

Leven leaned forward and pointed his right index finger at Dixon. "Well, you oughta be. We beat'em again like we did down at Fredericksburg and on their own land to boot. Hell, I reckon it will just plum demoralize the poor bastards," he replied as he leaned back and crossed his arms. "Old Abe Lincoln won't have no choice but to ask for terms of surrender. The war will be over. Like I said . . . I'm gonna miss spendin' evenin's around a campfire with the two of you."

"What if we don't beat'em, sir? You ever think about that?" Dixon took a swig of water from his canteen as he waited for an answer.

Leven jumped to his feet. "Lose the war? What kind of talk is that? And you bein' a first sergeant and all."

"I didn't ask you! I asked the Lieutenant," Dixon snapped at Leven.

"Well, forgive me for havin' an opinion."

"Bobby?" Dixon asked again ignoring Leven.

Robert turned his gaze toward the sky for a few seconds before looking Dixon squarely in the eye. "First off, all of the slaves would be free."

"That's nuts!" Leven exclaimed.

"Shut up! I don't want to hear another word."

"Looky here. I'm tellin' you . . . them Yankees ain't ever gonna whup our fine southron army. There ain't no way its gonna happen."

"Damn it, Leven, I said shut up."

"If that don't beat all. Here I is just tryin' to defend the honor of the army and you're yellin' at me. Well, if you don't wanna be respectin' me none—fine. I'm goin' to bed."

"Good. It'll shut you up."

Leven turned quickly and stumbled. Dixon glanced at Robert. He didn't seem to notice. Good. If the lieutenant had seen, he might have asked what the matter was with Leven. Dixon was afraid that in his condition Leven might have told him. The lieutenant really didn't need to know that Leven was a little drunk and that Dixon had also sampled a few shots of some exceptionally fine whiskey.

After Leven walked away, Robert turned toward Dixon. "What's with him?"

Dixon shrugged, saying, "So you think those no-account Yankees would free the slaves?"

Robert sighed. "They already did. That proclamation Lincoln signed freed all the slaves in Dixie. It doesn't mean anything now because our government is rightfully ignoring it, but if we lose the war, it will go into effect."

"Free Negroes? It don't seem possible. What in the hell would we do with them?"

"They can be educated. They can learn," Robert said. Dixon knew that Robert had taught his father's slave Isaiah to read the Bible, but he wanted to keep him talking.

"Hear tell. Free Negroes readin'." He shook his head. "It just don't seem possible. So, is that what you think we should do? Free'em all and teach'em to read?"

"I didn't say that. All I said was, they can learn. We could educate them."

"So, the North wins the war and all the Negroes go free?" Dixon scratched his head. "And just who in the hell's gonna pick the cotton?"

"Good question. The land surrounding Perote won't produce enough cotton per acre for the farmers to afford to pay anyone to pick it. I don't know what the Rumps, Rogers, and the other big growers would do without their slaves."

There was a loud thud and Leven started cussing. Robert pushed himself up.

"I got it, sir," Dixon said, jumping to his feet. He rushed off into the darkness after Leven.

Robert looked back to the fire. He liked to watch the red and yellow flames dance their fiery ballet. He started thinking about Isaiah. While he was almost like a part of the family, he was still a slave. Would he stay on the farm if he was free? No. He wondered what his father would do. The farm wasn't large, only 250 acres with over half of it a mixture of pasture and woods, but still, it was too much for just one man to work.

That was the reason his father had bought Isaiah in the first place. Together they grew corn, oats, peas, sweet potatoes, and, of course, some cotton. They both shared in tending the sheep, cattle, and pigs. His father needed Isaiah, and his family depended on him.

Dixon stepped back into the light.

"What's wrong with Leven?"

Dixon sat down and hunched forward. "He caught his foot in a gopher hole." After a moment of silence, Dixon said, "No lie, sir. So, you was sayin' if the slaves go free then big farmers around Perote are goin' to be in big trouble?"

Robert felt his jaw tightened as he spoke. "I don't remember what I was saying, and it doesn't matter anyway. They aren't going to beat us and no one is going to tell the free people of Alabama what to do with their slaves. That's why we're here. That's why we're fighting in the first place. The Union government has no right to tell us what to do with our property."

"Sho' nuff, Lieutenant. Tomorrow, we'll whup'em but good. But I've been wonderin' lately what our new country's gonna be like. You think the national government gonna protect states' rights?"

Robert braced his right elbow on his knee as he leaned forward and ran his fingers through his beard. He didn't speak, but instead just sat there staring at Dixon. "What're ya thinkin' about, sir?" Dixon asked after a silence.

"I'm just wondering why you keep getting me into conversations like this."

"You know me. I ain't had no fancy, formal education. Not like you, sir. I reckon I just like listenin' to one of you college boys talk such proper English and offer such mighty fine educated guesses."

"You smart ass."

"At your service, sir. You goin' back to college after the war is over?"

"I don't know. I hope so. This would have been my senior year. If it wasn't for the war, next summer I would be graduating from East Alabama Men's College."

"Hear tell."

"Yep, next summer. You know I really do miss school. Sometimes I even kind of miss old Professor Dunklin and his Greek Grammar class."

"You gotta be kiddin'."

"Yep," Robert laughed. "I hated Greek Grammar, but you know what I do miss most?"

"What?"

"Mrs. Stoudenmire's cooking," Robert said his smile widening. "She was a great cook."

"You boarded with Mrs. Stoudenmire?"

"Yes," Robert said, standing to stretch. "Her husband was the postmaster, and they lived close to school. I really enjoyed staying with them." Yawning, he then added, "Well, Dixon, this has been fun, but before it gets too late, you better relay our marching orders to the squad leaders. Also, make sure the men get turned in early. Tomorrow, I don't want to have any problems with stragglers."

"Yes, sir. I'll see to it."

"Thanks, Dixon. See you in the morning."

"Night, sir."

Robert knew he should take his own advice and go to bed, but he wasn't tired. Too many things on his mind, he walked down the road past a small church.

When he came to a large, two-story farmhouse, he paused. It wasn't the kind of building you would find back home. The red and white sands of central Alabama were useless for making bricks, but they did produce a very adequate building material—southern pine trees.

The brick farmhouse was more attractive than his family's log house, but he guessed it wouldn't be very practical during the long, hot Alabama summer. While his family's home wasn't necessarily eye-pleasing, it was functional.

With thoughts of home, he let his mind wander . . .

He walked up the steps to his family's front porch. He looked down the covered breezeway all the way to the back porch. The cool evening breeze felt good on his cheeks.

On the right side of the wide breezeway, there were three bedrooms: one for his parents, one for the girls, and one for the boys. On the left were the kitchen and living parlor.

He walked to his sisters' room. He slowly opened the door. His mother was sitting by the window in her favorite chair. She was bent over her knitting, softly humming. Martha and Jane were lying together in the same bed, both sleeping.

Robert walked to his sisters. Martha's face was taut, and her skin was an ashen color. Sweat beaded up on her forehead. Her breaths were quick and shallow. He had seen the look many times before. Death would be coming soon.

Hearing a chuckle, he looked at his mother. She was still knitting, still humming. He couldn't place the tune. He took a few steps toward her; then he recognized the melody. On many a night, he'd heard Yankee buglers playing it. It was their song of rest, but he also knew it was their song of death.

Laughter echoed through the room. Robert looked left. There was a man dressed all in black standing in the shadows of the doorway. Robert couldn't see his face.

You're next, the man said; then he laughed, a deep guttural, haunting laugh.

Robert shuddered, forcing the vision from his head. His hands shook. He clutched them into fists. *Was he next?* He turned and walked back the way he'd come. A bright, full moon rested just above South Mountain. Robert stopped when he noticed the man in the moon smiling down at him.

Raising his arms above his head, he stretched and exhaled. As he did, he noticed a faint light coming through the open church door. The soft dim light seemed strangely inviting. It had been awhile since he'd been in a real church.

Walking quietly through the doorway, Robert felt a peace sweep over him. His eyes caught the light of the candles near the altar, and from their shadows he noticed the vague outlines of other men sitting in the pews, heads bowed, caps removed. It was no surprise to him that the place was full, since every soldier knew they would fight tomorrow, and, for many, this could well be their last opportunity to make peace with their maker.

Robert slipped into a back seat and sat alone on the last pew. He bowed his head, praying, Lord, I haven't done this in a long while. *I'm not sure I even remember how. Please have mercy on my sisters and little William.*

Slowly raising his head, he tried to remember little William's face but couldn't. Swallowing hard, he tried pushing down the lump that had risen in his throat. It'd only been five years and already he couldn't remember the little boy's face. Quickly, Robert brushed away the tears as they rolled down his cheeks.

First William, now Martha and Jane. Robert prayed softly to himself, "Lord, please help my mother." He lowered his head. "My sisters are dead . . . God help me." His wet eyes gazed at the altar and then upward toward the simple wooden cross hanging above it. He wondered again why they had died. With a knot in his throat and his lips barely a whisper, he prayed: "Please tell me they did not die in vain. Tell me their deaths meant something."

Nothing but silence filled the darkened room. As Robert expected, there was no answer. Long ago he'd realized that God kept to himself the answer to the great, seemingly unanswerable question—why. Bowing his head, he placed his hands on his temples. Tears filled his eyes as the lingering question of why hung over him like a winter fog.

Rubbing his eyes, he suddenly felt weak, tired, and alone. He told himself that he wouldn't get the answer, not even in church. Painfully, he had learned long ago that yelling and screaming at God didn't do any good either. He had tried that when Martin died. It hadn't worked then . . . it wouldn't work now. He raised his head and gazed toward the ceiling of the church as if making one more attempt might provide an answer.

"Martin, you should have stayed home with your wife and six kids," he whispered as he felt a chill surrounding his body. His mind then raced to that dreadful night on the road to Winchester, Virginia. The regiment had been in pursuit of the Yankees retreating from Front Royal. As darkness fell, orders were issued to hold their position. A strong voice then called from the darkness. "Stand fast, boys. The Yankees are just up ahead behind that stone wall. Be ready. Them blue bellies might mount a counterattack." The officers were serious about standing fast, so they stood in the middle of the road and waited. It had been a cold night, but no one seemed to notice at first because of all the excitement and the threat of danger. As the hours wore on, the excitement turned to boredom. As the boredom settled in, so did the cold.

Robert was startled when he heard Martin's teeth chattering. He knew that something must be terribly wrong. Sure, it was getting colder, but it wasn't that severe. As he reached a handover and touched the side of Martin's face, he said, "I should have made you go on sick call. You're burning up."

"I'm fine, just a little feverish. Don't worry none about me."

"You're not fine. I'm going to -"

"You ain't gonna do nothin'," Martin snapped. "I've come all this way to fight them Yankees, and I'm not goin' to run from them just because I got a little old fever. I'm not gonna do it. You understand?"

Robert frowned as he nodded that he understood.

"Good boy."

They stood in the middle of the road all night waiting for the Yankees to attack. Foolish . . . they were so green.

Toward morning, Martin had trouble standing. Robert and Jacob, Martin's brother, took turns letting him lean on them.

"Martin, please. You got to go on sick call."

'No . . . I'm not goin' to . . . at least not yet. Maybe if I'm still feelin' poorly after we get through with them Yankees, I'll go see the surgeon but not before."

At dawn, the Twenty-first North Carolina, supported by troops from Georgia and Mississippi, advanced on the enemy.

The Fifteenth Alabama followed in a flanking maneuver. As they hurried through a waist-high wheat field, Robert lost sight of Martin. After the fight, Robert and Jacob backtracked through the trampled wheat, searching for Martin. After walking the field twice, they found him, face down on the cold, dew-covered ground, too weak to even turn over. Two days later, Martin was dead.

"No, Martin, I wasn't a good boy," Robert whispered. "If I'd told the first sergeant how sick you were, you might still be alive."

Pulling his mind back to the present, Robert rubbed his side. Although the wound healed and there was no pain, he rubbed it anyway. He knew it had become a habit born out of the constant nights of misery. It was the reminder of his brush with death, but that's all it had been, a brush with death.

Looking upward, Robert whispered a short prayer. "Lord, please, bless Marcena and her six children." Growing up without a father and for what? Even if Martin had lived, did the army need another forty-year-old private?

Robert then wondered what she told her children. Surely, she lied and told them Martin died fighting for their freedom.

Marcena and her children weren't alone in their loss. It bothered Robert that the company had lost forty-one good men due to illness before the regiment had seen their first combat. It tore at his heart to know that disease killed more men than the Yankees did.

Feeling fatigued, Robert yawned and quietly slipped out the back door.

As he walked, he gave a sarcastic look toward the moon. "I'm glad someone is happy." His own words made his jaw set tight as his facial muscles tensed. He scolded himself, knowing there was no time to wallow in self-pity. Too many men depended on him. He wouldn't let them down.

Turning his attention to other matters, his mind felt confused. Tomorrow the regiment would march into harm's way; the thirty-eight men in Company L would be looking for him and Hatcher to lead them into battle. He knew there was no room for error or indecision or doubt. The men depended on their officers to keep alert to what the rest of the regiment was doing. Hatcher would keep an eye peeled on the company to his right and the regimental battle flag.

During combat, the deafening sounds of shot, shell, and musket made issuing verbal orders to the regiment all but impossible. The companies out near the regiment's flanks couldn't hear the drummer boys' commands.

At times like those, it was up to the color guard to guide the regiment. The colonel marched directly behind the center of the color guard, with the drummer boys marching to his right and left. He would issue orders to the boys who beat them out on their drums. Being so close to the drummers, the color guard could easily hear the commands and respond accordingly.

When the battle sounds became almost deafening, the company commanders looked to the battle flag to be their guide. They followed the flag, and their men followed them.

Hatcher would be on the right of the front rank, and the rest of the company would be guided by him. Robert would be directly behind the second rank's left flank to make sure they stayed in line with the first rank.

As Robert started to cross the road, he wondered if the promotion board was right. Was he an officer who could lead a company into battle? Could he be like Captain Hill? Deep in his own heart, he knew the answer was no. He would never be the kind of leader that brave men would follow anywhere, but he wasn't ashamed. There were few men in the army like Captain Robert Hill.

Robert could almost hear the good captain's words ringing in his ears: "Follow me, boys. Come on. I know you can do it. Let's get after those Yankees." Robert knew then that he would have followed Dr. Robert Hill anywhere.

He'd followed him into the Perote Guards. Under the doctor's tutelage, Robert learned to become a soldier. When the guard was mobilized and became a company in the First Alabama Volunteer Regiment, the army sent them to Florida. When the then Lieutenant Hill returned home to Perote to raise a company for the Fifteenth Alabama, Robert followed him there too. The good doctor was his mentor, his friend.

Images of valiant advances crossed Robert's mind as he pictured the scene when they advanced at Cross Keys. The gallant captain, his sword raised high, urged his men forward and forward they went, right into a hail of enemy musket balls. The picture of his leader stood out vividly in Robert's mind, a man who looked so heroic, so honorable.

That was how Robert liked to remember him. It was like a painting frozen in his mind: his teacher, his friend, so handsome, and brave.

There were other pictures in Robert's mind—ones he didn't like remembering, and those scenes haunted him at times. There was the picture of his friend lying face down with his brains oozing from a gaping hole in the back of his head. Or the one of his lifeless face glaring with one eye, while nothing but a mass of flesh and blood remained where the other eye had been.

Robert wondered how long the crude stick headstone with the paper nametag had remained standing above the grave before the weather had beaten it down. There wasn't time for anything else. The regiment had moved on first thing the next morning. He still regretted that they had left him in that shallow grave.

He prayed that the civilians had given him a decent burial with a proper headstone after the fighting had moved on. He knew it was more likely that his friend still lay in what was now a shallow, unmarked grave in some farmer's field. The only reminder would be that the farmer's crops would grow taller and greener over the young captain's body.

Robert felt a sharp pain in his right side that doubled him over. He took several deep breaths as he waited for the pain to pass. "I guess you couldn't handle the soup," Robert said, patting his stomach. A sensitive digestive system was the only remaining physical problem from his brush with death. As the pain started to ease, Robert sat down in the tall grass that grew alongside the road.

His eyes followed the light in the corner of his eye back to the moon. It was higher in the sky now. He stared at the eyes. The moon seemed to be casting its gaze on the other side of the mountain.

"Tell me, old moon, how many bodies do you see lying in the fields around Gettysburg?"

He suddenly felt a cold, strange feeling crawl through his body. He tensed his shoulder.

"Tell me, dear moon, tomorrow night, will you be looking down on my cold body?"

Closing his eyes, it all seemed strangely familiar, with the next sharp pain; he remembered the last time he talked to the moon about death.

Reaching over, Robert grasped the stranger's hand. The man quieted down.

Casting his eyes toward Robert, the man weakly said, "How long?"

"I don't know," Robert answered truthfully, his forehead wrinkling. He had no idea how long they would have to lie and wait for the doctors to get to them. Cold Harbor had been a bloody battle.

In an instant, Robert watched as the man's grip tightened and sharp nails dug into Robert's palm. For a few moments, the soldier's whole body shook violently and then stiffened. Carefully, Robert lifted the man's fingers to loosen them. It was the only way to pry his hand from the dead man's grasp. For some time, Robert stared long and hard at the man's face, a face forever fixed in a horrible expression: eyes wide open, seemingly staring into the heavens. Robert let his gaze follow the man's, and the full face of the smiling moon coldly stared at him. Damn, Robert thought. Damn the moon.

Before the litter bearers carried Robert to the field hospital, he'd reached over and shut the soldier's eyes. Once at the hospital, the attendant sat Robert on a bloody wooden table in the middle of the tent and helped him out of his prized gray coat.

A burly doctor wearing a blood-stained uniform rushed over and apologized for running out of ether. A litter bearer pressed a leather belt into Robert's mouth as the surgeon made his first incision.

Opening his eyes, Robert glanced back toward the moon. "You thought you had me that night, and I cheated you," he whispered. Maybe tomorrow I'll do it again, he thought, grinning. As he slowly stood and brushed himself off, he said, "Goodnight, old moon."

Feeling more confident, he walked back to his tent. The small two-man tent was plenty big enough, but it was much smaller than the large officer tent he had all to himself until Hatcher joined the company last week. As the company's only other remaining officer, he had the right to share the tent with Hatcher, but Hatcher had asked him under the circumstances if he would mind sleeping in a different tent. He wanted to make it clear to the company who was in charge. "Maybe after my promotion to captain, we can work something out," he had said.

It was OK with Robert. He didn't want to share a tent with Hatcher anyway. Robert crawled inside and eased down toward his blanket. After tossing and turning a few times, his body's physical exhaustion soon took over. Forgetting his troubles, he drifted into a deep sleep.

Chapter 6

General Lee looked out Mrs. Thompson's front window. Even at this late hour, the street was still bustling with activity, and the lights in the headquarters tents shone brightly. He stepped away and walked over to the rocking chair, and sat down but couldn't get comfortable. Another sharp pain pierced his left side. It wasn't as bad as before. Maybe the cramps were finally going away. He then chided himself for not knowing better than to eat so much fruit.

Hearing a knock, he wasn't surprised when Armistead Long walked in. "I saw General Ewell leave," Long said. "I take it he wasn't happy with your order to leave his for him to pull back his corps."

"He took it as a personal insult and a vote of no confidence," Lee said. "He argued, very convincingly, that I should rescind the order and let them maintain their forward position."

When Lee felt another sharp pain, he felt his facial muscles tighten and then just as quickly relax as the pain eased.

Armistead shut the door behind him. "Sir, how are you feeling?"

"Fine."

"Sir, I can tell—"

"Armistead, we are not going to have this discussion." Lee didn't want his digestive problems to be of concern to others. "I want you to inform the rest of the headquarters that the Second Corps will be maintaining their position."

Armistead walked into the center of the room. "Sir?"

Lee pushed back the rocking chair. "You heard right. I'm leaving them in their forward position."

"Do you think that's wise?"

"I don't know what to think. Earlier this evening, I couldn't tell if it was Early or Ewell who was in charge of the Second Corps."

"Sir, it could be that General Ewell just happened to agree with Early's remarks."

"I hope so. I would hate to think Dick feels intimidated around Early. It would be bad for the morale of the corps."

"Maybe General Ewell just isn't up to leading a corps. We've seen it before—where a man is excellent at leading a division, but he just can't handle an entire corps."

"I pray that isn't the case. Just now, Dick seemed more like his old self, confident, surer of himself."

"Is that why you are rescinding your order to pull his corps back?"

Lee stopped rocking and leaned forward. "It was part of the reason. The other is I don't like pulling back from a forward position. The enemy is here, and I want to attack them." Armistead sat down in one of the kitchen chairs. "Does he still feel we should attack the enemy's left?"

"Unfortunately," Lee said as he resumed rocking. "And I'm afraid I might have to agree with him. It looks like the ground on the enemy's left is more suitable for a direct assault."

"Sir, that would mean Longstreet would have to lead the attack."

"I know, and old Pete feels it would be foolhardy to attack here. He had dreams of holding the high ground like he did at Fredericksburg.

"On the other hand, Dick thinks, and I agree with him, it would be bad for morale to fall back. What are the men going to think? We beat the Yankees; then we turn around and hand them the battlefield. The men aren't going to like it, and it leaves a bad taste in my mouth."

Lee slowly came to his feet and walked back to the window where he stood for a few moments looking at the street.

"The other consideration is that for a move like Longstreet suggests; I would have to have Jeb Stuart. The enemy is too close to try to maneuver around him without cavalry support." Lee lowered his head. "For all we know, Stuart could be dead or captured.

"The only thing I know for sure is that if we stay here, we must attack tomorrow. Our supply lines are much too vulnerable just to sit here and wait on the Yankees to decide what they want to do."

He returned to the rocker. "If we stay, Longstreet will have to lead the attack, and he advises me to search out better ground. If we pull back, then I risk demoralizing the army. I just don't know what to do."

"Why don't you try to get some sleep, sir? Things might be clearer after you've had some rest. I had a cot set up in your tent," Armistead said.

Lee patted the arms of the chair. "Thank you, but I'm quite comfortable resting here. Don't hesitate to wake me if anything comes up."

"Sir, I strongly suggest you try lying down in your tent. I think you would be more comfortable on your cot."

"I'm fine."

"Sir!"

"You're not going to leave me alone, are you?"

"No, sir, I'm not. It's my job to take care of you. You need rest, and you're not going to get it sitting up in that chair all night."

Feeling too tired and weak to argue, Lee got out of the chair and walked out the door without saying another word. Armistead followed him across the street and up to the tent.

Pulling back the flap, Lee looked over his shoulder. "You know, Colonel, you make a fine nursemaid."

"Thank you for the compliment, sir, and good night."

"Armistead, I expect you to get some sleep too," Lee said, ducking into his tent. Armistead went back to the command tent. Within minutes, the light in Lee's tent went out.

There was an air of excitement as the Fifth Corps of the Army of the Potomac marched from Hanover. Every man knew the situation was desperate. To lose a significant battle here in the North could signal the doom of the Union.

Colonel Joshua Lawrence Chamberlain took note of the pageantry. The marching men with flags unfurled seemed to almost glowing under the setting sun. Now, under the full moon, their shapes cast eerie shadows across the ground.

Somewhere back in the ranks, they started singing *The Battle Hymn of the Republic*. Lawrence joined in, "Glory, glory, hallelujah; His truth is marching on." He thought it was much better than the original *John Brown's March* with body lies amolderin' in the grave.

The Second Brigade was in the lead. The dust hung heavy over the Twentieth Maine. Lawrence wished they were still out front, but the two brigades had raced to see who would be first. The Third Brigade lost.

Shortly after they resumed the march, Vincent gave him the bad news: Gettysburg was thirteen miles away. It was going to be a long night.

The crowds lining the road seemed to grow as they got closer to Gettysburg. The Twentieth Maine hadn't seen anything like it. Most of their marching had been in Maryland and Virginia. There, they were the invading army, the enemy.

Here, they were the saviors. He wondered if the Rebels received this kind of treatment when marching through the South.

A loud cheer went up from the regiment in front of them. Lawrence stood in the saddle to see what the commotion was all about. There was a figure on horseback, waving his hat and yelling as the regiment marched past. Lawrence couldn't understand what he was yelling.

As he rode closer, he recognized Colonel Vincent.

"Good evening, Colonel Chamberlain."

"Evening, sir. What is all the cheering about?"

"I have the honor of informing the brigade that General McClellan is back in command of the Army of the Potomac."

A wild cheer went up behind Lawrence for General George McClellan.

"Thank you for the information, sir," Lawrence shouted.

McClellan in command? Could it be possible? No, probably not. Must be a rumor.

After the terrible defeat at the First Battle of Manassas, Lincoln turned the ragtag army over to McClellan, who knew the importance of training and organization. He also knew how to care for the enlisted men, and they loved him for it.

Within a short time, he had changed the Army of the Potomac into one of the finest, best-equipped armies on earth, but then it came time to lead them into battle. Unfortunately, he wasn't as skilled a fighter as he was an organizer.

At Antietam, Lawrence had witnessed McClellan's flaws. The attack began at dawn with the advance of Hooker's First Corps. Once Lee's men beat them back, and the enemy had a chance to get reorganized, then and only then was the Twelfth Corps ordered to attack. So it went, only after Lee beat back, a Corps would McClellan send another forward.

No coordination, no support, just each corps attacking alone. There was no battle plan, no organization. Lawrence shook his head. Lincoln wouldn't bring McClellan back. Not now, not ever.

He held us in reserve, thought Lawrence. It still bothered him. The Fifth Corps watched as one corps after another advanced on the heights above Antietam Creek. At 10 AM, it was the Ninth Corps' turn.

Lawrence felt sorry for the men of the Ninth Corps. McClellan had sent them forward; then Burnside had led them to slaughter.

In their front had been a narrow bridge. Around it, the creek was too deep to ford. The Rebels dug in on the heights above the bridge for three hours, used the Ninth Corps' men as target practice as they tried to cross the narrow bridge.

Bodies piled up along the approaches to the bridge.

Why? There were fords nearby. They didn't have to use the bridge. The attack on the lower bridge was desperate, senseless, bloody, and classic Burnside.

Thud, thud, thud. The sickening sounds still echoed through Lawrence's brain at just the thought of Burnside. The wall, the smoke, the horrible thuds caused by bullets smashing into the dead bodies he'd hid behind.

Lawrence heard the locals were now calling it Burnside's Bridge. He didn't see it as a compliment.

He wondered if they'd also named the heights above Fredericksburg for him as well. It would be fitting.

"Lawrence, did you hear?" Tom yelled as he rode up to join his older brother. "General McClellan is back in command."

"You should know better than to believe rumors."

"It isn't a rumor. Colonel Vincent told me himself. It must be true."

"Thomas, you expect me to believe that in the middle of a battle, President Lincoln would up and remove from command a man he put there just a few days ago?"

John joined his brothers. "What's all the excitement about?"

"McClellan is back in command," Tom said excitedly.

John laughed. "That's not what I heard."

"What did you hear?" Tom asked.

"I heard the ghost of George Washington is riding at the head of the column."

Lawrence laughed and looked at Tom. "Sorry, little brother. It looks like your hero was relieved of command, again."

"I don't think that's funny," Tom snapped.

"Lawrence, you don't like McClellan?" John asked.

"I wouldn't say that. I've never met the man, but I don't think he should be in command of the army."

Tom started to say something, and Lawrence cut him off. "The debacle at Antietam was his entire fault. Did you see the pictures in Harper's Weekly?"

"Yes, I did. They weren't particularly good quality. The ones I saw at the photo studio in Washington were much better. The clerk told me the photographs from Antietam were selling the best because they were the ones with the dead bodies in them."

"People are buying photographs of dead soldiers?" Lawrence asked.

"Yes. You didn't know?"

"No, I didn't. I guess I shouldn't be surprised. It sometimes seems that this war is nothing more than a way to make a profit. Have you seen what farmers along the roadside are asking for milk and butter? It's outrageous."

Lawrence's hands started to tremble as his voice grew louder. "Selling photographs of our dead? My God. And the people who buy them . . . why? Why would they buy photographs of dead soldiers?"

Lawrence noticed Tom nor John said anything. *What could they say?* The three brothers then rode on in silence. After a few minutes, the younger brothers dropped back into the darkness, leaving Lawrence time to ponder the photographs.

"Selling photographs of the dead," Lawrence mumbled. It was one thing to publish photographs in the newspaper. It was quite another to sell them purely for profit.

At least there are no photographs of the Twentieth Maine dead. The regiment never left a battlefield without first burying their dead, not even at Fredericksburg. The sickening thud, thud, thud once again echoed through his head.

It had been a cold, dreary December day. The smoke obscured the heights above Fredericksburg's and the belching, ravenous stone wall of death. It didn't matter. The lifeless forms scattered across the fields were a stark testament to the Rebels' defensive position's effectiveness.

The north wind blew gaps in the smoke, and he could see the stone wall. What are we doing here? Two corps and five charges hadn't driven the Rebels back; what made Burnside think the Third Brigade could?

"Forward!" Out into the open, they marched. Enemy artillery quickly aimed and unleashed their fury.

"God help us now," Colonel Adelbert Ames uttered. He turned to Lawrence. "Colonel, take the right-wing; I must lead here."

"Yes, sir."

Ames moved into the center of the line as Lawrence slipped over to the right-wing. They advanced over the ground littered with debris and the dead and unrecognizable parts of human flesh. Then there was the wounded moaning, crying, and pleading for help.

Lawrence slipped on a slick pool of blood. He quickly regained his footing. God help us. A shell exploded in the center of the brigade's line, and still up the uneven slope, they advanced. Excitement and dread pumped through Lawrence's veins. The Rebel fire slacked off as they moved down into a depression between the crests of two ridges. Here they were protected from the murderous wall. As they started up the incline, he held his breath.

A wounded man called out to them, "It's no use, boys. We tried that. Nothing living can stand there. It's only for the dead!"

Lawrence knew the man was right. This was the last crest. At the top, there was a slope up to the wall—gradual, open, unprotected—providing the Rebels with a perfect field of fire, a field of death, but what could he do?

Halfway to the top, he wondered if they had to do this. What was the point? They were just one small brigade. *We can't take that wall.* He put the thoughts aside. Orders were orders—they had to be followed.

He glanced to the setting sun. Soon darkness would cover them with a blanket of protection. *Darkness, come quickly.*

At the top of the crest, bullets whistled all through the air, and shells exploded in their midst, cutting the battleline into sections.

"Forward, keep moving forward." The cry came down the line, but the line didn't advance. To move forward was suicide, so the men held their ground and, in the fading light, returned the enemy's hellish fire.

As darkness settled in, the firing dwindled and finally stopped. The men crept back into the gully for protection. There, the Tweinth waited for orders to retreat to the warm army camps.

The north wind increased, and the temperature plummeted, and still, they waited for orders. Lawrence shivered. He'd left his overcoat tied to his saddle. The horses had to be left behind. There were too many fences to cross during the advance.

Lawrence felt cold and hungry, and he wasn't alone. The men were ordered to advance without their knapsacks to lighten their load, enabling them to rush the stone wall. Most of them had also left their blankets and overcoats behind. Maybe the generals had a point. Perhaps if they moved fast and light, it would make a difference. Possibly if the entire corps had advanced, who knows, maybe it would have made a difference. With one brigade attacking alone, it was just an exercise in futility.

The north wind blew stronger, bringing a biting cold that chilled them to the bone. Fatigue settled over Lawrence. He needed rest and protection from the weather. Two lifeless forms lay side by side; he dragged a third crosswise to form a makeshift pillow. It sickened him that he was using a dead man for a pillow, yet it was better than laying his head in the trampled, blood-soaked grass.

He settled into his makeshift shelter and used one of the dead men's coats to cover his face. There he rested, or maybe he slept. He wasn't sure. It didn't matter.

Softly at first, a strange sound settled over the battle-field. Cries, moans, groans of the wounded, and the dying all seemed to blend like a great orchestra's instruments playing a ghastly symphony of suffering and death.

The night grew colder, the orchestra played louder, and it seemed like the symphony was building to a great climax. But there was no climax, and around midnight Lawrence couldn't take it anymore. He rose from his bed and wandered the battlefield, helping those he could.

Other soldiers were up and about, and some helped those suffering. Others, like vultures, searched the dead for anything of value. Earlier several had pulled the flap off Lawrence's face, thinking he was dead. Some were quite rude when they found him alive. Lawrence went back up the slope to where the Twentieth Maine had left many good men, knowing it would be much quieter there. It wasn't in their nature to carry on. Reaching the top, Lawrence frowned together as he scanned the site, noticing how the wounded suffered in quiet dignity.

After a time, Lawrence returned to his bed. There a different kind of sound greeted him, a lonely repeat-ing sound of a window blind in a brick house to their right; blown by the wind, it beat out a rhythm against a wall. To Lawrence, it sounded like "never, forever; never, forever." It was a fitting reminder of the futility of their attempt to take the stone wall.

Slowly the eastern sky brightened, and still, the orders didn't come. Lawrence wondered how long they would have to stay here. The intensity of waiting grew more and more difficult.

With morning, the slope in their front now became their friend. It protected them from the Rebels behind the wall. Unfortunately, it didn't last. Many of the Rebels climbed over the stone wall and took positions at the top of the crest. Again, they had the advantage of position and once again rained death down on the Third Brigade's brave men and the men from Maine.

The bodies, which had protected Lawrence from the night's cold, now became a breastwork, protecting him from the deadly fire. Thud, thud, thud came the sickening sound of Minie balls smashing into human flesh and bone.

The sound penetrated deep into his brain. It was maddening, haunting, thud, thud, thud; yet, it also meant life. A man, nearby, slowly raised himself to peek above his wall of human debris. Lawrence blinked when he saw a hole in the man's forehead.

All-day, they lay under the cold December sky, and all day the thud, thud, thuds continued. By midday, a private from Company B let out a shout and jumped to his feet. He fired. His bullet had barely left the rifle barrel when several shots cut him down. *Why did he do it?* There was no answer. There could be no answer. His reasons died with him. Lawrence was relieved when darkness came along with the orders to pull back, but before they left, the Twentieth Maine's men had one more duty to perform. Though tired, they used their bayonets to dig shallow graves. They used fence rails carved with the names of the dead as tombstones.

"There are no photographs of our dead," Lawrence mumbled again. He patted his horse. "And there never will be."

He turned and glanced at the regiment. The men glowed under the light of the full moon. He then turned back around and yawned. His eyes felt heavy. He yawned again before closing his eyes.

"Lawrence, wake up," Tom said again. Lawrence grunted.

"Come on . . . wake up." This time he said it much louder.

After a few more grunts, Lawrence finally opened his eyes. "I'm awake. I was just resting my eyes."

Tom chuckled and smiled at his brother.

"What's so funny?" Lawrence asked as he stretched his arms above his head.

"You were resting your eyes so deeply that you were starting to sway in the saddle. I was afraid you were going to fall off your horse."

"I wasn't either. Was I?"

Tom nodded.

"Well, thanks for waking me up. How long was I out?"

"I don't know for sure, but I've been watching you for about half an hour."

"Where is John?"

"He's back talking to the Second Maine men. He thought that with the news of the defeat at Gettysburg, he should try again. I'm not sure if he is doing any good, but he is giving it all he's got. He almost sounds like he's giving them a sermon on duty, honor, God, and country."

Lawrence stopped his horse and dismounted.

"What are you doing?"

"I'm going to walk for a few minutes. I'm getting saddle sores."

"No more than a few minutes?" Tom asked.

"I promise."

Tom stopped his horse and dismounted. He walked on Lawrence's right. Each held a firm grip on his reins. It would be very embarrassing if the horses got spooked and ran off into the night. The two animals had no choice but to follow behind their riders.

"So, what is your opinion? Think John's having any luck with the Second Maine men?" Lawrence asked.

"I don't think so, but from what I overheard, he is sounding like he is going to be a good preacher."

"I'm glad. It would make Mother happy if he accepted a call into the Church. I think she is still disappointed I didn't."

"It's your fault. When you chose to go to Bangor Seminary, she was sure you would become a preacher. You should have told her you'd already decided you wanted to teach."

"I know I should have, but I didn't want to listen to her for three years telling me how disappointed she was going to be. It was better telling her after graduation."

"Lawrence, you never did tell her. Fannie let it slip out when she returned from Georgia."

Lawrence smiled. "Well, I was going to tell her."

"You miss being in the classroom?" Tom asked.

"Sometimes. I loved teaching, but now . . . I don't know. Maybe Father knew me better than I thought he did. Maybe I should have gone to West Point."

"You regretting becoming a professor?"

"No, not really, but I don't think I will ever be able to go back to it."

"Now you're talking crazy. Teaching is your life."

When Lawrence's horse then reared up, he pulled hard on the reins, and the horse settled down. "Not anymore. This horrible, wonderful, frightening, exhilarating experience has changed me . . . has changed us all. I just don't see myself going back into the classroom.

"Then there was the fight over me leaving. The College Board had no trouble with me going to Europe to study, but they fought my appointment as an officer."

"They changed their minds and voted their approval. They'll gladly take you back."

"I know, but there were hard feelings when I left."

"Sounds like there still is," Tom observed.

"They had no right defaming me to the governor. The nerve telling him I was too mild-mannered to be a soldier."

"No, they didn't, but they saw a bigger issue. If something happens to you, there's going to be a power struggle on the board, so your supporters didn't want you to join the army," Tom pointed out.

"I got more support from my enemies."

"Well, they have more to gain if you get killed."

Lawrence chuckled. "I guess you're right."

"Lawrence, you're going to have to get over it. They didn't cause you any harm. The governor didn't listen to them, and I even bet that he would have given you command from the start if he thought you'd take it."

Lawrence knew Tom was right. Just a few weeks before, the governor had asked him if he would be willing to take command of the next infantry regiment. Lawrence hadn't even considered the appointment. He knew his boarding school days at Major Whiting's Military Academy in Ellsworth hadn't given him the military training to lead a regiment into battle. Instead, the Twentieth Maine's command went to a regular army officer, Colonel Adelbert Ames, and Lawrence was placed second in the chain of command.

Ames, an 1861 graduate of West Point Military Academy, was wounded while serving with an artillery battery at the first Battle of Bull Run. After returning from sick leave, he commanded a battery during the Virginia Peninsular campaign.

"Your minds made up? You're not going back?" Tom asked.

Lawrence nodded.

"Does Fannie know?"

"I've written her about it. I'm not sure she understands."

"Brother, I'm not sure I do either. What are you going to do after the war? Stay in the army?"

"No, I don't know . . . maybe . . . but I don't think Fannie would appreciate army life— and besides, I want to go home to Maine."

"You could always try your hand at shipbuilding. As much as you enjoy sailing, it seems like a good profession for you."

Lawrence smiled at the thought of going into shipbuilding. It brought back memories from his childhood the thrill of hanging his hat from the top of the main mast of each of the new ships launched in Brewer. He loved shimmying up to the top of a seventy-foot mast. He wondered if he could still do the climb.

"Maybe, but I worry about the future of wooden ships," Lawrence said. With the fight between the ironclads Monitor and Merrimac, Lawrence knew the wooden sailing ship's age could be coming to an end.

Lawrence wondered what Grandpa would think of a ship like the Monitor. She was so different from the great sailing ships he'd spent his life building. Lawrence missed the old-man. Seven years had gone by since the death of the first Joshua Lawrence Chamberlain.

"You have any other thoughts?" Tom asked.

"I could go into public service. Maybe even run for political office."

"Politics?"

"I've been thinking about it."

"Lawrence, there's no money in it. The only reason Father could do it was because he had the farm to fall back on. Other than when he was county commissioner, he never made enough to support a family. What would you do?"

"I haven't thought that far yet. I still have plenty of time before I must make a decision. It doesn't look like this war is going to be over any time soon."

Tom nodded. "Lawrence, while you were a student at Bowdoin, did you get a chance to meet Harriet Beecher Stowe?"

"Yes." Lawrence smiled. "I was a student of her husband's. The Stowes used to invite a small group of us, students, over to their home. Mrs. Stowe even read to us from her manuscript. Why do you ask?"

"I heard some of the men talking. Do you think her book caused this war?"

"No, I don't think it caused the war, but *Uncle Tom's Cabin* did give the abolitionists a great deal of credibility and wide-ranging support. Still, I do believe the movement would have grown even without her book. Slavery is an immoral institution. It was just a matter of time before the abolitionist movement was strong enough to force a political end to the expansion of slavery.

"With or without the book, the mood in the North was going to turn against slavery. It was just a matter of time. If it wasn't Lincoln, it would have been someone else who shared his views against the explanation of slavery," Lawrence said.

"Do you think a different president would have let the South go?"

"I don't know, Tom, but I'm glad we aren't going to find out. With Lincoln as our guide, we will prevail and restore the Union.

"I think the South made a big mistake pulling out when they did. Lincoln wasn't going to outlaw slavery, just control its expansion."

Tom chuckled. "You still sound like a professor."

"Old habits are hard to change."

"But, Lawrence, the war has changed, hasn't it? And I'll tell you some of the men don't like it either. They say Lincoln was wrong to sign the *Emancipation Proclamation*. They say they volunteered to fight for the Union, not the coloreds."

"I've heard the same. Funny thing is, if we fail at Gettysburg, it might not matter. England and France will probably decide to join the Rebel cause and force Washington to sue for peace. Then the proclamation would become meaningless."

The war would end. With a permanently divided United States, slavery would go on. He glanced at his brother, but neither spoke.

They drudged on into the night, moving toward Gettysburg with each step just a little more difficult than the last. *How many more hours?* Lawrence wondered as he stopped and let his horse walk up to him. He grabbed the saddle horn, put his left foot in the stirrup, and flung himself up on the saddle. Tom walked to the side of the road and stopped. He waited for John and the Second Maine men and then rejoined the column.

For the first time today, Lawrence felt downhearted. He hated the feeling. Think about something happy, he told himself. *Home.* He smiled. He always smiled when he thought of their home.

He remembered the first time he'd walked through the place. He was following Fannie and Reverend Hitchcock through the one-story house. He liked the house's design, and it was just one block from campus, but he didn't know if they could afford it.

"Previous owners have rented this room out several times over the years," the Reverend was telling Fannie. "In fact, young Professor Longfellow even rented this very room. He and his wife lived here while he taught at Bowdoin."

Lawrence's interest in the house suddenly increased. "You mean Henry Wadsworth Longfellow, Bowdoin class of eighteen hundred twenty-five, lived in my house?"

Fannie flashed him a dirty look.

"Sorry, I mean our house?"

"So, are you telling me you are going to buy my house?" the Reverend asked.

Lawrence nodded, and the three of them laughed.

He could almost hear Fannie's laughter. *I love you. I've always loved you.*

He remembered how he had directed the First Parish Church's choir. As he gracefully flung his arms through the air, he glanced over at the young woman sitting on the church organ bench. His heart skipped a beat, and for a split second, he lost the rhythm of the music.

He quickly looked back to the sheet music and rectified his error. When they finished the hymn, he turned to face the congregation, but his eyes darted back to the young woman. She noticed his glance and smiled at him. He summoned all his courage and decided that this would be the day he would try and strike up an acquaintance with the minister's daughter, Frances Caroline Adams.

Lawrence smiled to himself. He was so young, so nervous. Their relationship developed slowly. It hadn't helped that Dr. Adams wasn't impressed with the young Chamberlain's advances toward his adopted daughter. He felt his Fannie could do much better than the farm boy from Brewer.

"Colonel."

The voice startled Lawrence. He looked down to his right. "Something wrong?"

"No sir," Captain Ellis Spears said. "Nothing is wrong, but I'm worried."

"About?"

"Stragglers, sir. It's been a long, hot day. I'm afraid we could start having some problems."

"Do you have any suggestions?"

"Call it a night, sir, and resume the march in the morning."

"I agree with that one, but I don't think the commanding general is going to like it. Any others?"

Ellis shrugged his shoulders.

Lawrence thought for a few seconds. "Ellis, I want you to take a squad to the rear of the regiment. Take Sam and Tom with you. Your orders are too strongly encourage the men to stay in formation."

"Yes, sir. That sounds like something we can do."

"Anything else?"

"No, sir. That should do it."

"Okay then . . . get after it."

"Yes, sir." Ellis saluted. Lawrence returned it.

"And, Ellis, thank you for thinking of it."

Ellis nodded before disappearing into the darkness.

Lawrence patted the horse on the neck. He was beginning to like this horse. He then wondered how long he would keep it.

Robert, why are you hiding from me? I'm your friend. I can take you to see Martha and Jane.

Robert Wicker recognized the voice. It was the same one that had laughed at him earlier in the evening.

I can take you to join them. William is there too. Come on, Robert. Let's go see them.

Despite a gnawing tightening in his chest, Robert didn't move, barely drew in a breath. He couldn't let death find him. As much as he loved his sisters and brother, he was in no hurry to join them.

Letting his breath out a little, Robert wondered if the vast darkness was a help or a hindrance. While it kept his pursuer away, it kept him from seeing what he was up against. Forcing his eyes to open wider, he tried to somehow gather in just enough light to get a glimpse of what was behind the voice.

Come, Robert . . . join your brother and sisters. They miss you so.

As the voice grew closer, he wondered if he should strike first, catching his foe by surprise, but would it do any good? Maybe it was better to stay hidden. It couldn't see him in the darkness. He told himself not to move, not to make a sound, and it would pass by.

Robert, why do you hide? You know how much you miss William, Jane, and Martha. They miss you too. Robert, come join them.

The voice was much closer now. Suddenly, Robert realized it was going to find him. He knew if he did nothing, he was a dead man. He wanted to stay and fight. Fear gripped him. How could he fight an enemy he couldn't see? How could he possibly win? He knew he would die; better dying facing his enemy.

Sweat poured down his forehead into his eyes. He felt his heart pounding in his chest. He wanted to stay and fight, but he was afraid. He wasn't ready to die.

His only chance was to run away. He started slowly feeling his way in the darkness. As he built up speed, his footsteps became louder.

There you are, boy. Now I have you!

The wind felt cool against Robert's cheeks as his legs drove him faster into the darkness. *You foolish boy. You can't outrun me. You're mine!*

Robert ran faster than he'd ever run before. He didn't know he didn't care where he was going. He had to escape the voice.

Suddenly, a sharp pain sliced his right ankle. With each step, the pain gave a deeper stab into his foot. Gritting his teeth, trying to fight the agony, Robert told himself that he wouldn't stop, regardless of how much it hurt.

Pushing forward, he then heard a loud crack as a bone in his ankle broke. A fraction of a second later, he screamed and went down, landing on his chest with a thud, the fall knocking the wind out of him. After a few seconds, he tried to get up but realized he couldn't move. It was as if an enormous weight pinned him to the ground.

You should have listened to me, boy. It would have been easier on you. You should have looked me in the face like your sisters did. They died bravely, not like you. You're nothing but a coward.

"I'm not a coward!" Robert cried as he sat up stiffly. Sweat poured down his face. *A nightmare? No, it wasn't all a nightmare. They were dead his sisters were dead.* Turning on his side, Robert pulled his blanket over his face to muffle his sobs as they drifted into the still night air.

Lawrence untied the blanket from his saddle before George led his horse away. He tried feeling for a soft place to rest. He wasn't too particular. Tom and John were already asleep.

He spread his blanket out on the dew-covered ground and lay down on his back. He was glad the general had decided to halt the march until morning. Gettysburg was just three miles away. In the darkness, there was a chance they could stumble into an enemy camp.

Lawrence closed his eyes. Good thing the general was cautious. He was too tired to do any fighting. He soon fell asleep. In his dreams, she was there waiting for him.

He wrapped his arms around her, pulling her body close to his. Her soft breasts pushed against his chest. He looked deep into her warm, brown eyes. *I love you, Fannie.*

I love you too.

Chapter 7

July 2, 1863

The moon, low on the western horizon, cast a warm glow over the pale white tents. The last remnants of dying campfires added a slight red tint to the glow. In the pale light, the sergeant had no trouble finding the tent belonging to the boys. He used the flat of his hand to beat on its side.

"Let's go, boys. Time to wake the brigade." The sergeant heard the tent occupants stir, but they didn't respond. He looked in. Shaded from the moonlight, the interior refused to reveal the movements of those inside its canvas walls.

Finally, a small head popped from the darkness.

"What's the time?" asked the high-pitched young voice.

"Time for you to go to work!" spat the sergeant. The young man crawled from the tent, pulling a large drum behind him. From the other opening, the guard saw a similar shape emerge. The boys hung their drums over their shoulders. Each took a moment to flex his hands before glancing at each other and nodding.

Robert listened as the drum roll's sharp, repetitive sounds turned the quiet valley of sleeping men back into a military camp. Before the drums stopped, Robert heard men stirring outside his tent. Already he could hear Dixon's strong voice barking at the men to get up. Robert rolled over on his stomach and used his elbows to push himself into a fetal position.

For a moment, he closed his eyes. The voice was still with him, still taunting him. *You ran, boy. You're a coward. You will die like a coward.* The voice had followed him back from his nightmare. *Was it a nightmare?* Whatever it was, every time he shut his eyes, the voice was waiting for him, reminding him of what he'd done and telling him what he was going to do.

With pounding heart, Robert tried hard to catch his breath. Tonight, it would be his body lying face down under the moonlit sky with a bullet in his back. Sitting by the campfire, the men would speak in hushed tones, saying it was a shame the lieutenant had turned out to be a coward.

"Lieutenant, you awake?" First Sergeant Dixon Bonner asked.

Tears welled in Robert's eyes as he tried to answer. No words came from his lips.

Then Dixon poked his head inside Robert's walled tent. "Bobby, you in there?"

Robert forced out a yes, barely audible over the sounds of the camp. Dixon crawled inside.

"Bobby, you sick or somethin'?"

"They're dead. My sisters are dead."

Dixon knelt beside Robert and rubbed his back. "Bobby, I know how you feel."

Reaching over, Robert patted Dixon on the arm. Dixon's two brothers had died of disease at Stanardsville, Virginia. "It's not the same."

"What else is it?"

"I'm scared."

"We all are."

"Not like this. I had a dream that I ran, and the Yankees shot me in the back. Dixon, I'm scared I'm going to die a coward."

"Bobby, it was just a nightmare. If you were a coward, you would have run away long before now, and I would have shot you down myself." Dixon laughed. "Now look. We don't want Hatcher to see you like this. You got to pull yourself together. I'm going to go finish getting myself packed up. I suggest you do the same."

Dixon quickly crawled out of the tent before Robert could say anything. Once outside, he cursed himself. He should have known better than to let the lieutenant sleep alone last night. How many hours had he been like that? How many hours had he been wallowing in self-pity and doubt? This was all his fault. It was his responsibility to look out for the men's welfare, including the company's officers. He'd failed miserably, and now he faced a huge problem. Hatcher would be looking for Robert, and if he found him in this condition, he'd relieve him of his duties, and Dixon couldn't let that happen. He had to keep the captain busy and pray that Robert could pull himself together.

Dixon found Bill and told him that Robert had a rough night. He didn't provide details. It wasn't necessary. Being the lieutenant's closest friend, Bill would understand. Next, Dixon found Joe Henderson and ordered Joe to get a detail together and get the lieutenant's tent taken down. He warned him Robert might not be finished packing and, if needed, he should give him a hand.

"Lieutenant Wicker, report!" Hatcher barked.

Thank God it's so dark, Dixon thought as he rushed over to the lieutenant.

"Lieutenant, sir. I saw Lieutenant Wicker,"—Dixon had learned the hard way not to call the lieutenant Bobby in front of the new company commander—"off into the woods to take care of some personal business."

"We don't have time to be messing around."

"No sir, and he and we ain't. I've got the men packing up, and we'll be ready on time."

Hatcher spat the words, "We better be."

Dixon was insulted and felt like slugging the bastard, but he held his temper and just walked away. *Who in the hell does he think he's talking to?*

Robert took a few deep breaths and then wiped his eyes on his shirt sleeve as he listened to the voices swirling outside his tent. There were shouts, cursing, and laughter, and the noise had a peaceful ring to Robert. At least these were the sounds of the living instead of the haunting voice of death.

Hoping the voice had disappeared, Robert again closed his eyes, but as he knew it would be, the taunting voice waited for him. *You're a coward*, the voice shouted in his head. Robert opened his eyes and looked at his hands. They'd never shook like this before. No, that wasn't true. They shook worse last summer.

Letting his eyes close again, Robert felt more peace, for this time, his father replaced the tormentor with kind and gentle words of love and understanding. *Son, only God knows when we're going to die, and in his infinite wisdom, he's not sharin' it with us. Someday death will come for all of us, but if we start looking for it, we're going to cater to our fears and miss out on livin'. And always remember—*

Robert laughed. "Only an idiot has no fears," Robert said softly as he opened his eyes. It felt good to laugh. His hands stopped shaking. Only God knows when death will come.

"Bobby, want somethin' to eat?" Bill asked as he ducked inside the tent. "Elisha fried up some pork. You want some to go with your coffee?" He handed Robert a tin cup full of hot coffee.

"Please."

"Be right back."

Taking a sip, Robert thought the coffee tasted good. He then set the cup down and pulled his boots on before taking another sip. Picking up his hat, he beat it against the tent side a few times to shake out the dirt before putting it on.

Then he carefully folded his blanket lengthwise into thirds. With the blanket folded just right, he spread out his meager possessions on it: chess set, skillet, tin cup and plate, fork, a deck of cards, extra flannel shirt, two extra pairs of drawers, the small wooden box where he kept his writing materials, and last, his little Bible.

As Robert held his tattered black Bible, his mind started to wander. What if Dixon is wrong, and maybe I am a coward? If I run and get gunned down in the back, what would Bill tell my father? If I run away and survive, where would I go? Would I become a laughingstock and embarrassment to my family, just like Alex Baugh?

"Don't do this to yourself," he whispered as he pressed the Bible to his chest and slowly, silently, recited the Lord's Prayer. The night's confusion, fear, and despair were temporarily pushed aside by growing confidence from within.

He placed his Bible with his other possessions, rolling them all in the blanket, and then he pulled a small leather strap from his coat pocket and tied the two ends of the blanket together. He held it above his head and shook it a few times to ensure the roll was secure. The blanket roll served the same purpose as a knapsack, without the extra weight.

"Damn, I forgot to get the letters out," he said to no one. Robert quickly untied his bundle and unrolled the blanket to pull the three letters from his wooden writing box. He stuffed them in his coat pocket with the letter he had received the day before.

Rolling up his blanket again, he pushed it out through his tent opening. He crawled out behind it, pulling along his uniform coat, canteen, haversack, and belt with his sword and pistol. Robert reached back in the tent and picked up the cup of coffee. Straightening, he took a long drink of the rapidly cooling liquid.

A voice called out from behind him, "Mornin', sir."

Robert turned and watched three shadows coming toward him out of the darkness. "Good morning, Joe."

"Sir, you ready for your tent to come down?"

"Yes, just finished packing."

"Let's get this thing down, boys," Joe Henderson ordered the two privates in his detail.

"Someone take down Lieutenant Hatcher's tent?" Robert asked.

"Yes, sir. We did." Joe replied as his detail quickly took down Robert's tent.

Robert saw another shadowy figure moving toward him, carrying something in both hands. He hoped it was Bill with some hot pork and a fresh cup of coffee.

"That you, Bill?"

"Yes, sir."

"Did you think to bring me a fresh cup of coffee?"

"Of course." With his free hand, Robert took the tin of coffee. He handed Bill the empty one. Bill handed over the pork.

"Thanks."

"The first sergeant asked me to pick up your canteen. He's sendin' out a detail to get them filled."

"It's over there," Robert said, motioning with his head.

Bill nodded. He grabbed the canteen and hurried off.

"We got your tent down, sir. You a needin' anythin' else?"

"No—and thanks."

"You're welcome, sir." Joe and the detail carried the tent to the regimental supply wagon.

Robert took a bite from the pork. As he chewed, he savored the flavor, knowing it might be the last piece of fresh meat he would get for a while. Being on the march, with the enemy so close, he knew he'd be lucky if he got anything else to go along with the hardtack, salt pork, and coffee he carried in his haversack.

Picking up his coat, he shook it vigorously. Various bugs, spiders, and sometimes snakes had been known to find shelter in a uniform. One morning, he'd discovered snakes didn't like sharing warm, comfortable sleeves with a human arm. One bit him three times.

He'd been lucky. It was only a small, nonpoisonous black snake. One man in the Forty-fourth Alabama wasn't so fortunate. He died within an hour of being bitten by a wood rattler that had taken refuge in his uniform.

As he buttoned his coat, he headed toward the latrine. He didn't like using the open pit for a toilet. There was something degrading about squatting over it, but he had learned the hard way that using the latrine was a necessary evil.

The poor sanitary conditions at the regiment's first camp had greatly added to the diseases that had swept through the men. Back then, it wasn't unusual for a man to climb out of his tent in the morning and piss next to it—or for men to find any secluded spot to shit. The smells of rotting human waste filled the camp and attracted every kind of pesky insect.

The situation wasn't much better on the march. One night, after a long march, Robert spread out his blanket on a pile of soft fallen needles under a tall pine tree. It was only after he stretched out again that he discovered someone had already used the spot as a toilet. Despite the smell of human excrement embedded in his nostrils, he fell asleep.

It had taken a few months for the officers and men to learn the importance of proper sanitation. Things were much better now. Whenever the regiment camped, one of the first orders of business was the digging of a latrine.

Robert finished and hurried back to the company just as Hatcher was calling them into formation.

"Nice of you to join us, Lieutenant Wicker," Hatcher spate.

Robert ignored the tone. He was late, and after last night, he knew Hatcher had a right to be mad at him.

Dixon reported to Hatcher. "All men present and accounted for, sir."

"Very good, First Sergeant. Have the men stand at ease."

"Yes, sir."

Dixon looked at Robert. "Bill has your canteen."

"First Sergeant, return to your place in the company," Hatcher ordered before turning his attention back to Robert.

Hatcher lowered his voice to make sure the company couldn't hear what he had to say. "Your lack of personal discipline is affecting the company, and it carries over to the way the men treat you—with a lack of respect."

Robert fought to control his anger. "You think they don't respect me?"

"I know they don't."

It was all Robert could do to keep from hitting his new commanding officer. "If you think the men's casual manner is a lack of respect, then you're a bigger asshole than I thought you were . . . sir." Robert regretted it as soon as he said it, but it was too late to do anything about it.

Standing his ground as Hatcher stared at him, Robert thanked God when the sweet sound of a tenor rose above the racket of the brigade:

"We are a band of brothers, and native to the soil, Fighting for the property we gained by honest toil . . ." It started with one man in Company B. Quickly, the entire regiment and the Forty-eighth Alabama Fife and Drum Corps joined in.

"And when our rights were threatened, the cry rose near and far; Hurrah for the Bonnie Blue Flag that bears a single star!"

Robert was surprised when Hatcher joined him for the chorus. The entire brigade filled the valley with the sounds of triumphant southern voices.

"Hurrah! Hurrah!

For Southern rights, hurrah!

Hurrah for the Bonnie Blue Flag that bears a single star.

As long as the Union was faithful to her trust,

Like friends and brethren, kind were we, and just;

But now, when Northern treachery attempts our rights to mar,

We hoist on high the Bonnie Blue Flag that bears a single star."

Silence fell over the valley. It seemed each man let the words reach deep into his soul. Northern treachery had brought them so far from home. They would soon beat them again, this time on the Yankees' own soil, which surely would bring an end to this war.

When the singing stopped, Hatcher focused his gaze on Robert.

"Report to the colonel; we're ready to march."

Robert just stood there dumbfounded for a few seconds before he responded with the customary "Yes, sir."

As Robert walked away, he was glad he wasn't in Hatcher's position. Taking over for a popular officer, while that officer was still assigned to the unit, had to be frustrating. Still, that didn't give him a right to take his frustration out on him, and Robert wasn't going to let Hatcher push him around.

As Robert walked through the cool early morning air, he hoped they'd begin the march soon. The early morning air hung heavy, giving a foretaste of what the day would be like: hot and very humid. It didn't take Robert long to find the colonel.

"Good morning, sir."

"Good morning, Lieutenant. How did you sleep?"

"Fine, sir, well, maybe not fine, but as good as can be expected. Thank you for asking."

"Good morning, Robert," came a voice from Robert's left.

"Good morning, John," he said to the colonel's younger brother.

Robert liked John Oates, a first lieutenant in Company G, the colonel's old company.

"I heard you had an interesting discussion with some privates last night," John said, looking at his older brother.

"You've been talking to the Sellers boys again. I'm going to have to get both of them sent to a different regiment. I can't have disrespect in the ranks!"

"Calm down; they were just teasing. They are both immensely proud to be serving under you. They were just havin' some fun. They know the teasing bothers you," John replied.

"I agree, sir," Robert joined in, "but if you would like, I'll talk to them about respecting their officers—even their cousins."

The colonel shook his head. "It won't help the other family problems they're causing me. Yesterday I got a letter from Mother asking me to take especially good care of Elisha. It seems Cousin Harriet wrote to her about how worried she is about her oldest son. She told Mother she didn't know what she would do if she lost another son to this war. Don't get me wrong—I don't want anything to happen to him either, but what am I supposed to do? We're in the middle of a war!" Robert smiled and looked over at John, who was also wearing a big grin.

"What are you two smiling about? I don't see anything funny about this."

"No, sir. Lieutenant Hatcher asked me to report Company L is ready to march."

"Very good. Tell the lieutenant we will be moving out shortly.

"Yes, sir."

The excitement of the march quickly waned into boredom. Left, right, left, right, left, right, head down, his eyes squinted to narrow slits. Robert stared at the heels of the man in front of him. The regiment's drummer boys beat out the rhythm, left, right, left, right. The heels moved, and Robert's eyes followed them, his eyes and his feet.

Robert became nothing more than a zombie. His mind drifted somewhere between sleep and consciousness, oblivious to anything around him, except the heels of the man in front of him.

It was the same with most of the company. Loaded down with their packs and rifles, the men of Company L dragged on through the morning darkness.

From Cemetery Hill's summit, General George Meade examined the dying campfires, outlining the Confederate positions west and north of town. He wished he'd gotten there before dark so he could have put together a battle plan during the night. No, this wasn't the time to second-guess himself. He'd made the right decision to wait at Taneytown until he was sure all the corps commanders had their men on the way to Gettysburg.

As he looked out across the fields north of town, Meade decided to attack Lee early in the morning. He would send his troops in on the Rebel flank, while holding his defensive position in their front. From looking at the campfires, it was clear that he would have to attack from his right. The town would be a significant obstacle if he tried to attack from his left.

Alpheus Williams' First Division of the Twelfth Corps was already on the right. The Twelfth Corps' other division, commanded by John Geary, was down near the smaller of the two round hills at the end of Cemetery Ridge. Meade looked to the south. In the moonlight, he could see the outlines of the two round hills that protected his left flank.

At first light, he would order Geary's Division to the right to reunite the Twelfth Corps. He would have the Third Corps take their place. Two divisions of the Fifth Corps were only a few miles from the right flank. He knew they would be in position shortly after sunrise, and the two corps could form the heart of his first attack against Robert E. Lee's Army of Northern Virginia.

The drum roll woke Robert from his sleepwalk. As his head cleared, he recognized the rhythm. After a short pause, the entire brigade erupted in the singing of what most of them regarded as the battle hymn of the South—Albert Pike's version of "Dixie."

"Southrons, hear your country call you,
Up! lest worse than death befall you,
To arms! To arms! To arms! in Dixie! . . .
Advance the flag of Dixie!
Hurrah! Hurrah!"

The song broke the monotony and boredom of the march. As the men sang, the pace of the march quickened. With the words ringing in their ears, their hearts and spirits soared, and their steps were longer and more rapid. The brigade was needed at Gettysburg. Their presence could make the difference between victory and defeat of the entire army.

As Robert sang, "If the loved ones weep in sadness" . . . a picture of his mother flashed in his mind. He kept singing:

"Victory soon shall bring them gladness,
To arms!
Exultant pride soon vanish sorrow;
Smiles chase tears away tomorrow."

Robert stopped singing. For the first time, he felt the powerful meaning of those simple words. A victory today could speed the end of the war and send him and his brother, Matthew, home . . . home to the loving arms of his mother. It would be good to be home again. *They're dead.* He shook his head as if to shake away the angry pain. *No, not all of them.* It would be good to see Nancy, little Henry, and William.

Another William. His father's idea was to give his fourth son the same name as his poor little departed third son. *If I die, will they name another son after me?*

Robert looked over the company. During the early morning darkness, the ranks had spread out, losing the look of a veteran company. "Tighten up the ranks," he shouted.

The stomach cramps were back again. Robert E. Lee tried shifting in the chair. It didn't make any difference. Another sharp one, almost like something was jabbing him in his lower back. He took several deep breaths until the pain passed. He pulled off the blanket from across his legs and laid it over the back of the rocking chair.

He'd gotten a couple of hours of sleep in his tent when he had another bout of the "Old Soldier's Disease." It had started early morning the day before but hadn't become much of a bother until late in the evening. Three times during the night, he was forced to visit Mrs. Thompson's outhouse. After the third time, he gave up on going back to bed and settled once again for a nap in her rocking chair.

He walked out the house's back door, noticing the full moon low on the western horizon. He looked up into the deep pale blue sky, which signaled the coming dawn. *Dawn already and I haven't decided what to do.*

He shook his head and walked to the outhouse. It was the one advantage of rank he genuinely enjoyed. He was grateful he hadn't had to spend the night hanging his backside over an open latrine pit.

He felt another hard cramp. He didn't think he'd eaten enough fruit to cause so much trouble.

When he finished, he walked east along the north side of the house. As he turned the corner, his eyes fell on the large dark mound southeast of town. In his heart, he knew the large, bald hill—he'd learned during the night the locals called it Cemetery Hill—was the key to the Union position.

He shook his head as he looked at the hill. Ewell should have taken it yesterday afternoon. He hoped Ewell's indecision was only a momentary lapse, not repeated when it was time to resume the attack.

Lee looked up at the stars. If only Jackson were here, he would have taken it yesterday. He shook his head. It did no good to dwell on the impossible. Ewell would lead any attack on those hills, not his dead friend, Thomas Jackson.

Neither one of his new commanders had served him well yesterday. Hill had gotten him into a fight he was neither ready for nor wanted. Then when the battle went surprisingly well, Ewell had failed to follow up the victory.

Longstreet was another matter that brought Lee cause for concern. His most reliable and experienced corps commander wanted the army to turn their backs on the enemy. Longstreet made a convincing argument for moving the army between Meade and Washington. He had shown up at headquarters, just after three in the morning, to continue presenting the views he had brought up yesterday. Lee had listened for a few minutes before retreating into the Thompson home to try and get some sleep.

Lee walked over to Traveller. A private, detailed to care for the general's horses, jumped to his feet.

"Mornin', General. Can I do somethin' for ya?"

"Good morning. Could you saddle Lucy Long for me?" Lee asked, already knowing the answer.

The private looked confused, but Lee was in no mood to explain that in his condition he would feel more comfortable mounting the shorter Lucy Long.

"Right away, sir. "The private said after a few seconds. Yesterday, when the cramps were terrible, Lee had found that riding seemed to ease the pain.

He heard footsteps coming from behind him. "Do you need anything, sir?"

"You're up early, Armistead," Lee said, turning to face Colonel Long.

"Yes, sir, I figure there will be time for sleep when this battle is over."

"I hope you're right," Lee said solemnly. "I've thought about what you said last night . . . I've decided . . . we will attack as soon as practical. Before we do, I'm going to need a reconnaissance of the enemy's position. I'm going to send out scouting parties to find out what the Yankees have prepared for us."

"I think that is a good idea, sir."

The private brought Lee his horse. He rubbed Lucy's forehead. "I want you, Major Venable, Captain Johnston, and General Pendleton to survey the enemy's positions, keeping in mind our primary objective will be to seize that hill," Lee said, pointing to the dark shape of Cemetery Hill.

"I understand, sir."

"I need you to find the others for me."

Armistead didn't move. "Sir, how are you feeling?"

"Is it that obvious?"

"It is to me."

"The cramps are back. I'm going to ride a little. It seemed to help the cramps yesterday," Lee said, mounting Lucy Long. "When you find the others, join me over on Hill's right."

"Shouldn't you have someone go with you, sir?"

"I will be all right, Armistead," Lee said as he turned Lucy Long in a circle before heading across the road toward the south.

As he rode, he could hear distant bugles. He patted Lucy on the neck. "Old girl, it sounds like the Yankees are waking up." The horse shook his head as if to say she thought so too.

Chapter 8

With the first sharp notes of the bugles, Lawrence sat straight up. His mind raced. *We're being attacked! They're flanking us.* He jumped to his feet. *We've got to counterattack.* He stumbled a few steps. *What's going on? Why are they blowing reveille? Shouldn't they be blowing charge?*

His head started to clear. No one was running, no shouting, no gunfire. *What happened to the attack*, he wondered? It took him several seconds before he realized that the attack had been nothing but a dream.

It had seemed so real: The Rebel battle cry coming from the woods in their rear. The sudden, horrible realization, the brigade had been flanked. Panic gripped the brigade. Men cried like babies, pleaded for help, and all of them threw down their weapons and ran—all of them except his men.

His Maine men hadn't run. They would never run. He was about to order a counterattack when his dream was rudely interrupted by the realities of war. He shook off the last remnants of sleep.

There was tightness in his lower back. Locking his fingers together, he stretched his arms out in front of him and closed his eyes, and reached skyward, arching his back.

Hearing someone call his name, Lawrence opened his eyes and greeted Captain Clark with a warm, "Good morning."

"Good morning, sir. Colonel Vincent sends his compliments. He regrets to inform you the brigade is to move out in ten minutes. The colonel understands the hardship this will cause, but we are needed at Gettysburg."

"I understand. Tell the colonel we'll be ready."

Clark saluted. Lawrence returned it. Then Clark hurried away.

"Sergeant Major," Lawrence yelled.

"Yes, sir," Sam Miller said, hurrying up to Lawrence.

"We march in ten minutes."

"Sir?"

"That's what the captain told me."

"Sir, you know we ain't goin' to be movin' out in no ten minutes. It's not gonna happen. We'll get the men formed up, and then we're gonna have to stand around until some general gets good and ready before we go anywhere. Maybe half an hour, but not in no ten minutes."

"I know, Sam, but just in case, pass the word to the first sergeants to hurry their men along."

"Yes, sir." Sam rushed off as John walked up to Lawrence.

"Morning."

"Good morning, little brother; how did you sleep?"

"Sleep. Is that what you call it? I thought it was more like I passed out for a few hours."

"I know what you mean. It's typical army life—long marches and little sleep."

"Excuse me, sir," Private Joe Tyler said, walking up next to John. "When do you want me to blow assembly?"

"Wait on the brigade buglers. I'm not going to call the regiment into formation until I have to."

"Sir, you want some coffee?" Joe asked.

"Please."

"How about you, Mr. Chamberlain?"

"Please."

"Where's Tom?" Lawrence asked.

"I saw him heading off into the woods," John said.

Lawrence realized he needed to do the same. "John, wait here for Joe and hang onto my coffee. I will be right back. You got your horse saddled?"

"George is taking care of it for me."

Lawrence smiled. Private Buck was making it a habit to be wherever the Chamberlain brothers needed him. The first opportunity, he'd have to get George his sergeant stripes back.

Lawrence tramped a few feet into the woods and found a tree to lean on. It was one of the few things he didn't enjoy about being in the army and at war. Last night it was too late to dig latrines.

So this reminded him of being a kid out on the back acres of his father's farm. It made no sense, walking back to the house to use the outhouse. Better and easier just to act like a bear in the woods.

He came out of the woods to find Tom, John, and Ruel standing together. Each was holding a cup of coffee. "Did Joe bring me a cup?"

"Yes, sir, he did," Tom answered. "It was getting cold, so I decided to drink it."

"Sorry, Lawrence. He pulled rank on me," John said as the two brothers laughed.

"Here, sir. This one is for you, and it's still hot," Ruel said, handing the tin cup to Lawrence. "Do you want me to get you your horse?"

"Is he saddled?"

"Not yet, sir."

"Take the lieutenant with you and have him do it."

"Lawrence!" Tom protested. "I'm an officer—I shouldn't have to saddle your horse."

"It's Colonel Chamberlain to you, Lieutenant, and you should have thought of that before you stole my coffee."

"Sir, the lieutenant's right. Brother or no brother, he shouldn't have to saddle your horse," Ruel said.

Lawrence smiled. "I guess you're right."

"Colonel, that wasn't funny," Tom fumed as Ruel walked away.

"Yes, it was." Lawrence laughed. "And it got you to address me as Colonel."

Captains Ellis Spear and Atherton Clark approached the group. "Sir, tell me I didn't hear what I thought I heard. The lieutenant called you Colonel?"

"Ellis—" Tom started to say.

"Ellis?" The captain quickly cut him off. "Ellis?" he questioned again as he came face to face with Tom. "Lieutenant, I don't ever remember permitting you to call me by my first name. In the future, you will call me Captain or, better yet, sir."

Tom opened his mouth and started to speak.

"Lieutenant, I strongly suggest the next words out of your mouth should be either yes, Captain or yes, sir."

"Yes, sir!" Tom snapped as his cheeks grew red.

What is he doing? Lawrence wondered. Executive officer or not, he has no business talking like that to my adjutant. Lawrence was about to say something when he saw a twinkle in Ellis's eyes. Immediately, Lawrence understood Tom had done something else to earn this butt chewing.

"Now, we're even," Ellis whispered.

Tom's jaw dropped open. "Who told you?" he whispered back.

"It doesn't matter who told me. They did, and now we're even, and you're going to help me get your younger brother."

Tom smiled. "My pleasure. It was his idea in the first place."

"What are you two talking about?" Lawrence asked.

"Military secrets," Tom said, glancing at John.

All the regiment's officers gathered around Lawrence and his brothers. Lawrence spoke up. "Gentleman, in a few minutes, we will be starting our march into Gettysburg. I wish I could tell you what General Meade has planned for us today, but I haven't talked to him yet." Everyone laughed.

"I know that no matter what the general has planned, the Twentieth Maine will be up to the challenge. We have come a long way together in the last year and farther in the last week than I thought possible. I want to tell you, and please pass it on to our men, how proud I am to be the commanding officer of the Twentieth Maine."

Bugles started playing assembly. Lawrence paused and waited for the special Third Brigade call. He only had to wait a few seconds.

He looked to his left, and Joe was standing with his bugle at the ready position. Lawrence nodded, and Joe joined in with the other buglers.

"Gentlemen, have your sergeants do a quick inspection before we march. Make sure your men are ready for combat. Upon reaching Gettysburg, there's a chance we will immediately be put into action. Are there any questions?" There were none. "Thank you. Please rejoin your companies."

"Regiment!" came the call from the front of the column.

Lieutenant Hatcher commanding Company L of the Fifteenth Alabama   followed with "Company!"

The corporals sounded "Squad!"

The order "Halt!" echoed throughout the brigade. According to the standing orders, rest and water breaks would be for only ten minutes. Robert sat down on the road and stretched out his legs.

He wondered what time it was. He looked up into the sky. It was much brighter, but the sun was still hidden behind the mountain, making it difficult to guess. He thought about asking someone but decided against it. Most of the watches didn't keep particularly good time anyway. If he asked ten different men, he'd probably get ten different answers, with none of them being correct.

"How ya doin', sir?" Dixon asked.

"I'm fine. Any word on water?"

"Not yet, sir. This here road's been heavily traveled. I doubt the detail will find any."

"I agree. You better warn the men. We might not find any water until we get to Gettysburg."

"Yes, sir," he said as he squatted down next to Robert. He reached down and drew a few circles in the dirt.

Robert could see something was bothering Dixon, and he knew what it was. He'd been foolish to think it was over. He thought about ignoring him. *No, it's better to get it out in the open.*

"What's wrong?" Robert asked.

"Nothin'," Dixon mumbled.

"Don't give me any crap. I want to know what's on your mind."

"I was wonderin' if you should go on sick call?"

"What?"

"Bobby, I was just thinkin' about what happened this mornin'. Maybe you're right. Maybe it wasn't just a dream— and if it wasn't a dream, it might be better for you and the company if you went on sick call. Hatcher and the colonel both know your leg's been botherin' you. Coupled with the news you got yesterday; they'd understand if you—"

"I'm not going on sick call."

"Bobby—"

Robert jumped to his feet. "It's Lieutenant to you. I told you once. I shouldn't have to do it again. I'm not going on sick call. Am I making myself clear?"

Dixon stood up. "Sir, we need to talk about this," he whispered.

"What is there to talk about? You're nuts if you expect me to let Hatcher take this company into battle without me because I had a bad dream. I think you're the one who needs to go on sick call. Not me. How dare you think that right before a fight I'd turn my back on . . ."

Robert stopped in mid-sentence. He shook his head. That's what he was thinking this morning.

Dixon smiled.

"What are you smiling about?"

"Nothin'. I'm just glad to see you feelin' better."

"You're an ass," Robert said sharply.

Dixon's smiled faded. "Lieutenant, after what happened this morning, I had to ask."

"It doesn't mean I have to like it."

"I'd be extremely disappointed if you did."

A smile slowly formed across Robert's lips. "You're still an ass," he said, his smiling spreading across his face.

Dixon grinned, shrugged his shoulders, and turned away.

Looking at the men, Robert saw that some had small fires going, trying to brew a quick cup of coffee. Others were playing cards. Poker was the game of choice. Then he looked up the road.

For a moment, he made eye contact with Hatcher. The older man seemed to look right through him before looking away. Good.

Looking past Hatcher, Robert wondered how far it was to the top of the mountain. Fortunately, the route through the gap had a gradual incline. With the building heat and the high humidity, a steep climb would have been challenging on everyone.

Pulling his canteen over his head, he shook it. It sounded about half full. He took a small sip. For now, it would have to do since he was going to have to stretch his water out so it would last until Gettysburg.

The drums and bugles sounded assembly. In a few minutes, the regiment was back in formation and ready to move out.

"Forward!" The command echoed through the regiment. "March!" Every left foot moved in unison. The entire column moved forward. The men, stacked tightly in columns of four with rifles at right shoulder arms, moved as if they were all connected.

"Oh God . . . they're unfurling that damn flag again," someone said.

"Quiet in the ranks!" Hatcher snapped.

"Lieutenant Hatcher, sir . . . permission to speak," Bill called out.

"Private Sellers, I said quiet in the ranks."

"Let him speak, sir," Robert shouted.

He said it just to piss Hatcher off and was surprised when Hatcher yelled back, "Go ahead, Private Sellers. Let's hear it."

"Well, sir, that flag has got my comrades and me all bothered up."

Robert was surprised to hear Hatcher yell, "So?"

"Looky here, sir. We want you to talk to the general about—"

"You want me to approach the general directly—jumping over the chain of command?" Hatcher laughed.

What the hell? Robert wondered.

"Yes, sir. I's already had this here talk with the colonel—"

"Oh, so you already went over my head—" Laughter cut Hatcher off. He waited until it died down. "Now you want me to go over the colonel's head." More laughter. "And why would I want to do that? So, I can open myself up to the same type of ridicule and disdain that you are now facing?"

"Well, maybe it'd be better if ya started with the colonel—" This time, the laughter cut Bill off.

"And what do you want me to bring to the colonel's attention?"

"Sir, the brigade's new color looks like a damn surrender flag. I talked to the color guard. They still got the old national color, and we want the general to fly it when we go into battle. We don't want to go attackin' them Yankees behind that damn surrender flag."

Robert caught a glimpse of the white flag waving above the troops in front of them. Bill was right. From a distance, it did look like a surrender flag. Sure, there was a hint of red and blue in the upper corner, but from a distance, you couldn't tell it was a small version of the Southern Cross battle flag.

"Private Sellers, aren't you the one who called the Stars and Bars a bastardized Betsy Ross flag?" Robert yelled out.

"Yes, sir. I hate to admit it, but I did."

Robert waited a few seconds to see if Hatcher was going to put a stop to it, but when he didn't, he spoke up again. "Didn't you also say something about there being too many cases of friendly fire because the men couldn't tell the difference between the Stars and Bars and that damn Yankee flag? Well, Private, it seems you got just what you wanted. No one is ever going to mistake the Stainless Banner for that Yankee flag."

"But, sir . . ."

It was Hatcher's turn. "There are no buts, Private. The white on the flag represents the purity of our cause, and I for one wish General Jackson would have had one with him at Chancellorsville." Several men uttered words of agreement. "Now, I want quiet in the ranks."

Robert stepped in a hole, causing him to stumble. He regained his footing and looked up. Colonel Oates was on his horse just off the road, watching the regiment march past. As Company L got closer, Oates dismounted. He greeted Hatcher first and then waited for Robert.

"Lieutenant, how's your leg holding up?" the colonel asked.

A shiver went down the back of Robert's neck. Does he know about this morning? If so, will he relieve me from duty? Oh God . . . please no.

"The leg's fine, sir. No problems."

"I hear you weren't the only one who had trouble with the fruit. By the way, how is old shit-for-brains this morning?" Oates asked loudly, his voice clearly heard by the entire company.

"Fine, sir," came Elisha's terse response, followed immediately by laughter from all those within earshot. "I appreciate ya showin' such concern for my welfare. Next time, why the hell don't ya stand in front of the entire regiment and shout it out?"

"That's 'nough. I want quiet in the ranks," the first sergeant snapped.

Robert smiled at Oates.

"Lieutenant, what are you smiling at?"

"You know everyone in the regiment is going to be calling him shit-for-brains, sir."

"I don't know what you're talking about, Lieutenant," the colonel said with a straight face. "Walk with me," Oates ordered. Robert stepped out of formation and followed Oates away from the road.

"How are you and Lieutenant Hatcher getting along?"

"Fine, sir," Robert lied.

"I know you're in a difficult situation. It's hard to being passed over for command."

"Yes, sir."

"Would you like a transfer to another company?"

Robert was instantly worried that Hatcher had bad-mouthed him to the colonel. "No, sir. I want to stay with Company L."

Robert was relieved when Oates's smiled warmly and patted him on the back. "Good . . . good. Hatcher's going to need all the help he can get."

"He can count on me, sir." He meant it too. The fate of the company was in Hatcher's hands, and no matter what he thought of him, Robert knew that when the fighting came, the men needed their officers to put their differences aside.

Oates jumped up on his horse and reached a hand down to Robert. "Come on. We better get you back to your company."

Chapter 9

"Lawrence, Lawrence." The voice seemed so far away. His mind, starved for sleep, tried desperately to shut it out. It's just another bad dream.

"Come on, Lawrence, wake up. Colonel Vincent wants to see you," Tom said, shaking him back and forth.

He opened his eyes, and the bright morning sun momentarily blinded him.

"Lawrence, you awake?"

"I think so. Did you say something about Colonel Vincent?"

"Yes. He wants to see all regimental commanders in five minutes."

"Okay. How long have I been sleeping?"

"Maybe fifteen minutes."

Lawrence lay back down. Only fifteen minutes, it seemed like hours.

"Come on, get up. You lie back down; you're going to fall back asleep."

Lawrence sat up and stretched his arms over his head. His back was already stiff, reminding him that he wasn't a young man anymore.

"I'm up." He stood. "Did you get any sleep?"

"Not yet. I was about to lie down when Vincent's aide found me."

"You better get some while you still have the chance."

"Good idea," Tom said as he lay down in the spot Lawrence had just vacated.

It took Lawrence a few minutes to find Colonel Vincent standing under an old oak tree. Colonel Rice of the Forty-fourth New York and Lieutenant Colonel Welch of the Sixteenth Michigan were already there. Lawrence exchanged greetings with them and Colonel Vincent, who explained the particulars about the geography in and around Gettysburg.

"This hill in front of us is called Wolf Hill. It is one of the highest hills in the area. To the north is a smaller hill. I'm sorry I don't remember the name of it, but it looks like that is where the Rebels have their left flank."

"Sorry I'm late, sir," interrupted Captain Orpheus Woodward of the Eighty-third Pennsylvania.

"You're not late, Orpheus," Vincent said. "I was just explaining a little about the ground around here. Have you ever been to Gettysburg before?"

"A few times, sir."

"Good. As I was saying, the Rebels have their left flank resting on a small hill just north of us. I don't know how far their line extends, but I did hear they control the town and the Lutheran Seminary to the west.

"From what I remember about Gettysburg, it seems that yesterday's battle wasn't as much of a defeat as we first heard. True enough. The First and Eleventh Corps were pushed back, but they held the Confederates long enough for the Twelfth Corps to join them on the high ground southeast of town.

"General Barnes tells me the commanding general is planning to drive the enemy from our front, and he expects the Fifth Corps to lead the attack."

"Excuse me, sir," Lawrence interrupted. "Did I hear you right? We have the high ground, and we're still going to attack?"

"Unfortunately, yes." There were several moans. "Don't ask me to explain it. I can't, but it isn't our place to question the commanding general's orders.

"Speaking of the commanding general, he wants all his commanders to speak to their men about the importance of this battle." Vincent made eye contact with Corporal Norton, standing a couple of yards away. "Go ahead and pass out the general's circular."

Vincent stood silently, giving them a chance to read it.

Circular. Headquarters Army of the Potomac, June 30, 1863. The commanding general requests that previous to the engagement soon expected with the enemy that corps and all other commanding officers will address their troops, explaining to them briefly the immense issues involved in this struggle. The enemy is on our soil. The whole country now looks anxiously to this army to deliver it from the presence of the foe. Our failure to do so will leave us no such welcome as the swelling of millions of hearts with pride and joy at our success would give to every soldier in the army.

Homes, firesides, and domestic altars are involved. The army has fought well heretofore. It is believed that it will fight more desperately and bravely than ever if it is addressed in fitting terms.

Corps and other commanders are authorized to order the instant death of any soldier who fails in his duty at this hour. By the command of Major General Meade

Lawrence reread the last line. It was the same order Meade had given him when he put the Second Maine men under his command. Lawrence couldn't shoot Maine men then, nor could he do it now.

"I have every confidence in the men of the Third Brigade," Colonel Vincent said. "I can't tell you when we are going to see action, so you had better take care of this as soon as possible. I know each of you will get across the general's point of view, in your own way. After you talk to your men, go ahead and try to get some rest. Dismissed."

Lawrence was glad Vincent hadn't ordered him to read the circular to his men. As he walked back to the regiment, he thought about what Vincent had said. While they'd been pushed back, the Army of the Potomac hadn't retreated and still held the high ground. It was almost the reversal of Fredericksburg, where the Confederates controlled the high ground on the other side of town.

Lawrence walked up to Tom, who had already fallen fast asleep. He hated to wake him. He looked so peaceful, but duty called.

"Tom, wake up. We have work to do," he said, giving Tom a couple of gentle kicks in the ribs.

"Quit kicking me, Lawrence," Tom said, sitting up. "I was careful about waking you, and how do you repay me—by kicking me."

"Quit your complaining. I didn't kick you that hard."

"That's not the point." Tom jumped to his feet.

Lawrence smiled at him. "You're right. I'm sorry I kicked you, but my back is bothering me, and I thought I would spare it by not bending over."

"It's not a very good excuse," Tom grumbled. "But I guess you old guys can't help yourselves."

"Who said anything about being old?"

Tom just grinned.

Lawrence shook his head. "I'm not old. I've been ordered to talk to the men about the importance of the coming fight. I want to keep this informal, so I want you to have Sam Miller gather the regiment into a circle instead of formation. Ask him to have the men ready in ten minutes."

"You want me to wake Sam so that you can give the men a speech?"

Lawrence's gesture indicated a yes.

"Sir, why don't you wake him yourself?"

"Because I don't want the sergeant major mad at me for waking him up over something like this."

"You'd rather have him mad at me?"

"You wanted to be my adjutant," Lawrence said, smiling. "This is the kind of thing that comes with the job."

"What's going on?" John asked as he joined them.

"Tom is going to wake the sergeant major and order him to wake the regiment so I can give them a speech about how important it is for every man to do his duty."

"John, you want to help me?" Tom asked.

"No thanks. I think this is a job for an army officer."

Tom lowered his head; he then walked over to where Sam Miller was peacefully sleeping under a small tree. As he bent over and lightly shook him a third time, Sam finally sat up. Even from this distance, Lawrence could see Sam's face flush red as he spoke rapidly to Tom. At this moment, Lawrence was happy he couldn't read lips.

Lawrence watched as Sam and Tom worked quickly, waking up the officers and sergeants who, in turn, would wake their men. As he waited, Lawrence decided to remain standing to avoid the possible embarrassment of falling back asleep.

"Why do you have to wake the men now, Lawrence? Some of them just got to sleep."

"Orders are for me to read this to them," Lawrence said, handing the circular to John, who quickly read it.

"You can't read this to the regiment, Lawrence. You can't tell them you're going to shoot them if they don't do their duty."

"I have no choice, John. All regimental commanders have orders to talk to their men and stress the sentiments in the circular. I'm too tired to think of anything to say, so I've decided to just read it to them."

"You are going to tell them you don't agree with the orders?" Tom asked.

"I can't do that. I can't read the general's circular and then tell the regiment that I disagree with it. No commander can," Lawrence said with a straight face. He gritted his back teeth to ensure he didn't crack a smile.

"You can't be serious. These men look up to you. They respect you. And you're going to stand in front of them and threaten to shoot them?"

Lawrence hadn't seen John this angry in a long time. "Keep your voice down," Lawrence said, smiling.

"You ass!" John snapped, realizing he'd been fooled.

Lawrence bowed his head. "At your service."

"The regiment is ready, sir," Tom reported back. "John, why is your face red?"

Lawrence chuckled as he walked into the middle of the regiment.

Tom tried to find out why John was mad, but the younger brother avoided the questions. Lawrence guessed John wasn't going to give Tom the satisfaction in knowing what Lawrence had done to him.

As Lawrence reached the center of the regiment, Sam ordered, "Attention!"

Lawrence immediately commanded, "As you were!"

"Good morning, men."

"Good morning, sir," came a scattering of replies.

Lawrence glanced at Sam. The sergeant major gave him a dirty look.

"I'm sorry I had to wake you, but the commanding general wanted me to talk to you. I will keep it short, so you can try to get more rest." He cleared his throat.

"First, I want to commend all of you on last night's march. It was some of the toughest marchings we've done yet, maybe except for last winter's little walk in the mud." Several men nodded in agreement. "I've just come back from talking to Colonel Vincent. He told me that our troops hold the high ground on this side of town." A cheer rushed through the regiment. Finally, after so many battles, they held the high ground.

"The colonel also told me that General Meade isn't content to wait for the enemy to come to us. He is preparing plans for us to attack."

Lawrence paused as complaints were shouted through the regiment. He ignored the grumbling and raised his voice, and continued.

"Of course, if ordered to attack, I know there will be no questions about whether the Twentieth Maine will do its duty, but I'm hopeful the general will let us have our turn on the high ground!"

Cheers and a sudden burst of enthusiasm poured out, brightening the tired and weary faces. This time Lawrence waited until the men quieted down on their own.

"While I agree with you that it would be nice to have the high ground, make no mistake . . . if ordered to attack, I expect all of us to do our duty with the same enthusiasm you just expressed," Lawrence said firmly, in an almost fatherly way.

"We must defeat the army of invaders. I'm sure when called upon, each of you will do his duty to assure Union victory here at Gettysburg." This time there were no cheers, but instead, a quiet sense of purpose fell over the regiment.

"Are there any questions?"

"Sir," Young Lieutenant Melcher spoke up. "You really think they're going to let us fight this time?"

Lawrence could see the frustration on the young man's face. He wasn't alone. They, along with the rest of the Fifth Corps, were held in reserve at Antietam.

Then, just before Chancellorsville, the regiment was given bad smallpox vaccinations, causing 73 men to come down with the disease. Instead of advancing with the rest of the army, the regiment's orders were to guard a line of telegraph poles. It kept them busy and away from the rest of the army.

"Lieutenant, I sure hope so. Are there any other questions?" Seeing there were none, he added, "All right then. I expect we will be moving out very soon, so stay in the area. Dismissed."

As the men started to disperse, Lawrence made eye contact with Ellis. "I need to speak with you, Captain Clark, and the sergeant major." Lawrence turned his back and moved several yards away.

John started to follow, but Tom reached out and caught his coat. "He wants to talk to his senior people. Let's you and I get some sleep while we still can."

"Come to think of it, that sounds like a good idea." John followed Tom a few feet to where the ground looked soft. They lay down next to each other.

"Hey, Tom. What did Lawrence mean when he mentioned something about getting stuck in the mud?"

"Oh, that," Tom yawned. "He was talking about the mess Burnside got us into after Fredericksburg. He came up with a brilliant plan for us to flank Lee. We were supposed to make a fast march down the river, cross the Rappahannock River, and get between Lee and Richmond.

"It seemed like a good plan, and the weather started wonderfully, but we hadn't been on the road more than a few hours when it started to rain. I've never seen anything like it."

"Was it worse than the first day I joined you? That seemed pretty bad to me," John interrupted.

"That was pretty bad, but nothing like this. In just a couple of hours, it turned the roads into mud pits. Artillery pieces and wagons sunk up to their axles in the middle of the road. It got so bad we had to move off the road and march through a swamp. We only made seven miles that first day.

"The next day, the weather wasn't any better. It just kept raining. We marched less than a mile. The whole army was literally stuck in the mud. Of course, by then, the Rebels figured out what was going on and shifted their position. Burnside finally gave up, and we marched back to our winter camp."

"It sounds horrible."

"It was. It was so bad I heard an artillery piece sunk out of sight in the middle of the road."

John rolled over on his side, facing Tom. "Fredericksburg was bad, wasn't it?"

"Yes. It was."

"Were you afraid?"

"Of course, I was. Anyone who tells you he isn't afraid is an idiot. Funny thing, though. I was more afraid during the withdrawal than I was during the fighting."

"You were more afraid during the withdrawal? That doesn't make sense."

"You weren't there. To cover the withdrawal, they sent three regiments back up to the heights above the town."

"Back up to the wall?" John asked.

"Yes. Colonel Ames had overall command, and Lawrence took over the regiment. The night was pitch black. You could hardly make out the face of someone standing next to you. We were under orders to whisper so we wouldn't give ourselves away, but all night I worried they were going to discover us— three little regiments up against the entire Rebel army."

Tom sat up, stretched his back, and yawned before he lay back down. "We dug in, but if the Rebs had found us, we couldn't have stopped them from overrunning us. It was cold, dark, and to make matters worse, the enemy was really close."

Tom chuckled. "Lawrence saw a man piling up dirt, facing to the rear instead of towards the enemy. He told the man to throw the dirt the other way. The man quickly replied, 'Golly . . . don't ye s'pose I know which side them Yanks be? They're right on us now.' "

"You're kidding," John said.

"No, I'm not. You can ask Lawrence."

"Ask me what?" Lawrence stretched out next to them.

"I told John about the Rebs digging the trench at Fredericksburg."

"Oh, that was a crazy night. Our lines were only a few yards apart. I'm so glad it was a new moon. If it'd been full, we wouldn't have made it off of those heights."

"Lawrence, Tom told me what the man said. What did you do?"

"I told him, 'Dig away then, but keep a right sharp lookout,'" Lawrence said, changing to a compelling southern accent.

"That was very good," John said. "Then what happened? The Rebels knew you were there? You'd been discovered, right?"

"Yes and no. I'm sure they heard us, but they didn't know who or how many of us there were, and, luckily, they didn't try to find out."

"Lawrence, if it weren't for you, they would have found out, and we wouldn't be here now," Tom said.

"What did you do?" John asked.

Tom didn't give Lawrence a chance to answer. "This captain was wandering the heights, calling out for the commander of the troops. Lawrence got his attention, and this man rushes up to him and yells out excitedly, 'Get yourselves out of this as quick as God will let you! The whole army is across the river!' "

"Did the Rebels hear him?" John asked.

"I'm sure they did. He all but shouted it out," Lawrence said.

"What did you do?"

Lawrence changed back into his southern accent. "I yelled, 'Steady in your places, my men! One or two of you arrest this stampeder! This is a ruse of the enemy! We'll give it to them in the morning."

"You are very good at that," John said.

"It isn't that hard. French and German are all much harder."

"Lawrence, I was wondering something."

"What, John?"

"I was just wondering how you got along with General Ames."

"Ames and I got along fine."

"Lawrence is the only man in the regiment who liked Ames," Tom said.

"That isn't true," Lawrence protested, but he knew Tom was right. No one else liked Ames, but Lawrence did. He guessed it had something to do with them sharing a tent last October on the banks of Antietam Creek.

The weather was horrible, cold, and wet. The camp was crowded and unsanitary, a perfect breeding ground for disease. Most of the men were farmers and loggers who'd spent their lives isolated from city folk and the infections they carried. They had no defenses against diseases like measles, diarrhea, dysentery, and typhoid. Over half the regiment took ill, and many died.

As bad as the weather was, the food was even worse. They only had salt pork, coffee, and maggot-invested hardtack bread. Lawrence shuttered just thinking about the maggots. Along with most of the regiment, he'd lost weight. Funny thing Tom was one of the few who seemed to thrive on the diet, gaining twelve pounds.

Hungry, wet, and cold, he and Ames pulled together to battle the elements. They ripped a seam in their small tent and used rocks and mud to build a fireplace. A flour barrel, with newspaper stuffed in its holes, served as a chimney. It had worked well—at least at keeping them warm. Unfortunately, the heavy, damp air dwarfed their primitive chimney. Staying in the tent was like living in a smokehouse, but they found it preferable to being wet and cold.

It had been during those long, dull days that Lawrence had gotten to know Adelbert Ames. Lawrence knew Ames had been hard on the men, and he didn't agree with many of his methods, but he strongly felt the regiment was much better off because of Ames. His strict approach to discipline had shaped the Twentieth Maine into a fine military unit.

"Well, I haven't talked to anyone else who liked him," John said. "The men all say he treated them like dogs."

"I don't think the men gave Ames a chance. It was a difficult job training these men to be soldiers and organizing the regiment. I don't think anyone could have done a better job."

"That doesn't change the fact he treated the men like dogs," Tom said.

"Well, maybe," Lawrence said, laying his head down. He knew Tom was right but talking about it wouldn't change the past. In less than a minute, he fell asleep, knowing that a few minutes later, his brothers would do the same.

"I don't see how I could attack them on their flank," said Major General Henry Slocum. "We would have to march through the woods, down into that steep creek bed, and then up that hill. I don't think I could keep a regiment together under those conditions, let alone two corps."

"Major General Meade is determined to make the first move. He feels an attack on the right has the best chance of success," Brigadier General Gouverneur Warren responded.

From his position on the summit of Culp's Hill, Henry Slocum, commanding the Army of the Potomac's Twelfth Corps, shook his head as he looked to the north. While not as high as Culp's Hill, the Confederate line on the next hill seemed almost as strong as his own position.

Slocum gritted his teeth. For once, his men held the high ground, and time was on their side. They had a good supply line and a superior position. This time Lee was the aggressor on foreign soil. His supply lines were long and vulnerable. Time was not on his side. He would have to attack.

We should wait for Lee to make the first move, Slocum reasoned. Strengthen our lines and wait. That's what we should do.

Slocum's First Division, commanded by General John Geary, had spent the night on the south side of Cemetery

Ridge down near Little Round Top. At first light, they'd moved to the wooded east slope of Culp's Hill. They were already busy chopping down trees and digging ditches to form breastworks.

He'd witnessed firsthand what it was like to attack a formidable defensive position. While the Twelfth Corps was held in reserve, he'd watched through his field glasses as the waves of blue troops crashed needlessly against the stone wall at Fredericksburg. This could be our Fredericksburg.

Slocum looked over at Warren, chief engineer for the Army of the Potomac. Meade had sent the two of them to examine the ground on the army's right so they could help him plan the attack. Meade would lean heavily on the advice of his engineer when finalizing his attack plan.

"The terrain would hide your advance. You might catch them unaware, like Jackson caught Howard at Chancellorsville," Warren said.

Slocum thought about it for a minute. Warren was right. The rough ground would mask his advance. Maybe he could get the jump on the Rebels. He took out his field glasses and examined the steep creek bank.

He doubted that even Jackson would have considered launching an attack under these conditions. Things were different at Chancellorsville. It wasn't a fair comparison.

The Eleventh Corps had held the western flank of the Army of the Potomac, the army's right flank, at Chancellorsville, supported by the Third Corps. When the Third Corps attacked what they thought was Lee's retreating army, the Eleventh Corps was left alone and isolated.

Instead of the retreating army, the Third Corps engaged a lone brigade from Jackson's Corps. Slocum knew others felt Dan Sickles should have known what he was up against, but he didn't blame Sickles. The ground west of Chancellorsville, for a good reason, was called The Wilderness. It was densely wooded and overgrown. It was rugged terrain in which to mount an attack.

There was no way Sickles could have known Lee had split his army and that Stonewall Jackson was making a daring, foolhardy advance. True, he'd routed Howard's men and carried the day, but it cost Jackson his own life.

He'd heard Jackson had ridden out ahead of his men, scouting for an opportunity to continue the attack. He had ridden in front of a North Carolina regiment on his way back, preparing for a suspected attack by Union cavalry. They mistook Jackson and his aides for the Union cavalry and had shot him down. A few days later, he'd died from his wounds.

The wooded ground in front of Slocum wasn't anything like the great expanse of The Wilderness. Still, its rugged nature and the problems it would cause concerned him. He kept thinking about Sickles. *What if I make the same mistake he did, and we get bogged down?* It could open an opportunity for Bobby Lee to make another Jackson-style attack. *It would be my fault.*

"Do you think you could take that position with two corps?" Slocum asked the engineer. Meade trusted Warren, and the engineer had the reputation of having a good eye for ground and blunt honesty. Slocum felt if Warren agreed with him, it would go a long way toward persuading Meade to give up his attack plans.

Warren took a deep breath. "No . . . I don't think I could," he finally answered.

"Well, we'd better go tell him," Slocum said. Warren nodded in agreement. They remounted their horses and rode back to Meade's headquarters.

Robert Wicker poured a little water from his canteen and splashed it on his face. The cool water felt good against his hot, sticky skin. He then ran a little more in his cupped right hand and poured it on the back of his neck.

The march up the gap had gone smoothly. It was a good road with a gradual slope. As they came over the summit, a pond surrounded by white cottages greeted them. They halted, and while the brigade remained in formation, a detail filled the canteens. Too bad they didn't have more time. The cool spring waters would have felt good on this hot, humid morning.

Robert noticed Dixon step out of formation as Hatcher went forward to talk to the colonel. Robert joined Dixon.

"Would the lieutenant like a drink?" Dixon whispered as he handed over a half-filled canteen. Robert pulled out the cork and smelled the contents: whiskey.

"Where did you get this?"

"I filled it up the day we crossed the Potomac. I've been drinking on it a little at a time. I thought you might want a shot."

"You better not let Hatcher catch you with this. He'd have your hide and mine."

"I ain't worried, sir," Dixon said, smiling. "I gave him a shot this morning. He just warned me not to get drunk."

"You like him?" Robert asked, putting Dixon on the spot.

Dixon looked away as he drew a deep breath. "I talked to some of the boys in Company D. They said he's good in a fight. I guess that's all that really matters."

Maybe he's right. Robert took a drink. It didn't matter if they liked him. The only thing that matters was how good of a leader Hatcher was in a fight.

"Have you told the company?"

"Some of them."

"Make sure the rest of them find out."

"Yes, sir."

Robert took another drink. "The Dutch do know how to make good whiskey."

"That they do, sir. That they do."

Robert handed Dixon back the canteen. "I wondered what you were doing carrying two canteens. I hope the other one has water in it."

"It does."

"You were only supposed to get one tin cup of that stuff."

"It didn't stop you."

"I didn't—"

"Bobby, I know all about it."

"Does Hatcher know?"

"Na, him and the colonel still think it was a bout of food poisoning. None of them expect that our college boy lieutenant was as drunk as a skunk."

Robert rolled his shoulders. "I got chilled to the bone wading across the Potomac."

"Hearing that Hatcher was coming over to the company had nothing to do with it?" Dixon asked.

Robert didn't answer. He was sure his expression said it all.

Dixon patted him on the back. "I would've got drunk with ya if you'd told me."

Hatcher came running back to the company as the drums started to beat again.

"The general got a message from General Longstreet. They're waiting for us before they attack again," Hatcher said. He looked to Robert. "There aren't going to be any more stops, so I need you to make sure nobody drops out of formation."

"Yes, sir," Robert pledged, and then he and Dixon took their places back with the company.

As they started again, Robert savored the dying flavor of the whiskey. He chuckled to himself as he wondered what Reverend Sasnett would think about him drinking whiskey. He guessed the reverend would be disappointed in him.

Reverend Sasnett was president of East Alabama College and also went by the title of Battle Professor of Moral Science. That was how the good reverend viewed the teaching of religion, a battle between good and evil. Robert wondered how Sasnett viewed the war. *Is this a battle between good and evil?*

Robert didn't know the answer, nor could he even guess. Maybe it was better that way. For himself, he decided it wasn't. To him, it was a war for personal freedom and human rights: the rights of all free white men. Still, he didn't see the Yankees as being evil.

While he didn't know what the good reverend thought about the war, he certainly knew how he felt about drinking. The reverend had been instrumental in writing the college's strict anti-drinking policy. Any student caught drinking anywhere in the town of Auburn would be immediately kicked out of school.

Robert wondered if Reverend Sasnett or any other instructors had followed the entire student body into the army. Suddenly, he missed Reverend Sasnett. Or maybe he just missed school. He wondered if it would reopen after the war.

He hoped so since he was looking forward to continuing his education.

As General Lee rode toward the Third Corps headquarters, he could tell it would be another hot day. He hoped it would be harder on the Yankees than on his boys from the south. Today he was going to need all the advantages he could get.

There still was no word from General Stuart and his cavalry. He wanted to follow up on yesterday's victory, but he still didn't have useful information on the enemy strengths, location, or the ground around Gettysburg. He needed Stuart, and he needed him now.

As he rode, he felt let down. He didn't like the feeling. Stuart had never let him down before.

He'd met James Ewell Brown Stuart, known to his friends and enemies as Jeb, at West Point Military Academy back in 1852 when Stuart was a cadet, and Lee was superintendent of the academy. It was a happier time so long ago.

After graduating from the academy, Jeb had served out west in engagements with the Indians and in "Bloody Kansas." It was the first stage of what would become the War for Southern Independence.

Congress voted to allow the residents of Kansas and the other parts of the Nebraska Territory to decide the fate of slavery in the new territory. There was no middle ground. The abolitionists and slave-holding interests came to blows, and the earth ran red.

It was in Kansas that Jeb had become aware of John Brown. Lee still remembered Stuart telling him about John Brown's abolitionist activities, including how he had supervised the killing of five pro-slavery settlers in a small Kansas town. Jeb had been in Washington on leave when he learned Lee would lead the troops against Brown at Harper's Ferry. He quickly volunteered to go along as Lee's aide. They'd been through a lot together since then, and James Ewell Brown Stuart had never let him down. *Until now, when I need him most.*

Every instinct told Lee to attack. He wanted to strike them and drive them from the field of battle, but he needed information—information that he'd always relied on Jeb Stuart to supply.

He had, of course, sent out scouts, including Captain Johnston. They'd come back with information that looked promising for an attack on the Union left. That presented a significant problem—in the form of James Longstreet.

If he attacked the Union left, Longstreet's corps would have to lead it. Longstreet wanted to fight a defensive battle. It was the type of action that suited him: take a position on a hill and dare the Union troops to knock him off. Fredericksburg was a perfect example. His men had held all day and into the night as the blue Union wave roared up against the stone wall.

Lee took off his wide-brimmed hat and rubbed his eyes. The two men he needed most weren't with him. Jackson was dead, and he feared for Stuart's safety.

With Stuart, his eyes, and Jackson, his right arm, there would be no indecision. The Army of Northern Virginia would attack quickly and decisively.

Lee was worried about Major Venable. He'd sent him to see General Ewell hours ago, and he hadn't returned. Lee wanted Ewell to look for an opportunity to attack the Union right. He had to know if that was possible before he finalized his attack plan. When Venable didn't return, Lee decided to visit Ewell himself.

Looking up at the bald hill, with the cemetery near its summit, he was certain Cemetery Hill was the Union position's keystone. Take that hill, and the Union army would run from Gettysburg. Captain Johnston had reported that the Union's left flank was somewhere short of the two-round top hills to the south. The small one's western face had recently been cleared of trees. It would make a strong defensive position.

He was glad Meade had chosen to leave it unguarded. From studying the map, it seemed clear: the Union flank rested somewhere on the ridge which extended south from Cemetery Hill. The ridge would be much easier to attack than the bald-faced Little Round Top.

A full-scale attack on the Union left would force Meade to pull troops from Cemetery Hill and the wooded hill to the east. Longstreet could start the attack. Yesterday, Anderson's Division of Hill's Corps was lightly engaged; they could follow Longstreet. They would force Meade to draw even more troops from his right flank. Then there might be an opportunity for Ewell to advance on Cemetery Hill and hopefully force Meade to retreat. He wouldn't make a final decision until he talked to Ewell. Maybe there was a better opportunity to start the attack on the enemy's right.

Lee realized it was going to be up to him to continue the fight. He'd met George Meade years ago when they both served in the other army. Meade was cautious, and being new to command, he would wait for Lee to make the first move, which was to Lee's advantage. Lee would decide where and when the fighting would resume.

Chapter 10

The closer Lawrence got to Rock Creek, the more hope-less the situation seemed. Thousands of men spread out along the road and through the woods, all looking for an open space along the banks. There was no way he would be able to find John and Tom in the growing crowd.

While others were gladly exchanging sleep for a chance to wash up in the shallow waters of the creek, Lawrence scanned the crowd that gathered along the banks and decided he wouldn't be one of them. With that thought, he turned and headed back up the Baltimore Pike.

As he walked, he chewed his upper lip. He knew that the men were restless. They'd gotten barely thirty minutes of sleep when the corps was called back into formation. Then they moved a short distance to the rear, near a sawmill on Rock Creek. When it became clear they weren't going to attack the Rebels' left flank, they moved across the creek to a crossroads. From that vantage point, they could quickly reinforce either the northern or western parts of the line.

Vincent assured Lawrence it would be their last stop for a while. Most of the men did their best to find soft places to catch up on much-needed sleep. Others couldn't resist the cool, clean water of Rock Creek, including John and Tom.

His brothers had wanted Lawrence to come along, but Vincent needed to see him. They said they would wait, but Lawrence sent them on ahead. He yawned. He was glad he couldn't find them. He looked up to see Captain Ellis Spear and Roland Howard coming towards him. Roland, another former student and brother of the Eleventh Corps' commander was visiting the army.

"Good afternoon, Professor Chamberlain."

"Hello, Roland. Good to see you."

"We're going down to the creek. Would you like to join us?"

"Thanks for asking, but no. I'm going to get some sack time."

"That's what Ellis said too, but I convinced him to join me."

"Sorry, Roland. I'm not going to change my mind. How's your brother?"

Lawrence noticed a funny expression sweep across Roland's face. He started to say something but quickly stopped himself.

"He's fine, sir. Thank you for asking," he finally said.

Lawrence noticed that a sad, tired look spread over Roland's face, indicating that all was not well with Major General Oliver Howard. "Tell him I said hello."

"If you get the opportunity, his headquarters is just a mile or so up this road. I'm sure he'd be happy to see you."

"If I get the chance, I just might stop in," Lawrence said, glancing at Ellis. His eyelids were half-closed and dark circles were hanging beneath his eyes.

Lawrence then turned attention to Ellis. "I'm going to need your help with something back at the regiment."

"Professor, can't it wait?" Roland asked in a slightly irritating tone.

Ellis didn't say anything.

"Sorry . . . no. I'm going to need the captain's services. Duty comes before pleasure."

"I was looking forward to having some company," Roland replied, trying to cover up his irritation.

"Tom and John are down at the creek," Lawrence said, straightening his shoulders.

"Oh, I'll go find them," Roland said softly. "See you both later."

Both men watched in silence as Roland walked into the growing crowd.

"You think he'll find them?" Ellis said, breaking the silence.

"No," Lawrence said.

"What do you need me to do, sir?"

"Get some sleep."

Ellis rubbed his chin and grinned. "Thanks for rescuing me."

"You're welcome," Lawrence said.

As they walked along, neither man spoke until they reached the crossroads. It was then that Ellis spoke up, "Sir, can I ask you something?"

"Of course."

"Do you think we're going to get into this fight? The boys aren't going to like it if we did all this marching just to be held in reserve again."

"I don't think you have to worry, Ellis. From what Colonel Vincent told me, General Meade placed us here so we would be in a position to support any part of the line. It seems General Meade's convinced Lee will have to resume the battle. He doesn't have the support in Pennsylvania to wait on us to do something stupid."

"Like attacking the heights above Fredericksburg?"

"Yes . . . like attacking those heights. For once, Lee is going to have to come after us, but this time we have the high ground."

"Sir, I hope you're right."

"Me too. Sleep well."

"Thank you, sir," Ellis said, heading toward an oak tree to stretch out under it.

Lawrence smiled as he left Ellis and walked toward his horse. Rubbing the animal's mane, Lawrence thought the poor horse looked tired too.

Lawrence gently patted the horse on the neck. He wondered how long this one was going to last. He'd lost a borrowed horse in shallow waters of the Potomac during their first battle at Shepherdstown Ford.

Before the advance, he'd had a bad feeling and decided to leave Prince behind. Lawrence then brushed his hand over the new horse's head. He was a pretty horse, big and strong, but he wasn't Prince.

Prince had made Lawrence the envy of every officer. Even the President, while reviewing the troops, had paused to admire the magnificent white horse. *I was a fool,* Lawrence thought.

At Chancellorsville, Lawrence couldn't stand being within earshot of the fighting without knowing what was going on. He'd ridden across the river and up on a hill to get a look.

Lawrence saw the artillery shells streaking across the afternoon sky, but he was slow to realize they were firing long. He quickly pulled the reins hard to the right, but it was too late. One of the shells hit just in front of them. The explosion threw Lawrence from the saddle.

Once his head cleared, he noticed Prince was down. As Lawrence edged toward the animal, he saw that the horse's chest was just a bloody twisted mass of flesh and bones. Even remembering the scene brought a lump to Lawrence's throat. Losing Prince had been hard on him.

As Lawrence rubbed his new horse behind his ears, he wondered why he hadn't bonded with the new animal the way he had with Prince. Regardless, the new horse would do for now. "Don't worry, boy," Lawrence said, smiling. "We're not going to ride just yet. I'm going to get some sleep too."

Lawrence scanned the area to find a good sleeping spot. He noticed that Ruel Thomas was curled up just a few feet away. Lawrence had to smile. He knew it was just like Ruel to be where Lawrence could easily find him. Lawrence eased next to Ruel and lay down. In less than a minute, he felt himself falling into a deep sleep.

"You wanted to see me, sir?" General Henry Hunt asked.

General Meade looked up. "Yes, Henry. I need your help. General Sickles is complaining about the Third Corps' position. He says it isn't suitable for his artillery. I want you to ride over and take a look. My thoughts are that his corps should extend its line down the ridge, with his flank resting on the smaller of the two hills to the south. George, what is that hill called?" General Meade asked his son.

"Little Round Top."

"Oh, yes . . . Little Round Top. Henry, do you understand which one I'm talking about?"

"Yes, sir, I was on that end of the line this morning."

"Good . . . good. If you agree with General Sickles that his position is unsuitable for artillery, report back to me with your recommendations. Otherwise, make it clear to General Sickles where I wish him to place his corps."

"Yes, sir," said Hunt as he spun around and left the room.

Meade returned to studying the map in front of him, confident his artillery chief could deal with the Sickles problem. What he saw helped ease the disappointment at not being able to go on the offensive. He didn't remember the Union army ever having such a strong defensive position.

The center and both ends of the line rested on imposing hills. Plus, he'd posted Buford's cavalry south of Little Round Top, eliminating the possibility of another Chancellorsville. Yes indeed. Things were looking very good for the Army of the Potomac.

Hunt reached up and pulled off one of the few remaining peaches from the tree. Only a few of the higher branches still held fruit. It was the same with the rest of the orchard. Though the peach wasn't ripe, he didn't care.

"Well, General Hunt, do you agree with me?" Major General Dan Sickles asked. "This is a much better artillery position."

Hunt twisted in his saddle and looked back to the east. He could follow the Union line from Cemetery Hill along Cemetery Ridge. About a mile to the south, in the middle of Sickles' position, the ridge flattened out into a small valley before rising again at Little Round Top's foot.

Hunt could understand why the low lying ground troubled Sickles. Five hundred yards to the west along the Emmitsburg Road, the ground here was much higher than Sickles' position on Cemetery Ridge. Sickles didn't like having high ground in his front, and Hunt couldn't blame him. If the Rebels put artillery on this rise, it could make things rough on Sickles' men on the lower ground to the east.

Sickles wanted Hunt to agree with him that he should move his corps forward. He proposed placing his Second Division along the Emmitsburg Road, with its left flank anchored in the Peach Orchard.

The First Division would continue the line slanting back from the Peach Orchard toward the Round Tops. Their line would run through woods along the edge of a wheat field and end on a small rocky hill, at the base of Big Round Top, called Devil's Den by the local farmers.

Hunt could see Sickles' reasoning for moving the corps, but he saw two significant flaws in Sickles' plan. First, the Second Division's right flank would be unsupported by the Second Corps, five hundred yards to the rear.

Second, the center of Sickles' line would almost form a right angle. While the Peach Orchard's elevation would give his men some protection from attacking infantry, the very nature of the slanted front would be a fundamental weakness in the center of his battle line.

"General Sickles . . . before you do anything, I strongly suggest you find out what's in the woods across the road. If the enemy is there, it could make things difficult if General Meade does approve -"

Cannon fire opened a few miles to the north, cutting Hunt off in mid-sentence.

"Dammit," Hunt said to no one in particular. His place was with the artillery. He didn't have time to deal with Sickles.

"General, I have to go," he said abruptly.

"Do I have your approval to move my men to this new line?"

"I'm sorry, sir. I do not have that authority. I will pass your concerns on to General Meade, but I would advise you to refrain from making any moves until you hear from him." Hunt turned his horse toward the cannon fire and galloped off with his staff of officers trailing behind him.

A ray of sunlight broke through the clouds and shone down on her face. It drew Lawrence to her, like a message from heaven. He leaned over and kissed her. Her lips were warm against his. He pulled her body closer.

A large wave crashed against the beach, its remnants spreading out across the sand and then rolling up to them. The water was warm. *That's odd*, Lawrence decided. The waters off the coast of Maine are always cold.

He turned back to her. His love. Another large roar. He turned back to the sea, but there wasn't a wave. Another roar. He wondered what was going on. He turned back to Fannie, but she was not there. He stood and looked around. She was gone.

Another roar. Again, he turned back to the sea, but it was also gone.

What's going on? Where did Fannie go? Where did the ocean go? Another roar. It dawned on him: it wasn't the sound of the surf. *What was it?*

As Lawrence opened his eyes, he heard another roar from the north. This time Lawrence recognized the sound—artillery. He sat up and scanned the ground around him.

Several other heads were also up, most with angry faces. After the long night's march, it was easy to get mad at the artillery.

John then raised his head, "Lawrence, what's going on?"

"Probably just an artillery duel. Nothing to worry about."

"Oh," John said, yawning as he stretched out on his back and thrashed a couple of times before rolling on his other side.

Lawrence laid back down, but his stomach churned as another volley thundered from the north. He wondered what they were shooting at as he closed his eyes. Another one, was the Rebels attacking? He knew he was silly. The artillery firing wasn't accompanied by the familiar pop, pop, pop of musket fire. Though his body craved sleep, he couldn't turn off his curiosity. Restless, he pushed himself up and stood.

Slowly, he walked to the Baltimore Pike. Less than a hundred yards to the north, the road went over the crest of a ridge. He decided he might be able to see something from there.

He started with small steps allowing his body to work out the kinks slowly. As he walked, he noticed how the division was spread out on both sides of the road. Many were showing signs of restlessness. "Damn artillery," someone shouted.

At the top of the slope, he could see a smoky cloud hanging low over the heights to the north. There were several flashes of light; then, a flurry of tiny black objects pierced the cloud, arching to the west. A few seconds later, the rolling thunder bombarded his ears.

In the middle of the Union artillery, there was a flash, and a mound of dirt exploded into the air. A Rebel miss . . . then three more misses in quick succession followed by a massive explosion that threw flames high into the air. The boom of the exploding artillery caisson reached him a second later. Someone had finally hit something.

It wasn't often they'd do any real damage to each other. To Lawrence, an artillery duel was always related to Shakespeare's play Macbeth—*the sound and fury, signifying nothing.* Lawrence felt that the duels were nothing more than a waste of perfectly good ammunition. He smiled, thinking that maybe that was a good thing. The more shells the artillery wasted on each other, the less they'd have for the infantry. Artillery was only genuinely effective against one target: massed infantry. Another flash, a streak of light, a shell's burning timed delayed fuse left a path across the afternoon sky. If the right length, the shell would explode twenty feet above its intended target, showering it with thousands of iron fragments. He didn't know how effective it was against other artillery, but Lawrence knew it was very effective against infantry.

For a soldier to see the streaking shell come arcing down was enough to make even the bravest man tremble. Sometimes it wouldn't explode but would instead hit the ground at speeds more than a thousand feet per second; pity to the unfortunate man who just happened to be in its path.

Impact shells were easier to handle. With no lighted fuses, they were harder to see. There was a measure of uncertainty about where the shells would land. Lawrence knew that the uncertainty brought hope and comfort for some. If they didn't know it was coming, they didn't know they were going to die.

He wondered if the Rebels had any solid shot with them. Primarily used for attacking fortified positions, but he'd seen it used against massed infantry with horrible results. The iron balls had a nasty habit of bouncing and skipping across the ground, mowing down anything or anyone in their path.

Turning his back on the duel, he retraced his steps down the road. After Fredericksburg, he realized that even with all its destructiveness, long-range artillery was little more than a nuisance compared to the tremendous power of cannons loaded with canister. He wondered what kind of sick mind had developed such a weapon. A canister was a tin tube filled with lead balls, each about the size of a large marble, packed in sawdust. When fired from a cannon, the canister immediately blew apart, and the balls filled the air like a blast from a giant shotgun.

With an effective range of four hundred yards, it was devastating to massed infantry. Between the six guns of a typical artillery battery, they'd fire a canister every six seconds. When the infantry got close, they'd pack the guns with a double load.

Lawrence breathed easy. If they stayed on the defensive, they wouldn't have to worry about facing Rebel canister.

As he neared the regiment, he noticed Sergeant Andrew Tozier, the regiment's color sergeant, sitting under a small fruit tree, flipping through the pages of a book. The sergeant looked up before starting to stand. Lawrence waved him down.

"I didn't mean to disturb your reading, Sergeant."

"You're not, sir. I was just thumbin' through it. I ain't even decided if I'm gonna read it. I saw it lyin' alongside the road this mornin' and bein' I was out of readin' material, I picked it up. You ever read it, sir?"

Andrew held the book up.

"*The Whale* by Herman Melville," Lawrence read. "I've read other books by Melville, but not that one."

Andrew nodded and then put the book down on his lap. He glanced up at Lawrence as if he wanted to say something, but instead, he looked back down at the book. "The whale in the story has a name. I never heard of whalers givin' 'em names, but this here Melville did. He calls him Moby Dick." Andrew shook his head. "Named the whale and gave him a funny one too."

He beat the top of the book with the flat of his hand. "It's kind of heavy, so I thought I'd skim through it to see if it was worth readin'. I hate to be carrin' it around if it weren't any good."

Andrew looked up at Lawrence. "Sir, shouldn't you be gettin' some rest?"

"I was having a wonderful dream until the artillery infringed on it," Lawrence said.

"It woke me too. Couldn't go back to sleep, so I decided to give Melville a look-see." Andrew then put the book on the ground and stood. "Sir, I've been meanin' to talk to you about somethin', and I'm wonderin' if this would be a good time?"

Lawrence motioned with his head for Andrew to continue.

"Well, sir, it's about the colors. I'm afraid it ain't lookin' none too good."

"I know."

"And, sir, it's time we had a flag with our name on it. I mean, how are people supposed to know who we are?"

Lawrence wanted to smile, but he set his jaw and gritted his back teeth. He didn't want to give Andrew the wrong impression, but inside he was jumping for joy. For the first time, he'd heard one from the Second Maine use the word we to describe the Twentieth Maine.

"I share your frustration. At the earliest opportunity, I will write to the governor and see if he can't give us a hand. We need a new flag."

"And, sir, we gotta have a battle flag. Can't have a new color without havin' one."

"I see your point. We don't want people thinking we're green."

"No, sir," Andrew stated firmly.

No. They didn't want to look like a green regiment. They'd been through too much for the men to put up with that. Andrew was right. They needed a battle flag. They were the only regiment in the brigade that didn't have one. All the rest had their battle honors painted around the eagle, which graced the center of the deep royal blue flag.

Still, so far, not having one hadn't been too much of a problem. The tattered and torn national flag issued when the regiment reached Philadelphia carried ample evidence that they were a veteran regiment even if it was missing their name.

Still, he knew Andrew was right—no one could tell who they were. The rest of the brigade's regiments had their names painted in silver on the national flag's middle white stripe. Not the Twentieth. Formed from companies all over the state, they didn't belong to any one town or village, so no one had bothered to present them with a battle flag or even a national color.

"You know, Colonel, while we is talkin' about flags, I was kind of wonderin' . . ."

"Wondering what?" Lawrence asked.

Andrew hesitated. "I was just wonderin' why you picked me to carry the colors. Why didn't you pick one of the regiment's original men?"

"I picked the best man for the job."

"Sir, ya couldn't h've. Ya didn't know me when you made me color sergeant."

"Are you saying you're not the best man for the job?"

Andrew rolled his shoulders back. "Of course not, sir."

"Then what's your point?"

"I was just curious, sir. Why me?"

"I was extremely impressed with the way you handled yourself. You quickly gained the respect of the regiment. It was a pretty easy decision." Lawrence didn't add that he'd purposely picked one of the old Second Maine men to carry the colors. He knew that having one of their own would help them feel like they belonged.

"Andrew, I need a favor."

"Name it, sir."

"I would like you to talk to the remaining six. I'm not going to be able to keep them under guard forever. Pretty soon, I'm going to have to do something with them."

"Colonel, I'm not sure they'll listen to me. They is pretty stubborn men."

"I know they are, Andrew, and I don't expect any miracles."

"All right, sir. I'll do what I can. Sir, shouldn't you be gettin' some rest?"

Lawrence nodded and then went back over to his soft spot in the grass. He sat down and let out a big yawn.

"What was that big explosion?" John asked.

Lawrence yawned again. "The Rebels hit a caisson."

"You were gone awhile."

"I stopped and talked to Andrew for a few minutes. He was looking over a book he picked up alongside the road this morning."

"Was it anything good?"

"I don't know. It was a novel by Melville called *The Whale*."

"He found a copy alongside the road?"

Lawrence wrinkled his forehead before lying down on his back and pulling his cap down over his eyes.

"That is strange. It wasn't one of Melville's better sellers, and there weren't very many copies printed." John rubbed his head. "Strange book to find alongside the road."

Dull pains radiated from Lawrence's lower back. He stretched, but it didn't seem to help. "You would be surprised what you find on the side of the road during a march."

"Well, maybe before I left home, but I was with the Third Corps when they broke camp. I've never seen so much waste before in my life. The ground was just littered with all kinds of perfectly good items. I helped gather up the remnants to be passed out to the sick and wounded. There were a lot of books too, and I hate to say this, but I was embarrassed by many of them. Some were so bad I just couldn't bring myself to pick them up."

Lawrence rolled over on his side. Maybe that would be better. "It's the same with all the corps. Nothing is more boring than to be stuck in an army camp. The men will buy just about anything to keep themselves occupied, and there is never a shortage of camp followers willing to help them spend their money. Unfortunately, many of the men find sin to be a good defense against boredom."

"Lawrence, you wouldn't believe the photographs and books I found."

Lawrence smiled.

"Well, maybe you would." John chuckled. "But why did they just throw it all away?"

"Weight. Twenty-mile marches are hard enough when you are carrying just the materials you need to stay alive."

"But what happens when the army goes back into a camp?"

"Everyone gets bored. The camp followers show up and it starts all over again."

John shook his head. "It's such a waste. Are the Confederates like that too?"

"I haven't seen any evidence of it. They don't have as many; I guess you could call them, luxuries. With most of the factories being in the north and the Union blockade keeping the imports from Europe to a minimum, the Confederate soldier has had to learn to do without many things we take for granted. There is something else too."

"What's that, Lawrence?"

"The men of the southern army are different than our men. We have many from the large industrial cities. Sure, we have our share of farm boys, but nothing like the Rebels. From what I've seen of the prisoners and when we've been close to them while on picket duty, the southern army is composed of mostly farm boys."

Lawrence sat up and stretched his arms over his head. It seemed to help loosen his back. "Another thing, we have a lot of foreign immigrants like the Germans. The foreigners and city boys help give us a kind of diversity that the Rebel army lacks. They are mostly native-born farm boys, who, I might add, are much more religious than our own. Most of the prisoners and dead have Bibles. While you're on picket duty, if you're real quiet, it isn't unusual to hear the enemy pickets praying."

"You get close enough to hear them praying when you're on picket duty?"

"We sure do." Lawrence yawned again and then lay down again on his back. "We better get some sleep while we still can."

"I guess you're right."

John closed his eyes, and within a minute, Lawrence could tell he was already asleep. Once again, he pulled his cap down over his eyes, and when he closed them, her face was there, waiting for him. He imagined they were home in their bed. He undressed her in his mind. His heartbeat faster and his breathing quickened.

God, he missed being with her. It seemed like a lifetime since they had made love, although it had only been a few months since they were together. In April, Fannie had come down to Washington, and they'd spent four glorious days together.

They toured the city by day and rediscovered each other by night. It had been only two months ago, but it seemed like a lifetime. It was different when they were younger before they were married. He had gladly waited four years for their wedding night before he knew Fannie in the biblical sense. Now, he had trouble going only a few months without the closeness of being with the love of his life.

It was much easier now than when he was at seminary in Bangor and Fannie had gone to Georgia to teach music. The three years apart were very troubling for him. She was busy teaching and going to social events that her employers expected her to attend. Plus, her eyes had given her so many problems. The southern climate had caused them to swell, giving her terrible headaches. It made writing letters difficult.

For a split second, the old doubts came rushing back to him; then, they were gone. Lawrence smiled to himself as he remembered the pages and pages of letters he had written her, proclaiming his undying love and begging her to write back. He also remembered how he thought his heart would break, as each day passed, without a letter from his love.

After eight years of marriage and four children, all the doubts were behind him. His smile faded as he remembered the other two little ones. Only a few hours old, his son passed into God's loving arms; then there was Emily.

Poor little Emily was only with them for one short summer. He felt a pain in his heart as he remembered watching her take her last breath.

Oh Lord, bless my family and take care of my poor little children. He found comfort in the prayer. He took a deep breath, and, in a few minutes, he was fast asleep.

Chapter 11

General Lee scanned Cemetery Hill with his field glasses. He had one objective. He wanted to drive the Union army from that hill, and victory would be complete. But before it could happen, one last remaining question had to be decided. Who would start the attack? Would it be Longstreet or Ewell? After talking with Major General Isaac Trimble, it became clear that Longstreet would have to lead the attack.

During the early morning, Lee went to the Second Corps headquarters. Ewell was out inspecting his lines, and while Lee waited, he found Trimble in a talkative mood.

"General, we could have taken that hill," Trimble said, his voice strained and his face red. "I asked General Ewell to let me lead a division against it. He refused. I asked him to let me have a brigade. Again, he refused. I pleaded with him to give me a regiment. When he refused again, I threw down my sword and walked away."

Trimble, at sixty-two, was one of the oldest officers in the army. He had just returned to duty after recovering from wounds he received at the Second Battle of Manassas. Trimble might look like an older man, but he was still a fierce fighter who wasn't afraid to speak his mind.

I pleaded with him to give me a regiment: the words confirmed Lee's worst fears about Ewell.

Lee put down his field glasses. Longstreet had become increasingly loud and adamant in voicing his opinion that the whole army should move to the enemy's right, getting between Meade and Washington.

No matter. The enemy was here. Lee would not leave Meade and the Union army in command of the battle-field. Longstreet would lead the attack. It didn't matter if he liked it or not. Lee knew Longstreet would do his duty.

Lee walked over and sat down on a log between Hill and Longstreet. He unfolded a map of the Gettysburg area.

"General Longstreet, I've considered your suggestion about moving the army between the enemy and Washington City," he said in a voice he hoped reflected he had indeed given Longstreet's plan careful consideration. "While the plan has merit, I'm afraid I cannot go along with it. As you know, I didn't want this fight, but fate has forced it upon us. Still, I have never left the enemy in charge of a field of battle, and I have no intention of doing so today.

"I cannot ask this army to retreat after the great victory we won yesterday." He glanced at Longstreet. "I'm sorry. I will not do it." He looked back to the Union position.

"We'll attack them echelon by brigades, from the right to the left of the line. General Longstreet, you will lead the attack. General Hill, you will follow, and when General Ewell hears your guns, he'll commit his corps."

Lee pointed in the direction of Cemetery Hill. "When the attack begins, Meade will have to pull troops from those hills to support his left flank. When he does, we will take them and force him to withdraw from Gettysburg.

"General Longstreet, I want McLaws' Division to lead the attack. I want you to place his division across the

Emmitsburg Road right here." Lee pointed on the map
to the crossroads of the Emmitsburg Road and the
Wheatfield Road. "You will put Hood's Division behind
McLaws' to provide support."

"General, do we know where the Union flank is to the
south?" Longstreet asked.

"We don't know for sure. Captain Johnston," he called,
"could you please join us?"

"Yes, sir."

"Captain Johnston, General Longstreet would like to
know the location of the Union flank," Lee said.

"I rode up that hill, sir." Johnston pointed on the map
to Little Round Top. "From there, I could see Union
troops on the ridge that extends south from Cemetery
Hill, but because of the trees blocking my view, I couldn't
see their left flank. If I had to guess, I would say they are
about here." Johnston pointed halfway between Little
Round Top and Cemetery Hill.

Longstreet looked up from the map. He quickly
scanned the ground to the south of the Union line. "You
didn't find any troops in the area of those hills?" he
asked, pointing south to the two Round Tops.

"No, sir," Johnston quickly answered.

Lee was not surprised by Longstreet's question.
He, too, had thought it odd Meade had decided not to
anchor his flank on the Round Top hills. They would
make a strong defensive position. He considered ordering Longstreet to take them but changed his mind. It
would divert troops from the task at hand—driving the
Yankees from Gettysburg.

Lee glanced at Longstreet; he then pointed to the map.
"General, you'll attack up the Emmitsburg Road and
press on the enemy's flank. General Hill, you will wait
until McLaws' and Hood's divisions are in contact with

the enemy. Then you will send in Anderson's Division on Hood's left flank. After Anderson is engaged, follow with Pender's Division. General Ewell will be instructed to advance at the sound of Pender's guns.

"Captain Johnson scouted a route to their left that will keep your divisions out of view until you are ready to attack. Are there any questions?"

"General Law's brigade will be here shortly," Longstreet interjected. "I don't want to attack without them."

"Very well. You can wait on Law. Were you able to save them some freshwater?"

"Yes, sir. I have enough put away for them."

Lee relaxed. For the most part, his job was done. The decisions were made. The attack plan was in place. The only thing left for him to do was ride over to Ewell's headquarters and go over the plan with him. After that, it would be up to his corps commanders to make it work.

Robert Wicker spread his fingers. His hands were shaking. He balled them back into fists.

Another wagon pulled off to the side of the road. This time, Robert averted his eyes. The wounded men in the wagons shouted out encouragement to the regiment. Under the circumstances, it was a very noble thing to do. Many in the regiment responded in kind, but Robert kept his eyes to the front.

It was only going to get worse. The men in the wagons weren't the most seriously wounded. Those would still be at the field hospital or worse—out on the battlefield.

"Hey, Yank. Where's ya shoes?" Joe Henderson yelled out. Laughter spread through the company.

Robert looked over at a group of prisoners standing behind the wagon of wounded men. None of them were wearing shoes.

A smile crept across his face. Shoes were the first thing Yankee prisoners were forced to give up. He'd just wished they'd been the ones to capture those Yankees. They all needed new shoes.

His stomach grumbled. He was hungry, but this was something else. He'd been through these many times before. The shaking hands, the upset stomach, and sweats were all typical by-products of his own fear, and thanks to his father, they had become almost like old friends.

The only difference today was that it had all begun much earlier than he expected. Usually, he didn't start getting scared until they'd formed a battle line. After last night, the fear was almost comforting yet troubling. If this is just the start, *what if it gets worse?*

As he went up another slope, the cramps came back, spreading up and down his right leg. He drank the last of his water. He wanted to fall out of formation, but that wasn't possible. He wasn't going to give Hatcher the satisfaction of seeing him fail. No matter how much his leg hurt, he wasn't going to break formation.

On the right side of the road stood a two-story brick building. Several men were lying on the front porch. Out of the corner of his eye, he noticed something come flying out of an open second-floor window. He focused on it as it fell. The severed leg landed in the middle of a wagon.

A lump rose quickly in his throat. He desperately wanted to look away, but he couldn't take his eyes from the open window, away from the bloodstained brick wall, or the half-full wagon of arms and legs. Clenching his hands into tight fists to hide his shaking, he tried to steady himself.

After a few seconds, he swallowed hard and looked away.

Runaway, a voice called out to him. He knew this voice well. It was like an old friend.

He suspected it was the same voice a deer hears when surprised in the woods. *Runaway, run for safety.*

The voice only meant to protect him, to keep him safe from harm. He understood its motives and took comfort in them. He understood the voice of his own fear, and he gladly accepted its advice, even though he could not follow it.

You should have gone on sick call; the voice from last night whispering in his ear startled him. He forced himself to keep his eyes glued to the front, resisting the temptation to look for someone or something that wasn't there.

Coward.

"Leave me alone," Robert whispered, and the voice was gone. Sweat beaded upon his forehead. He was thankful it was hot and humid. No one would notice. He belched, and a foul taste invaded his mouth. He shook his canteen, but there was no sound. He swallowed several times to flush some of the taste away.

As they came over the top of the ridge, his eyes scanned the long, shallow valley laid out before him. Runaway, his inward voice of fear shouted at him. His eyes darted over yesterday's battlefield torn up fields, downed fences, wrecked artillery, and dead horses. Wreckage of war littered the ground, but surprisingly there were no bodies.

A cloud passed in front of the sun, and for a few seconds the shadow cast a veil over the valley. Then a wall of sunlight swept the ground, spotlighting contrasts of color. Brown mounds of dirt stood out from the lush green of summer. The burial parties had been busy. The dead soldiers were already resting peacefully under the rich Pennsylvania farmland.

Here and there were larger mounds. Yankee dead. They didn't deserve a grave of their own. That much effort was reserved for the fallen brothers. "For the enemy," Robert whispered, "you just dig a big hole and stuff in as many as you can."

As he marched along, there were horses piled alongside the road. The bodies were already showing signs of swelling. As the regiment passed, the west wind brought the faint odor of rotting flesh. In a few days, the smell would be unbearable.

There were a white house and a barn with a stone face on the right side of the road at the ridge's crest. In front of them were the remains of a split rail fence. Scattered along the fence were Yankee dead. The burial parties hadn't gotten that far. With a sick feeling, Robert turned his eyes away.

As they crested the ridge, he could see into the next valley. He could barely tell there had even been a fight. Here and there were a few Yankee dead; otherwise, there was nothing but a few torn up mounds of dirt.

His eyes drew back to the fence. Many of the dead had long, narrow, bayonet wounds. They had stayed and fought hand to hand before being overwhelmed. It is evident that they had died honorable deaths.

Near the bottom of the valley, they came upon the body of a lone Yankee soldier. Lying face down, his head pointed like an arrow to the east, toward the Yankee line. A massive wound had turned his back into a twisted, unrecognizable mass of flesh and bones. His right arm lay nearby.

Coward? Robert wondered. Did he run while others fought and died bravely?

Another coward like you, the voice said.

"Not like me," Robert answered, realizing there was something more important than life. It was honor. For a while the men along the fence took their last breath, knowing they had done their duty; this poor fool had died knowing he was a coward.

"I won't die like that," he whispered.

They started up another slope. Troops were resting on both sides of the road, yet Law's Brigade kept marching. Between the resting men of McLaws' Division and the rest of Hood's Division, they marched.

Feeling another stabbing leg cramp, he stumbled, grabbed his right calf, and squeezed. It didn't help.

Cheers from the front of the brigade spread back through the regiments, toward the Fifteenth Alabama.

They followed three men riding on horseback. Company L joined in cheering as Generals Lee, Longstreet, and Law rode by at a trot.

Then the man in front of Robert abruptly stopped. Robert hadn't heard the order over the cheers. He doubted anyone else did either. Instead, everyone just stopped. They had made it, twenty miles—in less than seven hours. It was over, at least for now.

The cheers built as the generals retraced their ride alongside the brigade. Robert stepped to the side and saw that the regimental color was unfurled and moving. The rest of the regiment was following and falling out of formation.

Hatcher yelled out, "Company L, fall out to the side of the road." The men wasted no time complying with the order. Robert noticed some looked like they were about to collapse. Dixon caught his attention, and Robert joined him and Hatcher.

"Sir, all the men are out of water, and I'm afraid some are about ready to faint."

"I know, Dixon. Pick two men for canteen detail while I go check with the colonel," Hatcher answered as he pulled his canteen over his head and handed it to Dixon. Robert followed his lead and did the same.

"You want to come with me?" Hatcher asked Robert.

"Yes, sir," he said, but inwardly he thought: *Hell no.* He didn't want to go with Hatcher. His leg was killing him, and he was weak from a lack of water. All he wanted to do was to collapse alongside the road with the rest of the men, but he couldn't turn his back on what was an apparent gesture on Hatcher's part. As he followed Hatcher, he slightly favored his right leg, and he hoped no one noticed he was limping.

They joined the other company commanders gathered around Oates. "I want to congratulate all of you and your men on a fine march. I don't think anyone in this war has marched any further, any faster than we did this morning. We are not going to stack arms. From what I've heard from General Longstreet's staff, we shouldn't be here long.

"They are moving the division a few miles to the south. We should be going into battle within the hour. I'm sure the main question on all your minds is water." Robert and the other officers nodded. "General Longstreet has secured water enough for the whole brigade. Have a detail from your company meet the sergeant major at the front of the regiment. He will show them where the water is. Once again, congratulations on a job well done."

Robert and Hatcher hurried back to the company. Dixon was standing with Bill and Jacob Stough, both with canteens hanging from their shoulders.

"The Sergeant Major is waiting for you in the front of the regiment. Hurry back," Hatcher told them.

"Yes, sir," they said and hurried away.

Hatcher turned to Dixon. "Have the men keep their weapons. We're not going to be here long."

"They're not wasting any time," Dixon said.

"They've been waiting for us," Robert replied as he lowered himself to the ground.

"You all right?" Hatcher asked with a hint of concern that surprised Robert.

"I'm fine."

Elisha limped over to join them and collapsed next to Robert.

"Hey, shit-for-brains. You all right?" asked Dixon.

"No, and quit calling me that."

Robert leaned over to Elisha. "The detail will be back in a few minutes."

Elisha rolled over on his back, looked at Robert with a weak smile, and then closed his eyes.

"What's wrong with him? Is he dying?" Colonel Oates asked as he joined the group, carrying a canteen over his shoulder. Robert and Dixon started to stand up, but Oates waved at them to stay seated. Elisha didn't even try to move.

"Sir, you're not going to get rid of me that easily," Elisha said.

Oates took his canteen off his shoulder and knelt next to him. "Here, you better drink some of this," Oates said.

Elisha rose on one arm. "Thank you, sir," he said, taking the canteen from Oates.

"You're welcome, cousin. You better share that with your lieutenant. I noticed he was limping."

"Thank you, sir," Robert said. "I appreciate the thought, but I better wait."

Oates smiled approvingly. "Then why don't you share the canteen with some of the other men," he said.

"Thank you, sir," Robert responded.

"You're welcome, Lieutenant. I better get back to the front of the regiment in case somebody else needs my services. Get the canteen back to me when you're done with it."

"Yes, sir."

Hatcher followed along with the colonel as Elisha handed the half-empty canteen to Robert. He thought about sharing it with some of the other men who were also suffering badly, but he quickly changed his mind. He was an officer. The men might feel strange taking the canteen from him.

Robert handed it to Dixon. "See if you can't make good use of this."

"Sure thing, Bobby."

"You feelin' better?" Robert asked Elisha.

"I do believe so. I didn't think I was gonna make it. I was fixin' to fall out of formation back at that tavern they're using as a field hospital."

"Is that what the building was?"

Elisha nodded. "Herr Tavern—That's what the sign said. I hate to admit it, but when I first saw that buildin', I decided that was as far as I was gonna go, but when we got closer, I saw the wounded lyin' on the porch. I just couldn't do it. I couldn't bring myself to quit just because I's tired."

Robert's stomach grumbled. He dug into his haversack and pulled out a piece of salt pork and some hardtack bread. "You better eat," he said to Elisha.

"Not hungry."

"You need to keep up your strength."

"I'm feelin' better. I'll just wait until Bill gets back with my canteen, then I'll et somethin'."

"Why do you need your canteen? You having trouble with your teeth?"

"No . . . of course not."

"Liar. How long you been havin' problems?"

"Couple of weeks," Elisha admitted.

"You should have seen the surgeon. He could—"

"Yeah, he could all right. Prob'ly pull out half my teeth tryin' to find the bad one. You know he don't know the first thing about workin' on teeth."

"Here, sir. I got your canteen," Bill said, walking up to them. "Yours too, cousin." Bill handed over the canteens and then continued on handing out the rest of them.

Robert took a long drink. The water cooled his rough, hot, dry throat. He felt his energy start to return.

He took a bite of the hardtack. He didn't blame Elisha for wanting to soak it first. Even without teeth problems, it was hard to chew.

Elisha sat up and gathered a small pile of sticks.

"I don't think you're going to have time to make coffee," Robert said.

"I hope you're wrong," Elisha said, pulling out a match. As he struck it, the drums started sounding assembly. "Shit."

"You'll just have to soak it in water," Robert said.

"I hate it soaked in water."

"Then go hungry."

"Thanks a lot."

Robert smiled before standing. His leg felt better as he yelled, "First Sergeant."

"Yes, sir," came Dixon's reply.

"Have the company fall in."

There was a chorus of grumbles from the men. "Sorry, boys, but it's time to go to war," Dixon shouted. "You heard the lieutenant. Let's fall in."

Hatcher came back and gave Robert an approving look and then motioned for Robert to follow him. Now what? Robert wondered as he followed Hatcher.

"I've been thinking about what you said this morning," Hatcher began. "I was thinking of bringing you up on charges."

Charges? Shit. Robert started to protest when Hatcher cut him off. "But then I decided it wouldn't be good for the company. We get into a fight . . . they're going to need both of us."

"Yes, sir, they are," Robert agreed.

"For their sake, we need to appear as we get along," Hatcher said.

Robert could tell Hatcher was surprised when he stuck out his hand. "For the men," Robert said. They shook hands, and for the first time since they'd known each other, they both smiled.

The building pressure on Lawrence's bladder woke him. He sat up and rubbed his eyes.

"Good afternoon, Lawrence," John said.

Lawrence looked up. The sun was still very high in the sky. It might be afternoon, but it was no later than two. He hadn't been able to sleep very long. He scolded himself. He should have taken care of this sooner.

He glanced at John. He wasn't surprised to see his little brother reading his Bible.

"You couldn't sleep?" Lawrence asked.

"They woke me up," John said, pointing to an artillery battery parked across the road. "They moved in about a half-hour ago. They must have new horses. The gunners were having quite a time with them. I'm surprised you or anyone else could sleep through all that racket."

"You get used to it. Artillery and musket fire, bugles, and the smell of meat cooking will wake me up. I've learned to sleep through everything else."

"So what are you doing up? I didn't hear anything, and I don't smell any beef cooking."

Lawrence laughed. "Oh, I forgot to mention the call of nature."

John smiled.

"I'll be back in a minute."

John went back to his reading. Lawrence returned a few minutes later.

"What chapter are you reading?"

"Psalms 23."

"Yea, though I walk through the shadow of the valley of death, I will fear no evil: for thou art with me; thy rod and thy staff they comfort me. Thou preparest a table before me in the presence of mine enemies . . .." Lawrence quoted. "It takes on a different meaning, being around the army, doesn't it?"

"It does. It is one thing to talk about the valley of death while you're sitting in a church pew. It is quite another when you come face to face with it. Did I tell you what I saw at the Fifth Corps hospital?"

"I don't remember you saying anything about it, other than you visited some of the men from the regiment."

"After church one morning, I saw a detail of men digging two graves in the cemetery. I asked them who the holes were for, but they didn't know. Shortly after they finished, an ambulance drove up with two wooden caskets in the back. They lowered the boxes in the graves and covered them up. There was no service, no music, and no military honors. They just put them in the holes and filled them in." John closed his Bible. "As they covered the holes, some other men gathered around. I asked if any of them knew the names of the dead. No one did, nor did they seem to care. I counted over a hundred fresh, unmarked graves in that cemetery." John wiped his eyes.

Lawrence contemplated saying something but thought better of it. There was nothing he could say that would make this any better for John. The spectacle of war indeed was like looking into the dark reaches of hell.

"Lawrence, I never imagined such human suffering was even possible. I talked to one private. My God!" John said as he threw his hands into the air. "You wouldn't believe what he'd been through. He was a lad from Vermont who'd joined one of those three-month regiments."

John let out a heavy sigh and then clutched his Bible to his chest. "After their first battle, he came down with typhoid fever. He recovered enough to rejoin the regiment as they were about to be sent home. Before they made it, he had a relapse. The surgeon sent word to his family that he was dying.

"He recovered and enlisted in the Sixth Vermont. he was promoted to sergeant major. At White Oak Swamp, he suffered bullet wounds in the head, back, and hip. They left him for dead on the battlefield. The Rebels captured him and nursed him back to health.

"After being paroled, he returned to the regiment. They had appointed another sergeant major, so he was demoted to the second sergeant." John shook his head. "He was shot in the hip at Antietam. He came out of the hospital a private.

"At Fredericksburg, he suffered more wounds. This time he lay on the battlefield for four days and through a hailstorm before they gathered him up.

"Funny, he told me he feels lucky. Two brothers, an uncle, and three cousins are already dead. He's made his peace with God, and now he's just waiting to die."

"War is a cruel master," Lawrence said.

"I understand, but still, I just didn't know—"

"John, unless you live through it, there is no way you can know. For you, there is no comparison. No frame of reference. The only way to understand war is to live it."

John eyed Lawrence closely. "You're enjoying this, aren't you?"

"No . . . of course not. Only a fool would love to be around the suffering and agony of war."

"Lawrence, when you talk about the war, your face lights up. You look like you're having the time of your life."

"No... I'm not," he protested.

"You are too. This whole war is like one big adventure to you."

There was a long pause. "Well, in a strange way, it is. I've never felt so alive. Don't get me wrong—the suffering and horrors of this war appall me, but it is inspiring, and someday when I'm old and gray, I will be able to tell my grandchildren stories of this Great War and the small part their grandfather played in it."

"As Grandpa Chamberlain did with us . . . telling us stories about the War of 1812," John said.

"Well, not exactly. I mean Grandpa commanded the post at Eastport. They didn't see much fighting. I was thinking more of the old Indian warriors down at the camp near home. I used to listen to them for hours telling their stories. I especially liked the ones about their fights with the Mohawks."

"Is that how you see yourself? As a warrior?"

"I don't know how I see myself. All I know is this is the greatest adventure a man could ever have."

"You're going to have problems going back to the classroom."

"I know. I tried to tell Tom, but he didn't understand. After living through this great experience, I wouldn't be able to go back to teaching."

"What are you going to do?"

"Don't know. I'm thinking about politics, but it's too early to make plans. I've got to live through this adventure first." Lawrence said, laughing.

"You scared?"

"Not really. I have nothing to fear. If I die, I get to join Horace and God. What's so bad about that? Don't get me wrong—I don't have a death wish. I guess what I'm trying to say is I've seen the worst that can happen to me, and I don't fear it. I'm not rushing to it either. I guess you could say I have a healthy respect for dying, but I'm not scared of it."

Lawrence looked past John and made eye contact with Private Buck, who was walking toward the woods. George gave a nod. Lawrence returned the gesture.

John twisted his head to the right and caught a glimpse of George as the man disappeared into a thicket of trees.

"Lawrence, there's something strange about George."

"What do you mean?"

"Well, he just doesn't act like a private. He gives orders, and the men listen to him. I've even heard him giving orders to some of the sergeants. Even you don't treat him like he's a private."

Lawrence leaned toward John. "The army might have taken away George's stripes, but to the regiment, he's still Sergeant Buck."

"How did he lose them?"

"Back when we were in camp, Buck was ill and stayed behind when the rest of the regiment went out on picket duty. A quartermaster," he almost spit out the words, "ordered George to chop wood. Of course, he refused. He was on sick call, and besides, sergeants don't chop wood.

"George claimed the quartermaster knocked him down and kicked him when he refused. The quartermaster, an officer, and a so-called gentleman, said George attacked him."

"He hit an officer?"

"If he did, the quartermaster had it coming," Lawrence said sharply. "But the higher-ups disagreed, and George lost his stripes because of it. It wasn't right, but there was nothing I could do about it."

"Now it makes sense. I guess from the way the men treat him, you aren't the only one who thinks George got a -" The sharp sound of infantry fire interrupted John.

Lawrence listened for a few moments. John started to say something, but Lawrence put his index finger to his lips, and John stayed quiet.

The fire seemed rapid, but there wasn't much intensity to it. It sounded like a couple of regiments, no more. Lawrence guessed it was a few miles to the west.

Several men began to stir. The fire didn't intensify, nor had the artillery joined in on the action.

"I think it's just the pickets getting a little anxious—nothing for us to worry about. Well, brother, I'm still tired. I'm going to try and get some more shuteye."

"Sleep well," John said as he returned to his reading.

Chapter 12

Major General Dan Sickles rose in his saddle. "Well, gentlemen, it looks like Hunt's suspicions were correct. The Rebs are there in force," he said as he pointed to the woods on the other side of the Emmitsburg Road. He studied the area up and down the road before turning his attention back toward the three hills at his rear.

Brigadier General Andrew Humphreys set his jaw. He knew what was coming.

"The enemy has left me no choice. We'll be moving the corps forward, General Birney."

"Yes, sir."

"You'll place the left flank of your division on that small rocky hill," Sickles said, pointing to Devil's Den. "Place your right flank here in this peach orchard."

"Understood, sir."

"General Humphreys, you'll move your division up here to the Emmitsburg Road and extend the line from the Peach Orchard northward along the road."

Humphrey's frowned, "Sir, don't you think we should get the commanding general's approval before we move from our assigned position?"

"I don't feel it's necessary. General Howard agreed with me that the ground here is more suited for artillery. The commanding general has assigned me the left flank, and unless he tells me otherwise, I'm moving the corps forward."

"General Hunt said that General Meade was very clear that he didn't want you to move the corps forward," Humphreys argued, his eyes intense.

"But that was before General Meade pulled the cavalry from our left. The situation is now very much different. We have no cover on the left, and I have enemy troops poised to take this high ground and rain artillery fire down on the corps. I have no choice. I must move the corps forward.

"But, sir!" Humphreys complained bitterly.

"I had the high ground at Chancellorsville. The high ground and headquarters ordered me to pull back. Then the rebels put their artillery on that damn ridge and hammered my men. Not again, damn it. Not again. This time I'm going to have the high ground. You have your orders. Now carry them out!"

Andrew Humphreys gave his commander a quick salute. He turned his horse and spurred him back toward his division. For a moment, he thought about riding to Meade's headquarters so he could protest Sickles' orders directly with the commanding general. As quickly as the thought entered his mind, he dismissed it. I'm a West Point officer, and I follow orders.

Sickles' orders were putting his division in an impossible position. There was no way they could support him with a gap of several hundred yards between his right flank and the Second Corps. His right flank would be up in the air, and there was nothing he could do about it.

As he rode, Humphreys looked over at the bare rocky hill to his right: Little Round Top. He'd been up on the hill earlier in the morning and knew firsthand that from there you could look down upon the whole Union position on Cemetery Ridge. If the Rebels took that hill, the whole Union line would be in peril. He hoped for the army's sake Birney understood the importance of keeping it safe.

It was times like this that Humphreys hated being assigned to the Third Corps and being the only high-ranking general who had attended West Point. Both Sickles and Birney were lawyers. While they might be good lawyers, they didn't know a damn thing about being generals.

He looked back toward Cemetery Ridge. Meade's head-quarters was up there somewhere. He decided he would order all flags unfurled and make it obvious they were moving forward. That should get the general's attention.

A few miles to the west, things were not going well for James Longstreet. His orders were to move undetected to a position on the enemy's left flank. Unfortunately, the road they were on would make that impossible.

Where he stood, the road crested a small hill in plain view of the bare rocky hill to the west. He could see Union signal flags waving from the summit of the hill through his field glasses. There was no way he could move his troops over this road without being seen by that signal station, thus alerting the Union army of his advance and losing any hope of surprise.

He'd heard the gunfire and knew the Union troops had already discovered Anderson's Division hiding in the woods along Seminary Ridge. If they received warn-ing about his attack on their flank, chances were good; the whole attack could fail.

Longstreet couldn't control his temper any longer. "This is Stuart's fault!" he spat. "If he'd gotten back when he was supposed to instead of riding around the countryside, this wouldn't have happened. His cavalry would have easily scouted a route for us.

"Gentleman, I don't see that we have any choice but to do a countermarch. General McLaws, your division will countermarch back to Herr Ridge Road. I will ride ahead and personally scout a route from there to the Union position."

Longstreet turned his horse, and with the kick of his heel, he headed back the way he'd come. His staff followed. He would tell Hood to hold his division where it was until McLaws' men could make the countermarch. Then he would send a message to Lee, letting him know about the delay. It would take some time to countermarch McLaws' Division, but he had no choice. The attack must be a surprise.

Acting Captain Hatcher shouted, "Company!"

The squad leaders followed with "Squad."

"Halt!" Hatcher ordered what seemed to Robert like the twentieth time on what was supposed to have been a quick march to the Union's left flank.

Most of the men just sat down in the middle of the road. Several small groups resumed card games, which they had suspended just a few minutes before. Robert figured this time they had made some real progress. They'd traveled almost two hundred yards before ordered to halt. That was a significant improvement since last time they'd moved only fifty feet.

When Robert turned, he noticed Elisha already had a fire going. Good, he must be feeling better. Elisha pulled out a small coffeepot from his haversack and poured in enough water for one cup.

"How did you gather up those sticks so quickly?" Robert asked, his eyes watching the flames from the fire dance.

"I've been collecting and carry 'em with me. I figured the way this here march is goin' that I'd eventually gather 'nough for a fire. You want a cup of coffee?"

"Funny, as hot as it is, but yes, I think I would."

Elisha reached up for Robert's canteen, poured in water, and gave it back to Robert. He next placed the top on the pot and held it above the fire. "You got your cup out?"

Pulling his bedroll over his head, Robert relaxed and stretched. It felt good to have the weight lifted from his shoulder. He untied one end of the roll and reached in for his cup. He pulled it out and handed it down to Elisha.

"Bobby, I'll tell ya, this here army is all messed up. They just about kill us marchin' over here this mornin', and for what? So we can shuffle along this here road for a couple of hours like we got nothin' better to do?"

"I don't have an answer. The way the colonel talked the division was ready to advance. This was only supposed to be a short march. It doesn't make sense to me either. The only thing I can think of is they're having problems scouting the way. Stuart's still not back."

"True, and Jackson ain't here either," Elisha said.

Robert lowered his head and gave a slight nod.

"Clear the road!"

Robert looked up just in time to see a lone rider galloping directly toward him. As the rider approached, Robert jumped out of the way as the horse sped past.

"Bobby, ya all right?" Elisha asked, his voice ringing in the air.

"I'm fine," Robert said as he stood and brushed himself off. "Did you see who that was?"

"Nah. I only saw him from behind."

"It looked a lot like Pike Youngblood," Robert said.

"Couldn't 've been. They don't give horses to no count privates."

Robert then saw Dixon about fifty yards up the road. He was talking to Pat O'Conner of Company K. When Dixon looked in his direction, Robert waved at him. Dixon held up an index finger to signal that he'd be there momentarily.

"Coffee's done," Elisha said, handing the cup to Robert. Robert loved the rich smell of coffee. He let his nostrils draw in the rich aroma. He wished he knew where the Yankees got such good smelling coffee. Taking a sip, he felt his body's tension ease. The coffee tasted even better than it smelled.

When Dixon arrived, Hatcher joined them.

"Sir, you a needin' somethin'?" Dixon asked Robert.

"Did you see who that rider was?"

"Yes, sir. Pike Youngblood. He's a courier for General Longstreet. In fact, at this very moment, he's a carrin' a message to General Lee."

Robert sipped his coffee.

"You don't say?" Hatcher asked.

"Sho' nuff. I was standin' next to the colonel when he flagged Pike down. Pike told him that one of Lee's aides had led McLaws' Division down what was s'posed to be a secluded road. They is tryin' for another surprise attack on the Union flank, like what Jackson did at Chancellorsville, but the road went right over the top of a hill, in plain sight of them Yankees. Pike said Longstreet is hoppin' mad, and he's lookin' for a better route."

"Well, at least we know the reason for the delay. I saw you talking to Pat. How's he doing?" Robert asked.

"He's havin' problems," Dixon whispered.

When Robert stepped away from Elisha, Dixon and Hatcher followed.

"What's the matter?"

Dixon let out a breath and crossed his arms. "Pat told me Captain Bethune ordered him to make sure John Nelson doesn't run out on this fight."

"Did he tell Pat how he wanted it done?" Hatcher asked.

"Nope. He don't care. He's tired of Nelson fightin' with everyone in the regiment and then runnin' at the first sign of gunfire."

"What's Pat going to do?"

"He don't know. I told him he should just hold up the son of a bitch until the Yankees shot him dead. It would serve him right. He's the worst kind of coward. He picks on the young and weak then runs at the first sign of real trouble."

Robert took another sip of coffee. He wondered what kind of demon Nelson carried with him. Was it the same one that visited him last night?

Breaking the awkward silence, Robert said, "Elisha makes a good cup of coffee." Robert then rubbed his fingers on the side of his cup as his eyes raised to the men. "Either of you want some?"

"That's a good idea," Hatcher said, walking back to Elisha. "You two seem to be getting along better," Dixon whispered.

"We're trying," Robert said he and Dixon followed Hatcher.

"My mama wrote me that there ain't no more coffee in the shops in Perote anymore," Dixon said, changing the subject.

"No," Robert said in a quiet voice as he finished off the rest of the Yankee coffee.

"Yep. She says ya can still buy it over in Troy, but it's costin' sixty dollars a pound."

"I can't imagine my parents having a meal without coffee, but they can't afford to pay those prices," Hatcher said, frowning.

"Mine either," Robert said in agreement.

"Ya ain't gonna believe it, but they is roastin' okra seeds," Dixon said, his eyes twinkling.

Robert shook out his cup and stuffed it back into his bedroll. "They're drinking okra coffee?"

"That's what she says. Everybody in town is doin' the same. After we whup them Yankees again, I'm gonna scrounge up some extra coffee to send to my mama. I'm sure it'd be a real treat for her to get some real coffee again."

"That sounds like a good idea. I'm sure my folks would appreciate some of this good Yankee coffee," Robert said.

"You know what else she said?"

Robert shook his head.

"My pa is growin' goobers."

"You're kidding."

"No . . . serious."

Hatcher's face twisted into a frown. "Things must be bad if your pa is growin' peanuts."

"Ain't that the truth. I couldn't believe it either. She said they is grindin' them up with cottonseed oil and compressed lard in the place of kerosene and also feedin' them to the chickens. Funny thing . . . she says those birds fed on goobers are some of the best she'd ever et."

Robert tossed his bedroll back over his head. "I wonder if my pa is doing the same thing?"

"Probably so. Ma said everyone in the county is growin' 'em."

Robert's face tightened. His parents reduced to growing goobers and drinking okra coffee. No shoes. No dye.

What else are they running out of? He wrinkled his forehead. The northern blockade was causing as many problems at home as it was with the army.

A chorus of drums played assembly.

"If we beat them Yankees today, maybe they'll give up and leave us alone," Hatcher said.

Robert and Dixon nodded an agreement.

"First Sergeant, call the company into formation," Hatcher ordered.

"Yes, sir."

Robert stepped to the side as the men assembled. A knot formed in his stomach as he kicked the dirt, wondering what else his family was doing without.

It wasn't fair. He'd seen firsthand that the Northerners weren't suffering any drastic shortages. He stuffed his hands in his pockets. It wasn't fair, but then the North hadn't started the war. Everyone at home knew there would be shortages when Alabama joined the other southern states and seceded from the Union.

The folks back home had gladly faced the challenges and sacrifices. He remembered how the farmers planted crops, like wheat and corn, in between their fruit trees to make up for the northern grain loss.

"Sir, Company L assembled, and all men accounted for," Dixon said and then saluted.

Hatcher returned it. "Thank you, First Sergeant. Did you check the men's water supply?"

Dixon's frowned. "Most are runnin' out. We is gonna need to find some before we go after them Yankees."

"I was afraid of that. Pass the word for everyone to keep a sharp eye out for signs of water."

"Yes, sir."

Searching Robert's face, Hatcher drank the last of his coffee. "You're right. He makes a good cup."

"Best in the army," Robert said quietly.

The drums sounded again as the command "Forward" echoed through the regiment, followed by "March." As prescribed in the manual, Robert led off with his left foot, as did every man in the column.

The company stepped off together united through the discipline of their training, their years of combat, and their shared visions of the future, a future of a free confederacy of southern states unencumbered by their northern neighbors. Robert prayed today they would strike a significant blow to bring the vision to reality.

Boy, I'm waiting for you, the voice tormented him, but this time Robert didn't care. *You'll run;* the voice whispered.

"We'll see," Robert said under his breath, his voice full of determination.

The drums beat and a "Column left" command echoed in the air. Robert's heartbeat quicker as his body gave him a rush of adrenaline. He set his jaw, knowing that left would lead them to the Yankees. He knew that somewhere to the left, they would form into a battle line. Then they would advance. All too soon, the waiting would end.

The company then did a column left onto the cross-road as the pace quickened. Excitement spread through the brigade.

Approaching a small clearing, Robert sighed as he looked toward the southeast to see two hills a few miles away. Though the hills looked like excellent defensive positions, he was sure the Yankees would have them well guarded.

"Please God, no more hills," he said under his breath.

Captain George Meade took the message from the signal officer. He rushed down Cemetery Hill's southern slope to the small white farmhouse his father was using for his headquarters. Young George scanned the message.

A couple of hours ago, Little Round Top's signal station had sighted an enemy force in the woods west of the Emmitsburg Road. Now, it seemed more troops were using the Fairfield Road to move toward town. The message said the enemy column contained over ten thousand men, all moving northeast. It seemed the Army of Northern Virginia was preparing for an attack. When George walked around the house's side, he found his father standing on the small wooden front porch talking to Major General George Sykes, the Fifth Corps commander.

"Another message, George?" General Meade asked his son.

"Yes, sir." Young George gave his father and General Sykes one of his best salutes.

Both officers returned the salute. "General Sykes, I think that was for your benefit." Meade smiled at his son as he took the message from him. "He doesn't salute me like that when we're alone."

"How do you enjoy working for your father, George?" Sykes asked the younger Meade.

"Fine, sir. Except there never seems to be enough hours in the day."

"It's one of the hardships of serving in a staff position," Sykes said.

The older Meade unfolded the dispatch and carefully read it. He then handed the message to Sykes.

"We better study the map and make sure your corps is in a good position to reinforce the northern flank," Meade said. Sykes followed him into the house. They both examined the map of Gettysburg spread out on the dining table.

"The Fifth Corps is here on the Baltimore Pike. This road will enable us to support either flank," said Sykes, pointing to the corps position where the Granite School House Road ran west from the Pike. "I've checked this road personally, and it provides us quick access to the left flank while the Baltimore Pike proves us easy access to the right flank and the center of the line."

Meade studied the map. He would like to have the Fifth positioned farther to the north, but there weren't any other roads leading to the west. If he moved the Fifth Corps to the north, Sickles got himself in trouble; the Second Corps would be their only support, and they also were defending Cemetery Ridge.

Meade looked up from the map. His son was standing in the doorway. "Did the signal station report anything from the Third Corps?"

"No, sir."

"That is a pleasant surprise," the older Meade said.

"Dan been causing you problems this morning?" Sykes asked.

"He isn't happy with his place in line. He's been hounding me all morning to let him move to higher ground at his front. I think he's finally resigned himself to the fact that I'm not going to let him move his corps."

Meade went back to studying the map. He knew that Lee's attack would probably come from the north. It should be safe to move the Fifth further north. But that would limit support on the left of the line.

He looked up to Sykes. "For now, we will leave our corps where it is, but have the word passed down to prepare to move to the north."

"Yes, sir."

"Ahhhhh!"

Lawrence sat straight up. "What's going on?" he snapped.

"Something's in my pants," John yelled as he jumped to his feet.

Other heads rose. A few of the men uttered profanities at being awakened. As John unbuckled his pants and pulled them down, others started laughing. The laughter spread when John discovered a small black snake wrapped around his left knee. When he grabbed the snake by the head and threw it toward the woods, a chorus of hoots and hollers echoed through the regiment.

Lawrence noticed Tom and Ellis were still lying in the grass despite all the commotion, seemingly asleep. *Or are they?*

As John was pulling up his pants, he noticed them too. He kicked Tom in the ribs.

"Hey. What was that for?" Tom yelled.

"You told him," John snapped.

"No . . . I didn't," Tom protested.

"You liar."

"He didn't have to tell me. I already knew," Ellis said as he rolled over to face John. "He just helped me get back at you."

John kicked Tom again as another bout of laughter spread through the men.

"Hey, cut it out—that hurts. Why don't you kick him?" Tom protested.

"Because now him and I are even. But you . . . you traitor . . . I'll remember this," John said sharply.

"We got you good, didn't we?" Tom laughed.

John's frown lightened, and he grinned at Tom. "Yes, and I won't forget it."

"What's going on?"

The voice startled Lawrence. He jumped to his feet and spun around. "Attention!" he yelled and then saluted Colonel Vincent.

Vincent returned Lawrence's salute, and before any of the rest of the men could react, said, "As you were."

"Good afternoon, sir. Brother John was having a problem with the local wildlife," Lawrence said.

"I noticed he was in terrible distress. I guess he isn't used to dealing with those sneaky, vicious, baby black snakes."

"I can handle the wildlife just fine. It's my family I'm having trouble with," John snapped as he flopped down on the ground. More laughter spread through the regiment.

"Take heart, Mr. Chamberlain. It is our families that make life interesting and exciting."

"I thought it was the Rebels," a voice called out.

"Them too." Vincent laughed, and everyone within earshot joined him.

"Colonel Chamberlain, can I have a word with you?" Vincent asked.

"Of course, sir."

Vincent moved a few yards away from the regiment, and Lawrence followed behind. Vincent slowed, and Lawrence came up beside him.

"I've talked to General Barnes. The Rebels are massing troops to the north. They are expected to attack sometime this afternoon. At the first sign of trouble, get our men assembled and ready to move out."

"Yes, sir."

"Lawrence, how are you feeling?"

"Fine, sir. I've gotten some sleep, and I'm feeling good."

Vincent nodded. "Carry on."

Lawrence saluted. Vincent returned it. Lawrence went back and lay back down next to John. He closed his eyes, but he couldn't get comfortable. His throat was dry, and his stomach was growling. His horse was only a few feet away, and next to him were his saddle, canteen, and haversack.

He was hungry and thirsty, but he didn't want to get up. He lay there for a few minutes hoping that sleep would overcome him, but it didn't. Each breath of the humid afternoon air increased the irritation on his throat.

He sat up and wiped the sweat from his forehead. Glad they don't get many days like this back home in Maine, he thought.

He got up and went over to his horse and patted him on the head. The horse didn't move. Lawrence looked into his eyes; they were fixed, unmoving. The horse was asleep.

He flopped down next to his saddle, grabbed his canteen, and took a long drink of the tepid water. He reached into his haversack for a hardtack biscuit. He turned the biscuit over carefully, looking for any small holes. When he was satisfied that there weren't any maggots feasting on it, he bit into it.

The biscuit was surprisingly soft. Weevils. He looked at it and saw several of the small weevils scurrying for cover. Brushing them aside, he took another bite. Fortunately, he'd gotten used to eating the weevils. It was a good thing, too, since they infested almost all the hardtack, which wasn't bad. They were tiny, tasteless, and their tunnels helped make the tough biscuits a bit easier to eat.

Maggots—they were another matter. He just couldn't get used to eating them. The weevils were so small one couldn't see any details of their appearance. The same couldn't be said for the white, slimy, ugly maggots.

There was something else Lawrence detested even more than the maggots. Sometimes moisture would collect in the middle of the crate, causing the biscuits to be wet, soft, and moldy. Only starving to death would be worse than eating moldy hardtack. The commissary sergeant had standing orders to scrutinize every crate of hardtack for maggots and mold and turn back any that didn't meet his approval.

When Lawrence took another drink, he noticed that his canteen was starting to feel light. He guessed he wasn't the only one running low on water. He spotted Sam Miller lying nearby. It looked like he'd already fallen back to sleep. He hated to do it, but there was no way of knowing how much warning the Rebels would give them. Better to be safe and get all the canteens filled up now, while things were still quiet. Sam wasn't going to like being awakened, but duty called. He hated to think what it would be like if the regiment were to advance with near-empty canteens. Today wouldn't be a good day to get into a fight without any water.

With the way things had been going, Lieutenant General James Longstreet wasn't surprised to find that the enemy wasn't where they were supposed to be. Instead of being back on the ridgeline, they'd posted an entire division right up on the Emmitsburg Road. Through his field glasses, he could clearly see Yankee infantry and artillery posted in a peach orchard about 600 yards to the east, exactly where General Lee wanted McLaws to form his division. Longstreet knew he didn't have any choice. He was going to have to modify Lee's battle plan.

Anderson's Division, from Hill's Third Corps, was in position on the southern section of Seminary Ridge. A half-mile to the south, another ridge ran at an angle toward and eventually crossed the Emmitsburg Road, south of the peach orchard full of Yankees.

He decided to place Barksdale's Brigade from McLaws' Division on the second ridge in a position where Anderson would still be able to provide support during the attack. Kershaw's Brigade would extend McLaws' line to the south with his other two brigades giving support. Hood's Division would extend the line further to the south and cross the Emmitsburg Road.

Longstreet could see that the Union's right flank angled back toward the Round Top hills, but he couldn't tell how far. The hills looked like a formidable defensive position. He hoped the Union flank stopped short of them.

He called his staff together and began to issue orders. He sent one messenger to General Lee to let him know about the modifications he'd made in the attack plan. He sent another to General Hood.

It would take time for McLaws' men to get in position, and there was no longer a need for Hood's men to follow behind them.

He issued Hood orders to take to the fields so his men could push past McLaws' Division. It was getting late. He needed to get the troops into position as soon as possible if the attack would have any chance of success.

Walking was easier for Company L, the Fifteenth Alabama, now that they were moving through the fields instead of in the middle of the dry, rocky creek bed. The rocks had been hard on his feet and shoes. The hole in Junior Second Lieutenant Robert Wicker's right shoe was now much larger, and he now had a small hole in his left shoe.

The company marched through another row of fence posts. The division's advance guard was doing an excellent job of clearing the rails from all the fences. It made the marching much easier and quicker. Nothing was worse than trying to climb fences while attempting to maintain a column of fours.

When they came to a wooded area, Hatcher glanced over his shoulder. "Keep it tight as you can, boys," he shouted. When they came out of the woods, he directed the company to make a left turn.

Robert's heartbeat quickened. He knew there was just one more turn to the east. It shouldn't be long now.

The colonel called another halt.

"Stand at ease," Hatcher ordered as he stepped to the side of the road where Dixon and Robert joined him.

"Sir, did ya see that the Fourth Alabama sent out a canteen detail?" Dixon asked.

"Yes. Did you see signs of water?" Hatcher asked.

"No."

"Me either," Robert joined in. "They haven't made it back yet. Maybe it was just a wild goose chase."

"You have any left?" Hatcher asked Robert.

"Some . . . not much."

"I'm out, and so are most of the fellows," Dixon said.

Robert removed his hat and wiped his forehead on his sleeve. They had to get more water. He couldn't ask his men to attack without an adequate supply.

Just then, Robert noticed twenty men running toward him carrying several canteens.

"You find any?" Robert shouted, turning to face them fully.

A private stopped, gasping for air as he let out a "Yes, sir."

"About a half-mile back and a little ways to the west, sir. It's pretty warm and green, but it's all we could find."

Drumbeats suddenly filled the air.

"Shit," the private said as he hurried off.

"What are we gonna do?" Dixon asked, realizing it was too late to send a detail back to the pond.

"We're going to pray we find some water before we attack," Robert said. He glanced up at Hatcher, who was nodding in agreement.

Chapter 13

Brigadier General Evander Law paced back and forth. What's taking them so long? It'd been over fifteen minutes since he'd sent out a scouting party of six men to find the Yankees' flank. They should have reported back by now. The sun, moving through the western sky, was a sign that it was getting late, with only a few hours of daylight left. He thought about sending another party, but he was afraid there wouldn't be time.

As the general stood on the crest of a ridge just inside the tree line, he saw three hills on the other side of the mile-wide valley.

The closest, and smallest, was covered with huge boulders and Yankee artillery. Behind it was the second-largest hill, its western face was clear of trees exposing its rocky slope and summit. The general knew it would be a difficult position to take, but surprisingly, there, except for a signal station, there didn't seem to be any troops on it.

The largest hill was mostly tree covered and situated to the right of the other two hills. *Where is their flank?* Law wondered. He guessed somewhere on the largest hill, but it was only a guess.

Since his brigade was on the right flank of the entire Army of Northern Virginia, it was his job to find and turn the Union left flank. There was just one problem. He had no idea where it was. For now, his men were protected from view by narrow woods and the ridge line's crest. Soon the orders would come to advance and the brigade would start down a steep incline into the valley below. For almost a mile, they would be in the range of the Yankee artillery. Then they would have to attack uphill against what he assumed would be an entrenched enemy.

"Pure hell," he whispered to the wind. The Yankees had the rugged high ground, a place of excellent cover. He lowered his head, knowing he could lose half of his men.

From what he'd learned from a few Yankee prisoners, there might be a better way. They'd told him there was a farm road to the south that would give his men protection as they moved behind the largest hill.

While he didn't know exactly where the Yankees had their flank, he reasoned that it wouldn't matter if he got his whole brigade, undiscovered, into their rear. Of course, he needed to confirm what the prisoners had told him. He needed the report from his scouting party.

General Law mounted his horse. Time was running out. Confirmed or not, he would pass the information on to General Hood. He readied to kick his horse when he heard a man shouting, "General Law! General Law!"

A sergeant came out of a small patch of woods, twenty yards to the south. The general breathed a sigh of relief as he turned his horse and rode to meet him.

"Report, Sergeant," the general shouted.

"We found the Yankee's flank, sir," the sergeant said, half out of breath. He pointed to the guns on the smallest hill, the one the farmers called Devil's Den. "That's it, sir."

"No troops on the larger hill?"

"No, sir. A small stream cuts between them two hills. Ain't no blue bellies on the other side. No sir. And we found that road them prisoners told us about. Sho' nuff, sir. It leads right into their rear."

"If we took the road, could they see us?"

"No, sir. Not until it be too late. They even got a wagon train parked behind that one," he said, pointing to Big Round Top. "They're unprotected. They're ours for the takin', and that's not the best part. From the top of that hill, ya can look down on the whole dang Yankee line."

"What about that other hill? Are there any troops on it?" the general asked, pointing to Little Round Top.

"Nobody up there but them signalmen."

"Thank you, Sergeant. You better get some rest while you can. The brigade will be moving out shortly."

So they left the large hill uncovered, the general thought to himself, his face turning into a smile. Big Round Top dwarfed the other two. From what the general could see, it was one of the largest hills in the area. If a brigade or maybe even the whole division could take it, things could be tough for the Yankees.

The general knew too that the brigade could move farther to the right and come up from the south and take the hill without a fight. Once on Big Round Top, it would be a simple matter to chop down a few trees, opening the way for artillery. The hill would make a fine defensive position. Once in place, the Yankees would be forced to attack—or pull out of the area. He hoped General Hood would agree.

General Law looked back at Devil's Den just in time to see the battery let loose another volley. He watched the shells streak toward his left. They exploded in the trees above the Texas Brigade.

Those guns would make a direct assault complicated, the general thought. Law shuddered as he envisioned his men coming under canister fire from them. Attacking uphill against an artillery position would be suicide.

As he spun his horse around, he gave him several swift kicks. He had to talk to Hood. He had to convince him to take Big Round Top. Then they would have the high ground again.

"You wanted to see me, sir?" Major Homer Stoughton asked.

Colonel Hiram Berdan, in overall command of the First and Second U.S. Sharpshooters, looked up from his map. "Yes, Homer, I have orders from General Ward. The brigade is on the left flank of the division. He talked with General Birney, and the two of them agreed that since we lost our cavalry support, they needed to put a regiment out a ways to cover the flank."

"I'm surprised they thought of it," Stoughton said, without thinking. "Sorry, sir. I shouldn't have said that."

"At least not out loud," Berdan said. He agreed the citizen-soldiers of the Third Corps had a lot to learn. As one of the few regular army officers in Birney's Division, he saw it as his job to help them along.

"Homer, I want you to take the Second out a ways and cover the flank. General Ward thinks the Rebels are massing on this side of the Emmitsburg Road. I want you to make sure they don't surprise us."

"Yes, sir. We'll do our best."

"I know you will, Homer. Good luck, and keep your head down."

"Thank you, sir."

It took Stoughton a few minutes to walk back to the regiment.

"What's going on, sir?" Charlie Norton, his adjutant, asked.

"We're moving out front a ways. The general wants us to guard against a flank attack. He's worried Lee will try another flanking movement like he did at Chancellorsville."

"We going to have any support, sir?"

"No. We're going out there alone."

"Sir, we only have eight companies. What good are we going to be?"

"If nothing else, we can make a nuisance of ourselves."

Charlie smiled. "That we can, sir."

Things were getting worse by the minute. The woods, just a few hundred yards in front of Dan Sickles, were full of Rebels. Their skirmishers were already peppering his line with gunfire. He'd received reports from the Peach Orchard that the Rebs were crossing the Emmitsburg Road, a few hundred yards to the south. It looked to Sickles like Bobby Lee would be sending half the Rebel army down his throat.

To top it off, George Meade wanted to have a staff meeting. His whole corps would be under attack in a short while, and the commanding general wanted him to ride off to a staff meeting on Cemetery Ridge. *Ridiculous.*

"Sir, this is a direct order from General Meade. He wants you to report immediately to his headquarters," the colonel said again, emphatically.

"I heard you the first time, Colonel," Sickles said sharply.

He didn't understand Meade. He'd sent him a message saying the Rebels were massing in his front and that he needed additional artillery support. Meade sent him some of the reserve artillery and then sent a message requesting he report to headquarters for a staff meeting. The messenger told Sickles that Meade didn't think the Rebel threat on his front was serious.

Sickles asked to be excused. A short while later came another request that he report for a staff meeting. A second time he asked to be excused. Now Meade was once again ordering him to report.

"General Birney."

"Yes, sir."

"You have the corps until I return."

"Understood, sir."

Sickles mounted his horse and rode off toward Cemetery Ridge and Meade's headquarters.

General Law hated waiting. It'd been over ten minutes. *What is taking so long?* Hamilton should be back by now. After giving his report and recommendations, Hood had him repeat it to Captain Hamilton, who carried a message to General Longstreet. He should be back by now.

Two more shells came crashing down among the Texas Brigade. Law could hear several Texans shouting about the damn artillery—not the Yankees', but the Confederate artillery battery that set up right in front of them. The friendly battery let loose with another bombardment. Law watched the six shells streak toward the artillery position on top of Devil's Den. The Yankees fired an answering barrage.

Artillery commanders were notorious for having a habit of shooting at each other and sometimes firing long. Two more shells exploded in the trees above the Texans.

The Yankees hadn't seen the Texas Brigade come into line in the woods along the ridge's crest. For a time, everything was quiet; then the artillery battery showed up. They took a position in front of the Texas Brigade, and when they started chopping down trees, the Yankee artillery took notice. They weren't about to let their Rebel counterparts go unchallenged.

Of course, the Yankees hadn't yet done any real damage to the artillery other than killing a few horses. They were firing long. Two more shells exploded above the Texans. Law watched litter bearers carry a couple of men out of the woods. He heard a horse galloping toward him. He quickly turned to see Hamilton ride past and up to Hood. From the look on his face, Law knew the answer. They would attack as ordered.

Law walked up to Hood in time to hear Hamilton repeat Longstreet's order to attack up the Emmitsburg Road. Hood looked at Law. "You heard the order," he said.

Law started to say something but stopped himself. Arguing with Hood wouldn't do any good. Hood agreed with him. As Law walked over to his staff, he saw another rider coming up to Hood. It was one of Longstreet's staff telling him he needed to hurry the attack along.

Law turned to his staff. "We will attack as ordered."

"Canteen detail!" The sergeant major shouted the order. Bill Sellers and Jacob Stough broke formation and started gathering the company's canteens. Bill came to get Robert's.

"Who's got your weapon?"

"Wesley Smith."

Robert nodded his approval of Bill's choice. He'd been afraid Bill might have asked Elisha to carry it. With the way Elisha felt, Robert didn't think it would be wise for him to carry the extra nine pounds of the Springfield rifle.

"Hurry back—I don't know how long they're going to hold us here."

"We will," Bill said. They joined the rest of the twenty-two-man detail and hurried down the western slope of the ridge.

As Robert watched them go, he noticed Benning's Georgians taking up a position a couple of hundred yards to the rear of Law's Brigade. It would be up to the Georgians to provide support for the first wave of the attack.

Robert's hands started shaking again. He took a deep breath. It didn't help. Once again, he squeezed his hands into fists; then, he began to pace slowly back and forth behind the company.

He felt his heart pounding in his chest. He kept his chin down, tightened his jaw, and squinted.

"Bobby, it's okay to be scared, but it's not all right to act like you are," his father had told him last summer. When he rejoined the regiment, he had put his father's advice to practice and developed his battle face.

Others noticed his look. Some said he looked mad. Some said he looked determined. A hint of a smile crossed his lips. No one had ever said he looked scared.

He took his position three paces behind the left flank of the second of the company's two ranks—the spot reserved, in the manual, for the first lieutenant.

When the company organized bak in Perote, its formation looked like the diagram in Hardee's Infantry Tactics. They drilled for hours, with their four officers and five sergeants in their assigned places, helping to perfect the maneuvers of the company's one hundred enlisted men.

Less than two years later, with only two officers, three sergeants, and a third of the enlisted men, They'd been forced to improvise. Robert hated to think it, but after Hatcher joined them, things were easier.

Robert now had the first lieutenant's spot. Dixon's cousin, Sergeant Charlie Bonner, took the second lieutenant's place to Robert's right on the company's right flank. Sergeant Leven Vison filled in for both the third and fourth sergeants, marching in the company's center between Robert and Leven. Hatcher had the commander's spot, front rank right, with Dixon in the first sergeant position, right behind Hatcher.

You're a coward, boy. The voice was back.

Robert turned to face the hills in the front of the regiment.

You're going to run.

"I'm not scared of you," Robert said, smiling. Oh, he was scared, but only of dying. Robert took pride in the fact that he was no longer afraid of being a coward. If it were his time to die, he would do so, looking his enemy in the eye.

Robert walked around the flank and moved past the front rank into the narrow woods a few feet. His eyes were drawn to the large, tree-covered hill directly in front of the regiment. *Oh God, I hope we don't have to climb that.*

There was a rumble to his left. He turned his attention to the Union artillery on Devil's Den. Smoke hung low over the hill. A flash of light struck the sky. More smoke billowed in the air. From a distance, the hill looked like a miniature volcano throwing up smoke and flame.

Robert noticed a small cottage on the downslope of the ridge between the two lines. The stone house with the white picket fence looked so restful, so out of place. Robert then caught a glimpse of something moving behind the cottage's white picket fence.

Several small pockets of smoke rose in front of the fence, outlining Union pickets, and then came the pop, pop, pop from the muskets. Robert guessed they were engaged in a pickets' duel with the skirmishers from the Texas Brigade concealed in the woods in front of the cottage.

The pickets were the only Federal infantry Robert could see. The main Union line was somewhere in the woods on the next ridge. He wondered if the artillery marked their left flank.

Several companies from the regiment, to the left of the Fifteenth, moved past him and down the slope. *Skirmishers.* To his right, another group followed the first.

They would move out a couple of hundred yards in front of the brigade and clear away any Yankee pickets. He hoped the canteen detail made it back soon. He then hurried back to the company.

"It's almost time," Hatcher said, joining him.

"Yes, sir. Any orders yet?" Robert asked.

"No."

Robert gestured at the small hill covered with cannons. "I'd rather face them than climb that," he said, pointing at the larger hill.

Hatcher laughed and patted him on the back. "Me too."

When they came out of the woods, Dixon waved at them. As the two officers walked around the company's side, a snowstorm of little bits of white paper blew past them. The men knew it was almost time.

Robert pulled the letters from his coat pocket and put the letter from his mother on top, and kissed it. He quickly tore all of them up and scattered the pieces to the wind. Hatcher did the same.

"Sir, the skirmishers went out, and we don't have any orders," Robert said.

"Typical," Hatcher said, looking to his right. The drummer boys were already in position, standing three paces behind the regiment's center, surrounding the colonel. Several other officers were talking to the colonel.

"Come on," Hatcher said to Robert. Robert followed him over to Colonel Oats.

"Sir," Hatcher said. Then he paused and saluted. Oates returned his salute. "What are my orders?"

"Same as always, Lieutenant. Follow the colors," Oates snapped.

"Sir, can you give me an idea which way that might be?"

"I've had no word from General Law."

"Sir, what are you going do if the brigade advances and you still don't have any orders?" Robert asked, his voice firm.

"Do what we always do. Advance straight ahead until we get orders."

"Sir—"

"Lieutenant Wicker, you don't have to say it. I don't want to climb that hill any more than you do, but if we don't get any orders, that's exactly what we're going to do."

"Yes, sir."

"Return to your company."

"Yes, sir," Hatcher said. The two of them hurried away.

As Robert walked past the supply wagon, sweat rolled into his eyes. He pulled his bedroll over his head and threw it in the wagon. There was no way he could climb that big hill carrying his bedroll.

"Orders, sir?" Dixon asked.

"Same as always. Follow the flag," Hatcher replied.

"The colonel gonna go straight again?"

"Yes."

"Ain't he seen what's in front of us?"

"Unfortunately, yes. Let's just hope we get -"

A cheer went up to their left, cutting Hatcher off in mid-sentence.

"Damn it. The canteen detail isn't back yet. First Sergeant, take your place in line. Get the company ready to move out," Hatcher said.

"Yes, sir."

Hatcher turned to Robert. "Keep the formation tight."

"I will, sir."

More cheers.

Hatcher went quickly to the front of the company. There were more cheers as Robert took his place behind the left flank. Taking a deep breath and holding it, he listened as the drums sounded. It was time. The flag moved forward.

"Right shoulder arms! Forward! March!"

Colonel Lawrence Chamberlain sat straight up. He instantly recognized the sound of massed infantry. His men heard it too. Heads were popping up all around him.

He stood. The sound seemed to be coming from the west. That's odd. Vincent said the Rebels were moving to the north.

It took a few seconds before it dawned on him: *they're flanking us.*

"Sergeant Major!" Lawrence yelled at the top of his lungs.

"Here, sir." Sam Miller came running.

"Have the regiment fall in."

"Sir?"

"Let's get a jump on the rest of the brigade."

"Yes, sir."

"What's going on, Lawrence?" John asked as he let out a big yawn.

"It's begun. The Rebs are attacking, and it sounds like they're trying to turn the southern flank."

Lawrence squatted down next to John. "We're going to be moving forward soon. The corps will be setting up a field hospital. I want you to find it and make yourself useful."

"I'm coming with you," John protested.

"No, you're not."

"Lawrence, I could help with the wounded. I can serve as a litter bearer."

"No. You're not coming forward."

"Lawrence, you can't stop me."

"As colonel of this regiment, I am responsible for you. You have never seen combat. You don't know what to expect. This is not the time or place for you to get that experience."

"But, Lawrence—"

"There are no buts. Do I make myself clear?"

"Yes!" John got up and stomped away.

As Tom came over to Lawrence, he stared at him. "You were too hard on him."

"I don't remember asking you for your opinion," Lawrence snapped.

"Your horse is ready, sir," Sergeant Ruel Thomas said in a soft voice.

"Thanks," Lawrence said, taking the reins as he flung himself into the saddle. The gunfire was growing louder, and it was coming from the west. He kicked his horse in the flanks as he turned and rode to the Baltimore Pike.

Reaching the road, he heard the bugles as they started blaring. A few seconds later came the familiar call of Dan, Dan, Dan, Butterfield, Butterfield. Then came the call for assembly. Lawrence scanned down the road to the west. No smoke. The sound of gunfire meant the fighting was close but not that close.

He then turned his horse and galloped back to the regiment. As expected, Sergeant Major Miller had them in formation. Sam ordered the regiment to attention before giving Lawrence a crisp salute. Lawrence returned it.

"Sergeant Major, have the men stand at ease."

"Yes, sir." Sam did an about-face. "Regiment."

"Company, platoon, squad," echoed over the formation.

"Stand at ease," Sam ordered.

Lawrence dismounted his horse. "Nice job, Sam."

"Thank you, sir. Colonel, what do you want to do with the six prisoners?"

"Do we still have six?"

"Yes, sir."

"Well, we can take them with us or shoot them," Lawrence said with a smile.

"I guess we take them with us, sir, 'cause I know you ain't gonna shoot them."

Tom rode up, but he didn't say anything. Lawrence glanced at him and could see in his eyes that he still thought he had been wrong in the way he'd handled John. Maybe he was too hard on his younger brother. Lawrence looked over the area, but he didn't see John.

He did notice a group of horsemen thundering down the Baltimore Pike with General Barnes in the lead and Colonel Vincent close behind. Vincent pulled up in front of the Sixteenth Michigan, while the rest of the party turned down the road to the west.

Lawrence spun his horse and galloped over to join Vincent. The other regimental commanders did likewise. In less than fifth seconds, all four of them were with Vincent.

"Gentlemen, the division will be moving off at double-quick," Vincent said. "We're in the lead.

"The Third Corps has somehow gotten out of position, and they're isolated from the rest of the line. The general has gone ahead to survey the ground for us. They will put us in line as soon as we get there. Colonel Rice, the Forty-fourth has the lead. Let's get going."

Lawrence hurried back to the regiment. As he rode up, he waved for the company commanders and the sergeant major to join him.

"Gentlemen, we will be moving at double-quick. It looks like the Rebels are trying to turn the left flank. We will follow the Forty-fourth New York. Any questions?"

There were none. "All right then. Take your positions."

Lawrence waited for the officers to get back in place, and then he turned to Sam. "Get us ready."

"Yes, sir."

The sergeant major barked out the orders. "Attention! Right face! Order arms!"

Lawrence rode over to the regiment's new front, where Tom joined him.

"Tom, bring up the rear. Do what you can to keep everyone in formation."

"Yes, sir," Tom answered very formally.

"By the way, Tom, maybe you were right. I will say something to John when I see him."

Tom smiled, turned his horse, and headed to the rear of the column.

Lawrence looked back at the regiment aligned in a column of fours. All looked in order. The Forty-fourth moved out. It was time to go.

"At double-quick! Forward march!" he yelled. A shout rose above the Twentieth Maine as they followed Rice's New Yorkers down the dirt road.

General Gouverneur Warren gave his horse more kicks to encourage him to hurry up down the dirt road. The horse shook his head as if to say he was doing the best he could. He'd already galloped over a mile along Cemetery Ridge to get here, and now his rider was driving him up the steep, rugged road. Sweat cover the horse. Warren didn't have time to sympathize with the animal's plight. He had to get to the summit fast. It didn't matter how it affected his horse. The entire country's future might very well rest on what he found at the top of Little Round Top.

Warren and his two aides came out of the woods, looking southwest at Big Round Top's summit. He steered his horse along the western face of the summit to the south towards the signal station.

"Who's in charge here?" Warren demanded.

A captain stepped forward. "I am, sir."

"Report," Warren ordered as he jumped from his horse.

"Sir, it looks like the Johnny Rebs are starting to advance on the Third Corps line," he said, pointing to the west.

"Is that Sickles' left flank?" Warren asked, pointing down to the artillery on Devil's Den.

"Yes, sir. The center is up there on the Emmitsburg Road. Their right flank is anchored to the north along the road," the captain said as he pointed out the line to Warren.

There was a scattering of rising smoke. Pickets, Warren decided. Still it helped him follow the Third Corps' position, along the tree-covered ridge, past a wheat field, and up to the road.

Warren walked over to a boulder on the hill's western face. First, he looked north. He wasn't surprised by what he saw. The rocky hill looked directly down on the entire Union line on Cemetery Ridge. If the Rebels took this hill, Meade might not have any choice but to withdraw the Army of Potomac from Gettysburg. He wondered if the army or the nation could withstand such a defeat.

Turning back to the west, he noticed another tree-covered ridge, this one to the west of the Third Corps' position. It ran to the southeast, crossing the Emmitsburg Road south of the center of Sickles' line. It seemed apparent the Rebels were using it as their starting-off point. Warren wondered how far south their line ran.

Warren turned to one of his aides. "Lieutenant, go down to that battery," he said, pointing to the artillery on Devil's Den. "Have them fire some shots further to the left."

The lieutenant jumped on his horse and disappeared back into the woods. The hill's southern face was too steep and rocky, so he would have to backtrack down the road and then ride around the western face of the hill to reach Devil's Den.

Warren took off his hat and rubbed his head. In just a couple of minutes, his aide galloped past on his way across the valley floor. Warren easily followed his progress.

Why did Sickles move forward? Warren looked back toward Cemetery Ridge out to the Emmitsburg Road. Sickles was right. The ground out along the road would have been higher than the center of his line, but so what?

Moved forward, Sickles' right flank was unsupported, and he'd moved his left from this hill. He'd strengthened his center while weakening both flanks. Damn lawyer. He should have known better.

Warren put his hat back on. If the army was forced back from Gettysburg, it would be Sickles' fault, but the blame would fall on Meade. He should have known when Sickles stopped complaining that something was wrong.

Warren was surprised no one had told Meade the Third Corps had moved forward. Surely, the entire Second Corps had seen the move. Yet, no one had bothered to mention it to the commanding general. Maybe Hancock thought Sickles was under orders.

When Warren returned from surveying the northern section of the line, one of his aides, Lieutenant Ranald Mackenzie, had informed him that the Third Corps might be out of position. It only took a few minutes for Warren to confirm it; then it fell upon him to tell Meade.

Meade was shocked and outraged, but Warren didn't think he should have been. From what he had heard, Sickles had moved almost three hours before. Meade's headquarters was less than a hundred and fifty yards down the backside of Cemetery Ridge. From the top of the ridge, the Third's new position was clearly visible. Warren felt Meade should have known.

With word that the Rebels were advancing, Meade should have personally taken a survey of his line. But he hadn't. He'd stayed at headquarters, oblivious to what was happening on the other side of the ridge.

From the look on Meade's face, Warren could tell Meade knew it too. The look didn't last long. Sickles rode up, and Meade vented his anger on him. Then the Rebel guns opened fire in earnest.

Meade ordered Major General George Sykes to move the Fifth Corps to the left and Sickles back to his corps. Then Meade decided to take command of the entire left flank.

Warren had joined him on the ride toward the left, and it was he who pointed out the importance of Little Round Top to the commanding general. Meade ordered Warren to take command of the position. So here he stood on the most critical position on the left flank, and all he had to defend it was a detachment of signalmen.

He hoped the Rebels were more interested in attacking Sickles' position than taking an unguarded hill.

"Sir, they're aiming two of the guns to the left," Lieutenant Mackenzie said.

Warren turned back to Devil's Den. They were just finishing getting the guns turned—first one; then the other belched smoke and flame. A second later, the shells exploded on the next ridge. Immediately, a flash of bright light streaked through the trees to his left.

"What was that?" Then it dawned on him. Gun barrels— sunlight reflecting off thousands of gun barrels as the men turned toward the sound of the explosion.

Oh God, they're flanking us. There was no doubt. Their line would sweep past the Third Corps' flank on Devil's Den. There was nothing to stop them from sweeping right up the face of Little Round Top.

"Ranald."

"Yes, sir."

"I want you to go to General Sickles. Tell him to send a brigade to this hill immediately. If he can't—or won't—help, then find General Sykes. I'm going to write a dispatch to General Meade. In the meantime, I want you to get us some help."

"I will, sir."

"Hurry, Ranald. We don't have much time."

"Eyes front!" Robert Wicker ordered. The explosions were close, but there was no good reason to look. Looking couldn't change anything.

The colors moved out of the woods and into the open. The regiment followed them. Hatcher barked orders for the company to tighten up the formation.

They went down the slope, and as they did, the hill in front of them grew taller. Please, God, turn us, Robert prayed. He was thankful the artillery had gone back to blasting the Texas Brigade.

As Robert scanned the valley in front of them, he was certain that the regiment wouldn't be moving any further to the right. They were either going to advance up the big hill or turn and attack the artillery. Attack uphill against artillery or climb the bigger hill—to Robert, the choice was still clear: he'd rather face the Yankees than climb that hill.

Chapter 14

General Law pulled his horse hard to the right as he ducked under a large branch. The woods were thinning. Two more quick kicks to the horse's ribs and they broke into the open. He pulled back hard on the reins, and the horse skidded to a stop.

It took him but a few seconds to get his bearings. He quickly spied the rocky hill with the artillery. His brigade should be advancing toward it, but they weren't. He glanced hard to the right and saw they were moving straight ahead and away from the hill that marked the enemy's flank. Worse, the Fourth and Fifth Texas, the right flank of Robertson's Texas Brigade, were going with them.

Oh God, there's a hole in the line, and it's all my fault! He cursed to himself. Two more kicks, and the horse took off down the slope. He had to catch the brigade. He had to turn them.

Brigadier General Jerome Robertson's left flank had orders to remain anchored to the Emmitsburg Road, and his right was ordered to stay in contact with Law's Brigade.

General Law had become so preoccupied trying to get Hood and Longstreet to move the division to the right; he'd neglected to issue orders to his commanders. When his brigade advanced, they went straight, taking two of the Texas regiments with them. Robertson's other three regiments hung on to the Emmitsburg Road, causing a spilt in the Texas Brigade and a gapping and still growing hole in the line.

Law knew he had to get his brigade turned to the left. It wouldn't fix the hole, but it would keep it from getting worse. Then Benning's Georgians could be used to fill the gap.

He cringed, knowing they were supposed to be his support, but he had no choice. The hole had to be filled. His brigade would have to get along without any support.

He quickly rode up behind the colonel commanding the Fourth Texas.

"Colonel, gradually wheel your men to the left!" he shouted.

"Yes, sir."

He turned his horse and was off again. He issued the same order to the Fifth Texas and his own Fourth Alabama. Next in line was the Forty-seventh. They were a small regiment. To their right was the Fifteenth, one of his largest.

As he rode up to Lieutenant Colonel Bulger, commanding the Forty-seventh, he ordered, "Colonel, I want you to keep your regiment in close contact with the Fifteenth. If you become separated from the rest of the brigade, Colonel Oates will be in overall command."

"Yes, sir."

Three more to go, he thought, knowing he almost had it fixed. It was but a short ride to reach Colonel Oates.

"Colonel, I want you to take your regiment up the side of that hill," Law said, pointing to where Big Round Top sloped down to Devil's Den. "Get into the valley on the other side; find the Union flank and turn it."

"Yes, sir," Oates responded.

"Good luck, Bill."

"Thank you, sir. You too."

Law pulled the reins to the right. More kicks, and he was off again. He would order the Forty-fourth and the Forty-eighth regiments to wheel hard to the left and cross behind the rest of the brigade as well as the two stray Texas regiments. He would send them against the damned artillery position; he breathed a sigh of relief. It looked like his blunder wasn't going to be a significant problem after all.

After about fifty more steps, Robert's throat was dry. His muscles were already starting to ache. His body needed water, and fifty more steps, and the regiment would cross a small creek. He wondered if the colonel would call a halt. He hoped so.

He looked to his right. *Going left?* Robert stumbled and then looked back up at the flag. Yes, it was definitely shifting to the left. Thank God. He angled his steps. There'd been no command. Instead, it was just a subtle shift.

Glancing at the front rank, he knew that the men were adjusting nicely to the direction change. He smiled. No orders were needed. The men were all veterans—they knew what to do, follow the flag

Thirty steps. They were angling away from the large hill, and now they were almost to the water. Things were looking up. He looked back to the right. The flag was at the creek. It was hesitating; then it moved a few feet ahead and stopped again. Robert smiled.

Hatcher led the company toward the creek and then shouted, "Company halt!" as he stopped the front rank in the middle of the stream so they could scoop up handfuls of water.

"Forward!" Hatcher soon yelled. As the first rank left the creek and the second stepped into the water, he ordered another halt. Then it was Robert's turn. He scooped up three handfuls of water. It wasn't much, but it would have to do until the canteen detail caught up with them.

The flag started to move again. "Company forward," Hatcher ordered. The second rank center was ragged, so Robert yelled at Leven, "Sergeant, tighten them up."

"Second rank; tighten up!" Leven yelled. The men responded.

Robert turned to look back to the left. He was surprised to see the Forty-seventh wasn't turning. They were still going straight. They were crushing in on Company B, and soon they would play hell with Company L's formation.

"I see it, sir," the Sergeant Major yelled as he rushed by Robert. Good. The sergeant major would get the mess cleaned up.

Colonel Homer Stoughton peeked over the stone wall. They were still coming. Two Rebel regiments were in front of him. One was angling to their left, and the other was crowding in on them. Perfect. It would make it harder for them to return fire.

"What're we waitin' for?" A private next to him protested.

"Shut up," Homer snapped. He was waiting for the regiment on the left to get a little closer and more

angled. This would make it even more difficult for them
to respond to his regiment's attack. *Two hundred yards.*
Almost time. This is going to be too easy, he thought.
With his men on a rise above the creek and a stone wall
for cover, they should be able to get off two or three volleys before the Rebels would be able to press upon them.
He noticed that the Rebels' back rank had just cleared
the creek. He knew it was time. Bravely, he stood and
held his sword high in the air.

"Ready . . . aim . . . fire!"

Robert looked back to the right and was pleased to see
all was back in order. He made eye contact with Leven
and gave him a nod of approval. Leven gave him a slight
wave of his hand and smiled. Suddenly, Leven's face disappeared into a red misty cloud. Leven's body fell face
first as the sound of the Yankee volley reached them.

Run, you idiot . . . run while you still can. Robert
ignored his inner fear. Smoke was rising above a stone
wall to their front. With the turning movement, the
regiment wouldn't be able to return fire. It would be
up to the next regiment in line to drive the Yankees
from the wall.

Robert yelled at Joe Henderson, marching in the second rank. "Joe, take Leven's place."

"Me, sir?"

"Yes, Corporal, you. It's time you earned those stripes
you sewed on yesterday."

"Yes, sir!"

As the second rank shifted to the right, Robert noticed
there were no other casualties. Too bad about Leven. He
was right. They wouldn't be sitting around any more
campfires.

He glanced back to his right and was shocked to see
the Forty-fourth and Forty-eighth regiments doing left

wheels. They're cutting behind us. "Damn . . . that puts us on the flank," he said under his breath.

As he pulled out his sword and waved it over his head, he caught Colonel Oates' attention and pointed at the regiments maneuvering behind them. The colonel waved back.

Another volley. Robert spun back around. This time his company hadn't taken any fire. He gave a quick glance toward the flag. It had stopped. He noticed several men down in the middle of the regiment.

The drums were sounding, but in the growing fury of the battle, he couldn't hear the command. He kept his eyes glued on the flag. He knew where it was going, but still, he prayed he was wrong.

"Damn," he said as it moved to the right. After ten feet, the line went up the slope, and he and the company followed. He knew the colonel had no choice. They were now on the flank. There was no way they could continue to the left and leave the Yankees in their rear.

Robert had a sickening feeling in his gut as they went up the slope. The large, tree-covered hill loomed above them. *God, please . . . I don't want to climb that thing.*

"Where the hell we goin'?" someone in the company yelled.

"Quiet in the ranks—keep the formation tight!" Hatcher ordered.

As they started up, the hill's slope protected them from the Union fire, but it was only a temporary reprieve. A few seconds later, they reached the top. The Yankees greeted them with another volley. The regiment's right flank felt the brunt of the fire.

A company in the center of the line got off a volley. Hatcher ordered, "Front rank . . . ready . . . aim . . . fire!" The line exploded. The sound hammered Robert's ears.

More drums. "Fix bayonets," Hatcher ordered. The clangs echoed across the company. "Order arms!" came next. They were ready.

The flag darted ahead. It was time. "Let's go, boys!" Hatcher shouted, waving his sword toward the stone wall.

"Fall back. We've done enough for now," Homer ordered his four remaining companies. I hope this works, he thought. "Make it obvious, boys," he shouted. For his plan to work, the Rebels had to follow them.

His other four companies had already fallen back, but they didn't go far. They'd sulked away into the woods to the left. They had orders to stay hidden until the Rebels passed by; then, they were to blast them from the rear.

He checked his positon. All the living were already gone. Only a few dead remained. Hopefully, they'd get a chance to come back for them later. He didn't like leaving anyone behind, even the dead.

Homer followed his men up the slope of Big Round Top and disappeared into the trees. Once he was sure they could no longer be seen, he turned them to the right —no reason to go up the hill any further than they had to.

Twenty yards from the wall, it was obvious the Yankees had fled. But how far had they gone? Just behind the wall, the ground was heavily wooded. They could be lurking just inside the tree line.

Where am I . . . that's what you're wondering, isn't it, boy?
"No," Robert lied.

Ten more yards. The voice was no longer frightening, just irritating. "Let's get this over with," Robert demanded, but there was no answer.

Over the wall went Hatcher and the front rank. Robert followed the second rank over. There were only a few dead Yankees, all with gunshot wounds in the head.

"First Sergeant . . . dress the company," Hatcher ordered.

As Dixon barked out orders, Robert looked for Elisha. He was still in line, although he looked pretty haggard. Elisha smiled at him. Robert nodded.

He glanced back at the flag. It was moving again, moving uphill. He made eye contact with Hatcher and pointed at the flag with his sword.

"Forward!" Hatcher ordered, pointing his sword to the front.

"We can't climb . . ."

"Quiet in the ranks!" Robert snapped. If he couldn't mouth off about climbing the damn hill, no one else in the company was either.

As they went up into the tree line, the woods thickened, preventing him from seeing past thirty feet. As a further hindrance, the ground was so full of large boulders that it made it difficult for the men to maintain formation.

Sweat escaped the band of his hat and trickled down his forehead and into his eyes. He used his sleeve to wipe it away. His breathing became labored. The muscles in his right leg tightened up again. *Hurry back, Bill. We need water.*

A rustling noise swept through the leaves. *What was that?* An instant later, the sound of the Yankee volley reached them. "Damn, they're behind us," Robert said under his breath.

He glanced to his right and saw that Dixon was down. Robert rushed to him.

"How bad?"

"I don't know," Dixon replied, in obvious pain. He rolled over slightly, revealing a small hole in his right hip.

"You're going to be fine," Robert reassured him. He looked up to see the company pulling away.

"I'll be fine. Get going."

Though Robert wanted to do more, his duty required him to stay with the company. As he hurried after them, there was another blast from the right. This time it was friendly fire. The regiment's right flank was giving them a taste of their own medicine. It looked like the colonel was dispatching a company to deal with the Yankees in their rear.

Through the trees, Robert caught a glimpse of the flag. It was still moving, still moving up. Then the ground flattened out. The flag stopped. Hatcher ordered another halt.

Go left . . . go left . . . Robert silently pleaded. Surely the Yankees had circled the mountain. They wouldn't have continued up the steep slope in front of them. The flag waved back and forth, then forward, and it disappeared in the thick, leafy canopy. "Forward!" Hatcher ordered.

"And keep quiet in the ranks," Robert yelled, deciding to get a head start on the complainers.

Colonel Strong Vincent glanced back at his brigade; all looked in order. The Forty-fourth New York was on his left. On the right was the Eighty-third Pennsylvania, with the Sixteenth Michigan and Twentieth Maine in the center. He considered the Eighty-third his regiment.

He knew he wasn't supposed to feel that way. All the regiments were his now, but the Eighty-third—they were special. He'd started with them, serving as their lieutenant colonel. Last June, Colonel McLane was killed at Gaines' Mill, and he assumed command. While Captain Woodward had taken his place, they both knew the regiment still belonged to Vincent.

He looked back to the front, out across the Wheatfield. Soon General Barnes should be coming for them. When the brigade reached the edge of the field, Barnes and General Sykes were waiting for them. They had told him to hold his position until they returned.

"Colonel Vincent," Lawrence Chamberlain called out.

Vincent smiled. He liked the way the stately professor from Maine pronounced his name. The e took on the character of a long a.

"Yes, Colonel Chamberlain."

"Sir, are we going to make a stand here?"

"No. General Barnes ordered me to hold here until he could find a place for us. I expect he should be back shortly, and we'll move forward." Vincent pointed to the woods on the other side of a wheatfield where the gray smoke was steadily rising above the trees.

"How are you feeling?" Vincent asked.

"Fine, sir. Much better."

"You don't look like you're feeling well, does he, Corporal?" Vincent said, turning to his color bearer, Oliver Norton.

"Well, sir, I've seen the colonel look better."

"Lawrence!"

Vincent turned, wondering who was, breaking military discipline, by shouting out Colonel Chamberlain's first name. He smiled when he saw the youngest Chamberlain brother riding between the New Yorkers and the boys from Maine.

"I thought you told your brother to stay behind."

"I did, sir."

John pulled hard on the reins, coming to a stop next to his brother and Vincent.

"Lawrence, don't be mad. I had to come. I couldn't let you go into battle thinking I was angry with you. I'm sorry I got upset. I shouldn't have—"

"John, it's fine. I'm glad you came."

John smiled.

"But when things start to get rough, I want you to get back to the rear. Do you understand?"

"Yes. I do," he said and then paused before asking, "Lawrence, where are the Rebels?"

"Attacking uphill against the woods in front of us," Lawrence said.

"How do you know they're attacking uphill?"

"'Cause, if you listen really close, you can hear their bullets flying over our heads."

John got a funny look on his face. Vincent smiled, thinking that it was an eerie sound, the swoosh of bullets just a few feet above their heads.

Vincent then noticed an officer riding out of the woods to their left. Squinting, he recognized the man as being a captain on General Sykes' staff. Vincent wondered where the captain was going in such a hurry.

Vincent flicked his horse's reins and kicked him in the ribs. His horse responded immediately and leaped forward. Norton holding the brigade colors, followed, leaving the Chamberlain brothers behind.

Vincent cut in front of the lieutenant. "What are your orders?"

"Sir, do you know where I can find General Barnes?"

"No, Lieutenant; I don't. What are your orders?"

"I have a message for General Barnes."

"Damn it, man. I say again . . . what are your orders?"

"Sir, I have orders for General Barnes to take a brigade to that hill." The lieutenant pointed to the rocky face of Little Round Top. "The Rebels are flanking us."

"When you find General Barnes," said Vincent, "tell him that's where I'm taking my brigade."

"Sir, my orders—"

"I know what your orders are. I take full responsibility for moving my brigade. Now get going."

"Yes, sir."

Vincent spun his horse around and headed back to the brigade with Norton close behind. The rest of his commanders were waiting with the two Chamberlain brothers.

"We're moving the brigade to that hill," he said, pointing. "I'm riding ahead to scout the ground. Colonel Rice, your regiment is still in the lead, and bring the rest of the brigade with you."

"Will do, sir."

Vincent yelled "Git up" at his horse. As he glanced over his shoulder, he saw that Norton was right behind. He cut over to the dirt road and headed for the rocky hill. The horse's hooves shook the wooden bridge over the small creek.

Vincent cut off from the road and tried to ride up the hill's western face, but the horse stumbled and slid back. Vincent yelled again and gave the animal a couple of kicks. It leaped forward, but once again slid back. "Damn," Vincent swore.

He pulled hard to the left and steered the horse back down the hillside. They went around the north side of the hill until they found a dirt road. The horse galloped up between the trees. It wasn't long before they broke out into the open on the southeast side of the hill.

Vincent gasped. The hill commanded all the ground in the area. If the Rebels took it, the unthinkable would happen. The Union army might have no choice but to retreat.

Vincent frowned as he glanced toward the woods to the west. It seemed to be on fire. Smoke from volleys of musket fire engulfed the trees. In his front, a few regiments and an artillery battery were engaged in a desperate fight on a smaller composed of massive boulders. They must be the flank of the Union army.

Further to the left, he saw nothing but the tree-covered slope of a hill, even larger than the one he was on.

He remembered the captain's words: "They're flanking us."

They must be maneuvering through the trees. Since his brigade was too small to cover the entire hill, he decided to post it on the southeast slope.

Suddenly a shell exploded nearby, then another. He turned to Norton. "They're firing at the flag," he said, dismounting. "Get the flag and horses out of sight," he said, handing his reins to Corporal Norton, who hurried away.

Vincent wondered how long Sickles' flank could hold. Would it be long enough to cover his right flank until more troops arrived? He hoped so.

Another shell exploded near the summit. Vincent climbed down the face of the hill about twenty yards. The ground was rockier. It would provide better protection for his men, plus it wouldn't be as easy of a target for the enemy artillery. He would put the New Yorkers there.

He looked out to the valley floor. The Rebels were going to be seeking the left flank. If they turned it, the thought made him shudder. They'd march right up the backside of his brigade. He knew he had to find a good place to anchor his left. With the tension upsetting his stomach, he walked across the face of the slope to the east. The hillside curved back toward the north. Soon, he came to a narrow gully that gradually sloped down to the valley floor. It would provide the enemy troops an easy approach to his line.

He then climbed down into the gully and up the other side, passing large boulders. He turned to look back over the area. He determined that the boulders would provide his men with a commanding position, and the gully wouldn't be a problem.

He continued east, cutting across the face of the slope. Once again, the hill curved to the left. After a minute, he came to a ledge where the ground dropped off from a large boulder, almost ten feet to the valley floor. He smiled, knowing that the ledge would provide an excellent defensive position for his left flank. He could have one regiment cover the gap between the gully and the ledge. Thanks to the Second Maine, the Twentieth now had close to four hundred men. They would fit nicely.

The three Chamberlain brothers were riding in front of the regiment as they started up the dirt road. Lawrence was in the middle with John to his right and Tom to his left.

When an artillery shell exploded to their right, John's horse reared up. "Boys, I don't like this. Another shot, and it could be a hard day for Mother. Tom . . . go to the rear of the regiment and see that it's closed up.

"John."

"I know, Lawrence . . . time for me to go to the rear."

"They'll need you at the hospital. Do what you can for the wounded."

"I will, and Lawrence, good luck."

"Thanks, John."

The two younger brothers turned their horses and quickly rode away. When another shell exploded nearby, Lawrence glanced back at the regiment. He saw John galloping along a wood line toward the rear. "I hope I see him again," he whispered.

Chapter 15

Dixon Bonner slid down the slope and crawled over to Leven's body. "You was right, old friend. I'm gonna miss sittin' around the campfire with ya." Wiping tears from his eyes, he patted Leven's shoulder.

He dragged himself over to the creek bank and dipped his cupped hand between the streaks of red, and drank much-needed water.

"First Sergeant."

Dixon looked up. The canteen detail came running toward him. Bill Sellers stopped while Jacob Stough and the others splashed across the creek and up the slope.

"I got your canteen," Bill said as he handed it down to him. "You hurt bad?"

"Na. They got around behind us, and I took one in the ass. It ain't serious, but it hurts like hell to walk."

"You want me to help you back?"

"No. I'll make it. You better get goin'. The company needs the canteens."

Bill smiled. "Shot in the ass."

"Shut up!" Dixon snapped.

Bill laughed, saying, "See ya soon."

Dixon gave a slight nod, and Bill took off up the slope. When Bill got to the top, he turned to see Dixon waving. Bill gave a hearty wave back before taking off again.

When Bill reached the stone wall, he stopped. Except for a few dead Yankees, he was alone, and he couldn't tell which way they'd gone. Suddenly to his right, a man dressed in gray limped from the woods carrying a canteen.

Bill crawled over the wall and shifted the canteens, getting them back upon his shoulders. Then he was off again. He trotted by the wounded man and up into the woods. After fifty yards, he had to slow down. The weight and heat were getting to him.

Taking a drink from his canteen helped a little. As he put the lid back on, he heard a cough coming from the trees ahead and heard a voice say, "I think we should go toward the sound of the fighting."

Bill didn't recognize the voice, so he proceeded cautiously.

"Corporal, you got to make a decision. We can't just stand here."

Bill then recognized the voice. He yelled, "Jacob, where are you?"

"Over here."

He followed the sound through the branches. "Where's the regiment?"

Jacob shook his head. "We don't know."

Charlie Norton peeked from behind the tree. There looked to be no more than twenty Confederates. Damn. He only had twelve men with him. After laying down fire into the Rebel regiment's rear, his flank had become disorganized and separated in the heavy underbrush.

Twelve against twenty. Not particularly good odds. He reached up and carefully pulled back a branch. It took him a few seconds to realize the Rebels were unarmed. *A canteen detail.* He crept back and eased over to his men.

"It's an unarmed detail," he whispered. "Form a single rank . . . weapons at order arms."

The men crept into position. When all looked ready, Norton signaled them forward.

"Did ya hear somethin'?" Bill asked.

"Yeah," Jacob answered. "What was it?"

"You men . . . stand where you are," came a voice from the woods. "We have you covered."

"Should we run?" Bill whispered.

Jacob nodded. Bill shifted his weight and started to turn.

"You there . . . take a step, and we'll gun you down." Bill froze. They were too close. The blue line stepped into view. There weren't many of them, but they all had rifles at ready. To run would be suicide.

"I'm sorry, Bobby," Bill whispered.

"Drop the canteens and put your hands on your heads," Norton ordered.

Bill did as he was told. The cork came out of one of the canteens as it landed on the ground. The water rushed out and flowed down the rocky ground. Bill shook his head. What a waste.

Second Lieutenant Robert Wicker dropped to his hands and knees. He felt lightheaded and couldn't catch his breath. Collapsing face-first on the ground, he struggled to suck air into his lungs.

He rolled onto his back. That was better. He took off his hat and waved it back and forth in front of his face, but the effort wasn't worth the slight breeze it produced. Using his sleeve, he wiped the sweat from his face. It didn't help. Almost as fast as he could wipe it away, the moisture beaded up again. Within minutes, his breathing slowed, and his head cleared. He pushed himself up and saw that Elisha was lying next to him.

"I didn't think you would make it up the hill."

"I didn't either," Elisha agreed.

Hatcher, looking worn and tired but still on his feet, came over. "You going to make it?"

Robert sat up. "I think so."

"Sir, we gonna stay here a while?" Elisha asked.

"I hope so. At least until the canteen detail catches up with us," Hatcher answered. He then squatted next to Robert. "Who's next in line for First Sergeant?"

Robert looked to see who was still with them. Ten feet away sat Charlie Bonner with his back against a tree.

"Charlie Bonner."

"Have him get the company organized, and we better get a headcount."

"Yes, sir."

Robert forced himself to stand. "Charlie . . ."

"Yes, sir."

"Let's get our men back into formation and get me a headcount." There were several moans and groans from the troops lying around them.

"Sir?" Charlie asked.

"Acting First Sergeant, you heard me. Get the company into formation," Robert snapped.

"Yes, sir!"

"We're going to check with the colonel and see how long we're going to be here. After you get them lined up and counted, have them sit down," Hatcher ordered.

Charlie nodded. Hatcher headed up the slope, and Robert limped behind him. It wasn't as bad here—none of the huge boulders to climb over. They soon found Colonel Oates near the summit.

"Sir, do you have any orders?" Hatcher asked.

"How many of your men made it up the hill?"

"Not sure, sir. I'm having the acting first sergeant get a headcount."

"Dixon?"

"Wounded, back at the stone wall," Robert reported.

"Any sign of the canteen detail?"

"No, sir," Hatcher responded. He hesitated before asking, "Are we going to wait for them?"

"Lieutenant, I intend to dig in here. Take a look," Oates handed his field glasses to Hatcher, who, after a few seconds, passed them on to Robert. Robert had trouble focusing through the trees, but it looked like they were looking down on the Union line that ran all the way up to town.

"We can control their flank from here." Robert smiled.

"That's what I was thinking. We can clear a field of fire, drag some artillery up here, and this hill could become a fortress. It would make things difficult for them."

One by one, the regiment's other officers joined them. Robert passed the field glasses to his right. They all agreed that the regiment was in a perfect defensive position—even better than Fredericksburg's heights.

"Colonel Oates."

Surprisingly, a rider on horseback was weaving his way up to the summit. It was Captain Terrell of General Law's staff.

"Colonel Oates, why have you halted your regiment?" Terrell asked.

"We just climbed up this mountain, Captain. My men needed rest. Also, we're waiting for our canteen detail to catch up with us. Have you seen them?"

"No, sir. General Law sends you his compliments. He wants you to advance against the next hill, find the Union flank, and turn it."

"Captain Terrell, this hill commands all the ground around the area. I would like to have my men fortify it. Within half an hour, I can convert this hill into a Gibraltar. Captain, the two regiments under my command could hold against ten times their number. I believe my men should remain here and be reinforced with artillery."

"Colonel, I understand your position, but I have no authority to change General Law's orders," the captain answered flatly.

"Captain Terrell, where is General Law? I'm sure if the general could see our position, he would agree with me that my men should stay here and be reinforced."

"I'm sorry. It would be impossible for the general to come here. Hood was wounded by artillery fire. Law is now in command of the division. You're too isolated from the rest of the division. It would be impossible for him to make the climb up here. Colonel, I urge you to waste no time in pressing the attack."

"Tell the general we'll be moving out in five minutes. I got to give the stragglers a chance to catch up."

The captain saluted and headed back down the hill.

"You heard the order," Colonel Oates told his officers. "Have your men ready to move out in five minutes."

Robert followed Hatcher back to the company. Through the trees, he could see heavy firing below. The other regiments were attacking the artillery position on Devil's Den. Robert looked ahead to the next hill. He hoped it was just as empty as this one.

Charlie was ready when they got back. "We still got twenty-eight men with us, sir. Better than I thought," he reported to Hatcher.

"The regiment is moving out in a few minutes. Any sign of the canteens?" Hatcher asked.

Charlie shook his head. "Where are we going, sir?"

Robert looked through the trees and pointed at Little Round Top. "We're going to take that hill."

"Oh God. . .not another hill," Charlie whispered. "The colonel . . . he can't be serious."

"I'm afraid so. You better get them ready," Hatcher replied.

"Yes, sir." Charlie turned to the company. "Company L, on your feet. We got another hill to climb."

As the Forty-fourth New York left the road to the right, Colonel Strong Vincent rushed up to meet the Twentieth Maine. Lawrence jumped down from his saddle.

"Colonel Chamberlain, I'm putting your regiment on the left flank of the brigade. Place your right flank there," Vincent said, pointing to the rocks above the gully. "You're on a foot of the bald hill. It crests about fifty yards into the trees. Extend your line across the face of it as far as you can. You might want to familiarize yourself with the ground before you bring your regiment into line. Colonel, your regiment is the left flank of the entire army. You understand . . . you are to hold this ground at all costs."

"Yes, sir."

"Good luck, Lawrence."

"Thank you, sir. You too."

Lawrence turned and faced the regiment. Hold at all costs. Ruel rushed forward and took his horse. Sergeant Major Sam Miller was right behind him.

"I guess we ain't got to worry about missin' this fight, sir."

"It looks that way, Sam. Captain Spear and Captain Clark, report," Lawrence shouted. Both men came running.

"Before we put the regiment in line, let's the four of us go inspect our assigned position."

Lawrence went up past the boulders. The ground continued to slope upwards. He followed it until he came to the crest, another summit, much lower than the first. They would be defending their own little hill.

As he stood for a minute examining the ground in their front, he asked, "Any suggestions?"

"Sir," the Sergeant Major spoke up, "I suggest we place the regiment along the face of the hill down along those boulders. It'll give the men some protection."

"I agree, sir," Ellis said.

Lawrence scrutinized the ground. Sam and Ellis were right. The boulders would give the right and center of his line some much-needed protection, but the left would still be pretty much out in the open. It couldn't be helped.

"It's agreed then," Lawrence said. "The valley is pretty open across our front, so I'm going to put a company of skirmishers out there." He pointed to the densely wooded area off their left flank. "I would hate to think what would happen if they got past us.

"I'm going to use the command 'on the right file into line' to get the regiment into position."

"That's going to take time, sir," Ellis said.

"It'll take time to get the entire regiment into line, but it's the quickest way to put guns immediately on the firing line. The main threat is going to come from our right, so even if the Rebels advance before we get everyone in line—"

"We'll have the right flank ready to greet them," Atherton Clark cut in.

"Exactly. Ellis, I want you to take the left flank. Atherton, the right. I'll command the regiment from the center of the line. Everyone clear what we're going to do?" They all nodded. "Get the men ready."

The three others walked back toward the regiment. Lawrence hesitated. For the first time, he truly felt the full weight of command, and he loved it. This was what he and his men had trained for. For the first time, the Twentieth Maine was in a position to make a difference in the war. He was determined that neither he nor his regiment would fail. He took a deep breath and headed back to his men; with each step, excitement pulsed through his veins. This was why he had joined the army in the first place: to play an essential role in a critical battle. With one frustration after another, he had begun to wonder if it would ever happen. Held out of the fights at Antietam and Chancellorsville and wasted in the futile attempt against the wall at Fredericksburg, he had wondered if his time would ever come. Would he get the chance to lead his men when it counted?

Lawrence gritted his teeth to keep from smiling. Their time had come. His time had come.

Then the weight slowly started to settle over him. He began to get nervous.

"Hold at all costs" were his orders. He knew it meant only one thing: there would be no retreat. They would stay and fight. They would stay and die, but they would not fall back. They would not run away.

As he watched his men come up the slope, he was proud and nervous. They were his men. They would look to him. There could be no indecision on his part. No hesitation.

"Regiment, halt," Captain Ellis Spear ordered.

The sergeant major came forward. "We're ready."

Then Lawrence barked out the command. "Regiment!"

"Company, platoon, squad" seemed like an uncanny echo.

"On the right file into line. Guide right. March!"

The men moved smartly, and within a minute, Company E was in line, ready for action. Next came Company I, then Company K.

Lawrence looked over each company as the men got ready to take their places in line. He still had to pick one to serve as skirmishers, but which one?

Company B was next. Perfect.

"Captain Morrill, report!" he shouted.

Morrill sprinted forward. "Yes, sir."

"Captain, we're on the left flank of the brigade. I don't want the Rebels sneaking by us. Take your company out there," he said, pointing to the left, "out past the big boulder. Find some cover, and don't let them surprise us."

"I won't, sir."

Lawrence watched as B Company disappeared over the ledge and into the woods. He then turned back to the rest of the regiment.

Company G was coming into line. It was the last of them. Lawrence realized I don't have enough men, as the line fell short of the large boulder by almost twenty feet. Maybe he shouldn't have sent out all of Company B.

He pounded his fist on a tree. *No doubts, no regrets*, he told himself. He'd made a decision—one he couldn't change.

There was no sense rehashing it. Better to deal with what is instead of worrying about what could have been.

Within minutes, he realized there was another problem. Company G's left was out in the open where there were no boulders or trees for protection.

The men of Company G were doing what they could to solve the problem on their own. They were quickly gathering rocks, branches, and even some logs to pile up in front of them. The slope of the hill and their makeshift breastworks, along with firing from a prone position, would provide them with some measure of cover.

Fortunately, for most of the rest of the line, several large boulders and trees provided a some protection for a large number of the men. The rest were doing the same as Company G, piling up whatever they could find for cover.

"Sir, the regiment is in position," Sergeant Major Miller reported.

"Very good. I'm sure glad the farmer decided not to clear this part of the hill of trees. We would be pretty exposed without them."

"Most of them are scrub oak, sir. No good for timber."

Lawrence glanced up into the stately oak trees with their wide expansive branches. Scrub oak. It'd been a long time since he'd heard the term. A good oak for lumber was tall, straight, and had few branches. These were short and wide with lots of branches. Scrub oaks, but he sure wouldn't mind having one like them in his front yard back home.

"Anything else, sir?"

"Yes, Sam. Send the drummer boys to the rear. The line is compact. I don't think I'll need them. No sense in putting them in danger for no good reason."

"Yes, sir. One more thing, Colonel. What are we gonna do with the prisoners?"

"I'll see to them myself. Where are they?"

"Up there," Sam pointed toward the summit of their little hill.

Lawrence walked quickly up the slope. The corporal in charge of the detail gave him a crisp rifle salute. Lawrence returned it with a hand salute.

"Corporal, I'm releasing you and your men back to your companies. Take your places in line."

"Yes, sir," the corporal responded enthusiastically. The detail hurried away, leaving Lawrence alone with the six Second Maine prisoners.

"Gentlemen, would any of you care to join us? If you do, I'll make sure all charges are dropped."

"Colonel, I ain't never run from a fight," one of the privates said. "No sense in startin' now." A couple more nodded in agreement.

"For those of you who want to join us, just find a place in line. We don't have any extra rifles, but as you know, there will be some available soon enough. As for the rest of you, I expect to find you here after the fight. You're still under arrest."

Lawrence walked back down the slope and found Sam by the large boulder. "Sam, some of the prisoners have decided to join us. Make sure they find a place in line."

"Sure thing, Colonel. I have a feelin' we'll need the help."

"Colonel Chamberlain!" The voice came from up the slope. Lawrence was surprised to see Jim Rice walking quickly toward him. Brother Tom hurried over to join them. "Lawrence, just past my regiment, the hill is pretty open. I thought you might want to come to see what we're going to be up against," Rice said.

"That's a good idea. Tom, let Ellis and Atherton know where I'm going."

"I want to come too," Tom said.

"Better not, Tom. The shelling still looks pretty heavy up near the summit. I don't want to take the chance . . ." Lawrence didn't feel the need to finish the sentence. Tom looked disappointed. He didn't care.

Lawrence walked past him as he followed Rice back up the slope. As they went past the Pennsylvania regiment, Lawrence was surprised to find the New Yorkers next in line.

"Jim, I thought Colonel Vincent put your regiment on the right flank. Where's the Sixteenth Michigan?"

"The Eighty-third was large enough to fill the gap between our regiments, so he moved the Sixteenth over to the right flank."

"Why didn't he shift your regiment to the right? It'd been easier than moving the boys from Michigan."

"He thought about doing that, but I talked him out of it. You know we always fight next to the Eighty-third. I didn't think it was a good time to break with tradition."

"I didn't know you were superstitious," Lawrence said.

"To tell the truth, until now, I didn't either."

As they walked up the slope, the sounds of the fighting grew louder—boom, boom, boom. The artillery thundered and vibrated across the hillsides. The musket fire was almost a constant pop, pop, pop.

As they got closer to the summit, the sounds blended into a roar that thundered like an angry sea. They came into the open and, to Lawrence, it seemed like a dense, dirty fog had settled across the valley below. Yellow flashes from the barrels of thousands of muskets twinkled and beamed like miniature lighthouses shining through the mist.

Artillery shells exploded up near the summit. Thankfully, they were firing long.

A lone Union regiment stood on the valley floor, its two blue lines in perfect formation and their colors waving proudly above them. They rushed forward and quickly disappeared into the smoke. The yellow lights swept across in front of them as if they were lighting the way to death.

One man came running out and threw down his musket. His cap flew from his head. Then there was another and another. It quickly turned into a flood of men fleeing for their lives. The last regiment had broken.

More flashes. Then they came into the open. The men in gray streamed out into the clear air. They were coming, and there was nothing between them and the Third Brigade.

"Time to go," Lawrence said.

The two men hurried back the way they'd come, with Rice in the lead. As they reached the Forty-fourth, Rice turned and stuck out his right hand.

"Good luck, Lawrence."

"You too." They shook hands, and Lawrence continued past the Eighty-third, down into the gully, and back up the slope. He paused and surveyed his right flank. There were several large boulders his men were already taking refuge behind.

"Boys, the Rebels are coming. We got to keep them from taking this hill."

"We will," several men shouted.

Lawrence found his company commanders standing at the crest of the hill. James Nichols, Charles Billings, Joe Fitch, Sam Keene, and the others all looked to him with eager faces.

"Gentleman, we're going to have guests very shortly. They've overrun the Third Corps' line. We're the only thing standing between them and the rear of the army. I'm sure everyone knows by now that we're the left flank of the

Army of the Potomac. Colonel Vincent ordered me to hold this place at all costs. We will not withdraw from here."

Suddenly, the shelling stopped. Everyone knew that it meant the Rebel infantry was close. Less than a minute later, the brigade's right opened fire.

"As soon as your company has targets in its front, you can have them fire at will. Good luck to each of you."

The company commanders hurried away. Lawrence walked down the slope and took a position in the middle of the line next to Color Sergeant Andrew Tozier.

"Sergeant, you can unfurl the colors."

"Yes, sir." Andrew pulled the protective sleeve from the flag and quickly unrolled it. The tattered national flag hung limply from the nine-foot pole.

"Andrew, have you seen Joe?"

"Yes, sir. He begged the sergeant major to put him back into the line. He told him that he was sure you weren't gonna need him to blow that damn bugle."

A deep gray smoke rose from the trees to their immediate right, and then the thunder from the volley crashed in on their ears. It was the Eighty-third Pennsylvania. They were next. Lawrence couldn't see them yet, but he knew the Rebels were there. With each second, they were getting closer, and at any moment, his right flank would open fire.

Even though he was ready for it, he still jerked when companies E and I let go with the first volley. The firing spread to the left; then Lawrence saw them—a jagged battle line weaving between the trees.

The center of the line fired. The volley hurt his ears, and the smoke made his eyes water. As the sulfur smell flooded his sinuses, Lawrence smiled, and his heartbeat stronger.

Yes, this is what he'd waited for . . . what he had trained for. They were finally in a position to make a difference. Today no one would die in vain.

Suddenly, a stray artillery shell exploded in front of the line and knocked Lawrence back against the hillside.

"You all right, sir?" Andrew shouted.

"I think so, Andy. I don't think I'm hit."

Lawrence looked down at his feet. There was a gash in his right boot, and though he didn't see any blood, suddenly his foot hurt like hell. He'd been lucky. The shell had exploded just in front of a boulder, helping to defect away most of the explosion. Lawrence noticed a piece of shelling at his feet. He went to pick it up, but it was too hot, so he took out his handkerchief and wrapped the piece of shell in it, and stuck it in his coat pocket as a souvenir.

As he stood back up, he noticed a Confederate regiment crossing the valley in their front. Their battle flag floated majestically above the grayline. The Twentieth's line exploded in another volley. Through the smoke, he could see several of the Rebels fall as the rest ran for cover.

"Colonel Chamberlain!" Lieutenant Jim Nichols, commanding Company K, yelled as he ran over from the regiment's right.

"Report, Lieutenant."

"Sir, I think a Rebel regiment is trying to get around our flank. They're moving through the trees over on the next slope."

"Very good, Lieutenant. Return to your company."

"Yes, sir."

Smoke obscured the valley. Lawrence couldn't see what the lieutenant was talking about. He wondered what he should do. He had to see what was going on. Seeing a large boulder to his left, he had an idea. He knew it was crazy, but he jumped up on it just the same.

From his vantage point, his eyes caught a flash of red and blue moving through the trees on the next hillside. There was something else: dark shapes moving through the foliage. The lieutenant was right; it was a full regiment and a big one too.

As his eyes followed their line of march, he knew they were heading past the left flank. "Oh God," he whispered. "I sent Morrill out there."

Praying that God would look out for Company B because there was nothing he could do for them, Lawrence jumped down from the rock and climbed up the slope. It wouldn't be long until the Rebel commander did a left wheel of his regiment. When he did, they would come crashing down on his flank.

When he looked back at them, more shapes moved through the trees. He realized that it was indeed a large regiment much larger than his own.

Lawrence knew that he had to do something. His first thought was to pull his regiment away and change front, but the shooting continued across his line's center and on the right flank.

Lawrence spotted Sam Miller and Tom and waved them over to join him.

"The Rebels are moving past our left flank. Tom, go see Captain Woodward. See if the Eighty-third can give us any help. Hurry, Tom."

Lawrence then turned to his sergeant major. "Sam, pass the word to have the company commanders join me."

What am I going to do? For a few moments, his mind went blank, but he didn't panic. It would come to him. The other officers rushed to join him.

"Gentlemen, we're about to get flanked. I've sent for help, but I don't expect to get any. We're going to have to extend the line. Have your men keep up the fire as they shift to the left. We're going to stretch the line out to one rank. Sam, pick a spot on the left. As the men reach you, I want the left flank to slant back at a right angle."

Lawrence remained firm despite moans from his officers.

"I don't like this any more than the rest of you, but we don't have any other options," he said sternly. "We will hold this ground. We will not retreat. Tell your men to keep up the firing during the move. I don't want to give the Rebels in our front an opening to charge us in the middle of the move. Captain Spear, you're in charge of the extended line. Now all of you get going."

"Colonel!" Tom yelled as he came running from the right. "They couldn't spare anyone," he panted.

"I'm not surprised. We're going to extend our line to one rank and form another front on the left." Lawrence scanned his eyes over the slope.

"Colors to the left flank!" He wanted the colors to move to the new center, near the large boulder.

He drew a deep breath. There was nothing else for him to do. He'd issued the orders. It was up to his commanders to carry them out.

"No doubts," he muttered. It was risky maneuvering a regiment in the face of the enemy. What if they charge while we are in the middle of the move? And he'd purposely put the center of the new line on a slant. It was going to take fire from two fronts. No choice. No doubts.

Lawrence watched as the men started to move. The firing continued up and down the line. They showed no weakness. The Rebels weren't advancing. This might work, he thought, as he watched Ellis guide the extended line into position.

Lawrence walked toward the left. The center of the line was on a slant. It would be the weakest part of the line.

Fortunately, the boulder on the end of the line would help. If the center started to show weakness, it would be difficult for the Rebels to exploit it.

A private suddenly cried out in pain and fell to his knees. Blood splattered from a wound in his thigh. Two slender shapes rushed past Lawrence to the wounded man. *Drummer boys. What are they doing?* The two boys helped the man to his feet and helped him to the rear.

Sam rushed over to Lawrence. "Sir, they wanted to help. I didn't have the heart to tell them no."

Lawrence said nothing but gave a slight nod. He knew how the boys felt. He briefly thought about joining them with the detail but quickly changed his mind. It wasn't his place.

Instead, he would have to put up with his own inactivity, the curse of command. He pulled out his sword. It made him feel like he was doing something in some way contributing.

The extended line was in place. The Rebel regiment would wheel about any second now and come crashing in on them, and when they did, the Twentieth Maine would be ready for them.

Chapter 16

I'm over there, boy, waiting for you, the voice taunted him.

Second Lieutenant Wicker tried to ignore the voice. A bullet whistled past his head.

That wasn't me. When I come after you, I won't miss, the demon whispered.

Robert clutched his hand tightly around his sword and prayed, "God, help me." His nagging fear returned . . . the same fear he'd felt the night before. *I'm not a coward*; he reminded himself.

When the drums sounded ordering a left wheel, the regiment swung to the left. Smoke from the Yankees' fire against the Forty-seventh hung low across the ridge's face, plainly pointing the way to their flank.

As Robert glanced to his left, he saw that they were coming in at an angle to the Yankee position, and half the regiment would be rolling up into their rear.

Eyes front, he told himself, as he noticed dark shadows moving through the smoke. *What are they doing? Are they running?* More shadows. The Yankees were retreating! Relief swept over him. He couldn't believe his eyes. They were running. The voice would go with them. In triumph, he waved his sword above his head. "They're running, boys," he yelled. A cheer spread through the company.

A gust from the south wind blew between the hills and caused the smoke enveloping the Yankees' flank to swirl and dance. Robert swallowed hard when a tattered red, white, and blue flag appeared amid the smoke. The flag flapped majestically, defiantly. The color bearer stood firm, unmoving. Robert lowered his sword as he realized the horrible, awful truth: the Yankees weren't running.

The smoke swirled more and revealed an officer with a sword standing next to the color bearer. He was tall, almost regal in appearance, with a large mustache.

You're a coward.

Had his demon taken human form? He didn't know didn't care, but that officer became the target of Robert's anger and frustration. He planted his feet and shifted his sword to his left hand. He then reached for his pistol. *You idiot . . . run . . . run for your life,* the voice of his own fear screamed at him. He pulled his pistol from its holster. I won't run. He raised the weapon and took aim. He knew he was too far away, but he didn't care. He slowly squeezed the trigger. It fired.

A second later, the Yankees fired a volley. The officer disappeared into the angry, swirling, gray smoke.

Bullets whistled by Robert's head. *Run, boy,* his fear demanded. "I can't," he muttered through the screams that now echoed through the valley. He pulled the trigger two more times, firing blindly, madly into the smoke.

When Robert lowered his pistol, the Yankees fired another volley. The top of a small tree behind him crashed to the ground. He didn't move. He couldn't. A battle raged within his mind, a struggle for his very soul. *Run away . . . stay and fight . . . run away . . . stay and fight.* With his mind tormented, he just stood there seemingly transfixed on the smoke, staring, waiting.

"Lieutenant," Joe Henderson snapped at him.

More bullets, more screams, and still Robert just stood there, with angry bullets screaming past him. Joe grabbed Robert's shoulder and spun him around.

"Lieutenant, what's wrong?" Joe yelled.

Robert didn't respond. His eyes were fixed. Joe took him by the collar and shook him. "Lieutenant, snap out of it. The company needs you."

Joe's words penetrated his mind, invaded upon his own inner conflict. *My company. They need me. Think about the men*, he told himself. He blinked his eyes. Lord, if it is my time to die, please let me die like a man.

"My God, Bobby, snap out of it," Joe pleaded.

There were yells to the right. The regiment was advancing again. Robert looked over the men. Most, including Hatcher, had their eyes fixed on him. He looked back at Joe. "Take your place back in line."

"You all right?"

"Yes. Take your place in line."

Robert met Hatcher's gaze and nodded. Hatcher waved his sword and pointed to the front. "Forward," he shouted.

The smoke stung Lawrence's eyes. When he wiped them on his sleeve, he felt a little relief. He then turned his gaze toward the right flank; all seemed in order. The Rebels weren't pressing on this section of the line. He decided it would be safe to pull a company from the right flank and move them to the left if it came to it.

He started back toward the center of the line when a yell rose from the valley floor. The hairs stood up on the back of his neck. They're coming again. He raced up to the crest of their little hill to get a better view. Through the smoke, he saw jagged lines dodging between the trees. There were so many of them. The enemy far outnumbered his regiment. *We have to hold . . . we can't retreat,* he told himself.

As his men increased their fire, several of the enemy dropped to the ground, but the rest kept coming. Looking to his left, he saw that Ellis was calmly standing behind the line urging his men to keep up their fire, but Lawrence knew it wasn't going to be enough to stop the enemy's advance.

As the Rebels moved up the slope, his men in many places along the extended lines had restored to hand-to-hand combat. One private fired his rifle at point-blank range, and with no time to reload, he picked up rocks and hurled them at the attackers. Others used their rifles as clubs.

The desperate men's shouts and screams were drowned out by the constant pounding roar of musket fire. Men fell to the ground—some dead, some wounded. Grudgingly the line fell back, moved upslope, but not far; then it stiffened. They'd bent, but they hadn't broken. After a few minutes, the Rebels retreated, but they took positions behind nearby trees and rocks and continued to pepper his men with musket fire.

Lawrence moved back down to the center of the line, giving his men encouragement and praise. He looked out into the trees and smiled. His men they'd held. Finally, they'd made a difference.

Robert ducked behind a small boulder. Elisha Sellers settled in next to him.

"They're pretty stubborn," Elisha said as he bit off the end of another cartridge and dumped the black powder down the barrel. He pushed down the minie ball and rammed it home. He cocked the hammer and carefully placed a primer under it. Elisha peeked from the side of the boulder. "I can't see anything. Too much smoke."

"Give it a minute. It'll clear," Robert said as he looked over the top. They were stuck in front of a ten-foot embankment formed by a large boulder. It made Company L's advancement extremely difficult. Further to the right, there was more of a gradual slope. The colonel was moving the regiment to take advantage of the ground. So far, it hadn't helped his men. Hopefully, the regiment would swing farther to the right where his men would have an easier time getting at the Yankees.

A hole opened in the smoke, and he was there again—the tall officer with the sword, the root of his torment. This time Robert didn't hesitate. He raised his pistol and fired. A private next to the officer dropped to the ground. Damn pistol, it wasn't much good past twenty-five yards.

"Shoot, Elisha," he yelled, just as the smoke swirled back around the Yankee. Elisha fired, but it was too late.

Elisha reloaded his musket, and Robert searched the smoke, hoping he'd get another chance to shoot down the Yankee demon.

A private standing next to Lawrence fell to the ground, and he knelt next to the young man. A bullet had torn a path across his forehead.

Surprisingly, the dazed boy sat up. Blood was pouring down his face, and jagged pieces of white bone protruded from the wound.

"Son, can you walk?" Lawrence asked.

"I think so."

"You need to get to the rear."

"I'm fine, sir. It ain't that bad."

"I'm ordering you to the rear."

One of the drummer boys ran up and grabbed the young man by the arm, dragging him to his feet and helping him up the slope. Lawrence wished him well.

"They're coming again!" The shouts spread up and down the line.

This time the Rebels were more careful. They were using the trees and rocks for cover. Also, they were moving even further to the left. They were reaching, searching for the flank. If they turned his flank, they would march right up the brigade's rear, and all would be lost.

Lawrence was startled by an increase of firing coming from the brigade's right flank. If they overran the right, the Twentieth Maine would be cut off.

There was an artillery blast and then another. He breathed easier. Someone had dragged artillery to the summit of Little Round Top. The right flank should hold.

From the left came more shouts. The Rebels were making a desperate dash. Once again, the two lines clashed. Men fired their rifles literally in the face of their enemies. With no time to reload, once again, their rifles became clubs.

Again, his men fell back. The Rebel battle flag floated up above his line.

A ramrod streaked through the smoke, and Lawrence knew the Rebels weren't their only enemy. His men were also battling fear, excitement, and dread, all fighting to cloud their minds. Their hours and hours of training were the only defense against the second enemy, the one that rested within every man.

He knew other mistakes were being made too. The ramrod was just the most glaring example. He knew some of his men would load their weapons time after time and never fire a shot, ramming one minie ball down on top of another until the barrel was completely full. Others would cock the hammer and fire their rifle over and over, never remembering to load it.

He took solace in the fact his men weren't alone in battling the enemy from within. The Rebels would be fighting it too.

When a few of the Rebels broke through his line, Captain Billings raised his sword high and urged his Company A to follow him. They rushed forward and disappeared into the smoke of a Rebel volley.

Lawrence saw Billings' silhouette in the smoke, so brave, gallant; then he fell to his knees. For a moment, he seemed to be praying before he fell on his face. Another man was dead, this one an officer, a friend. Lawrence bit his lip, but he didn't grieve. There wasn't time. For now, he had to turn all his attention to the living. After the fighting, there would be enough time to mourn for their dead.

Again, the Rebels retreated. The musket fire slacked off, relieving the pounding in his ears. He took a deep breath and enjoyed the peace of the moment. His men, outnumbered, outgunned, had held again.

Sam Miller rushed over to him. "Sir, some of the men are running low on ammunition," he reported.

Already? Had they been fighting that long?

"Have them strip the dead and wounded," Lawrence ordered. "The second wave should be coming along soon."

"Yes, sir. I'll see to it."

When the smoke started to lift, Lawrence was stunned by what it revealed. Over half the men on the left were already down. It's time to move a company from the right, he decided.

Lawrence immediately rushed over to Atherton Clark.

"Captain, I want you to pull Company E out of line and move them to the left. Have the other companies spread out to cover the gap."

"Yes, sir."

Lawrence set his jaw to keep from smiling. He figured his men would not understand and think him batty. How could the colonel in the middle of a desperate fight start grinning like a schoolboy? They wouldn't understand, and he didn't know if he could explain it to them—explain how he'd waited his whole life for this one glorious moment in time.

There were shouts from behind, and when he looked over his shoulder, he was stunned to see the entire right flank retreating up the slope.

Lawrence took off at a full run, cutting across the face of the slope. "Reform the line! Reform the line!" he yelled.

Sam Miller was coming from the left, yelling the same. Clark was waving his arms for them to stop.

After moving ten yards up the slope, thankfully, all the men stopped. Lawrence waved all the company commanders over to join him.

"Reform the line where the men are," Lawrence said. "Captain Clark, increase Company E's spacing. Extend the line to the left. The rest of you do the same. We have got to shift the line over. We have to get more men on the left flank."

The company commanders hurried away, but Clark hesitated.

"Sir, I'm sorry. I don't—"

"No apologies necessary. It was my fault. I should have known better than to pull a company out of line. Carry out your orders."

"Yes, sir."

Lawrence stood behind the new line as the men reformed and shifted to the left. He knew full well that they'd been lucky this time. The enemy hadn't taken advantage of their mistake. He knew they might not be so lucky if they made another one.

The last charge had breached the Yankee line. It looked like the right flank was in the enemy's rear for a short time, but they couldn't hold. Maybe, hopefully, next time.

Hatcher crawled over next to Robert.

"You all right?"

"Yes, sir."

"The heat is worse than the Yankees. We've lost half the men already. When we go forward again, we'll go as one rank. You take the left, and I'll have the right."

"Sounds good," Robert said.

"We've got to carry that hill," Hatcher said with a sense of desperation.

Robert's adrenaline rush was rapidly wearing off. His mouth was so dry he couldn't suck up enough saliva to spit. He'd stopped sweating. Every muscle in his body cried for water.

His pistol was beginning to feel like a lead weight. He quit trying to use it. At this range, even on a good day, he'd be lucky if he hit anything, but now it would take a miracle. He decided to save his ammunition for when they got in close.

"I hope Bill makes it back soon. I'm getting mighty thirsty," Elisha said.

"He's not coming back! None of them are," Hatcher snapped.

"Sir, Cousin Bill won't let us down . . . he'll be here."

"If he were coming, he'd be here by now. I'm afraid the Yankees got him and the rest of the detail. They were all good men. Either they were captured, or they're dead. There's no other explanation," Robert said.

"Damn. I hope he's not dead."

"Me too," Robert said.

"Well, Benning's Brigade was lined up to support us. Some of them should be coming along soon. Maybe they'll share some—"

"The advance was messed up. I'm afraid they used them to fill in holes in the line," Hatcher said.

"Sir, you don't know that."

Robert glanced behind and saw there was no movement in the darkening woods. "They were only five hundred yards behind us. If they were coming, they'd be here by now," Robert added.

Robert looked over the company and noticed that Charlie and Joe Henderson were the only remaining noncommissioned officers.

Rubbing his forehead, he had to admit that Hatcher was right. Time was quickly running out for the Fifteenth Alabama. Heat and exhaustion were claiming even more casualties than the Yankees. If they didn't take the heights soon, all would be lost. They wouldn't have enough men left even to try.

Maybe the company could do more good if they moved away from the damn boulder. *But which way? To the left or the right?* While most of the regiment was angling to the right, the left was becoming vulnerable.

The Forty-seventh Alabama had already retreated, and their own Company B had been decimated. Which way should we go? The shouts, screams, and gunfire increased on the regiment's right. Colonel

Oates decided for them. Once again, he was pushing them forward.

"Here we go again, boys," Hatcher shouted to the men. "This time, we're going to take that ledge."

Lawrence paced back and forth just behind his right flank. He knew Clark would see it as a lack of confidence, but it couldn't be helped. After what had happened earlier, he had to make sure all was in order on the right flank.

The Rebels facing his right crept forward, using the trees for cover, but they didn't make a serious effort to advance on his line.

From the left, once again, the Rebel yell pierced the heavy afternoon air. They were coming again. The angry gray and white smoke danced and swirled, giving Lawrence only glimpses of the fighting. A hole appeared near the center of the line. Lawrence was shocked to see only two men were left to defend the colors.

Everyone else was down. With the staff planted in the ground, Andrew Tozier had an elbow hooked around it. He flung up a rifle, aimed, and fired. Without hesitation, he reloaded the weapon. The private next to him fired his musket.

Lawrence noticed brother Tom was nearby. "Lieutenant take some men and protect the colors," he yelled.

"Yes, sir." Tom went down the line, picking out men from three different companies. Then the group rushed toward the flag as the smoke once again enveloped it. They were gone. God help them.

When Lawrence turned, he was face to face with Ruel Thomas.

"Sergeant, there is a gap in the center of the line. I sent Tom and some men to go fill it. Take some more and go help him."

"Yes, sir!" Ruel tapped Private George Buck on the shoulder. "Come with me," he said. The two men rushed into the smoke.

There was another hole, this one more to the left. The Rebel battle flag floated above his line. One of his men reached for it. As a rebel raised back his rifle, there was a flash of light. A rare beam of sunlight found its way through the trees and smoke and flashed off the man's bayonet.

Lawrence fixed his gaze on the bayonet as it came down into the head of the young private from Maine. Lawrence had to turn away as blood spurted from the wound.

More and more men went down, and slowly, grudgingly, his line fell back, then the smoke closed in and settled over them. The Rebels in front of his right flank increased their fire.

Colonel Vincent's words echoed in his brain: "You understand, Colonel, this ground must be held at all costs!" Lawrence understood. If necessary, they would all die before they would retreat or surrender.

He had no problem with his orders, but that wasn't the point. The point was to hold the ground, and it was beginning to look like they wouldn't be able to do it alone. The smoke lifted again along the left flank.

His line was intact but rapidly thinning. They'd pulled further up the hillside. What had started as an L-shaped line now looked much more like a narrow V, as the line was beginning to bend back upon itself. If they didn't get some help soon, he would once again have one line—a line being attacked from two sides at once.

"Colonel Chamberlain! Colonel Chamberlain!" Lawrence turned to see a lieutenant running toward him.

"Sir, Captain Woodward sent me. We're getting fire in our rear. Has your flank been turned?"

"We're holding, but barely! We've got an entire regiment coming in on our left flank. Tell Captain Woodward I have got to have some help—and fast!"

The lieutenant rushed off in a hail of bullets.

For a moment, Lawrence felt like he was in the audience of a great outdoor theater, watching the performance of a Greek tragedy unfold. The swirling smoke, the screams of desperate men, and bullets flying through the air and finding their targets with a sinking thud whirled all around. There was nothing he could do except watch and pray that his men could somehow drive back their gray-coated foe.

"Colonel Chamberlain!" The officer from the Eighty-third was back.

"Sir, Captain Woodward says he can shift our line to the left. He advises you to do the same."

Lawrence took a deep breath. "Tell the Captain, thank you."

"Yes, sir."

Lawrence waved for Sam and Atherton to join him. They both came running.

"We're going to shift the entire line to the left. The Eighty-third is going to cover the gap. Get it done."

They both hurried away. Everything is going to be all right, Lawrence said to himself, as if the words would make it so. He took a step forward when something slammed into his left leg. Lawrence dropped his sword as he spun around. Then he fell to the ground.

His leg throbbed, but as he reached for it, he found there was no blood.

"You all right, sir?" Sam Miller asked as he knelt next to him.

"Do you see any blood?"

"No, sir."

As Lawrence sat up, his leg throbbed, but when he reached for the spot, there wasn't even a hole in his pant leg.

"Sir, look at your scabbard."

Lawrence was surprised to see it smashed. He smiled as he shook his head. The scabbard had deflected the bullet and entirely possibly saved his leg.

Sam stood, reached down, saying, "Give me your hand." Lawrence took his hand, and Sam pulled him to his feet. Lawrence then braced himself on a tree as he tried to put weight on the leg. Even though it hurt, he could stand the pain.

Sam bent to pick up the sword.

"Here, sir. You might need this."

"Thanks," Lawrence said, grasping the handle.

When a man's figure then ran past them, Lawrence glanced over. It was the boy with the head wound rushing to the left. Two more men scurried by. The last of the Second Maine men were joining the fight. Behind them were three more who'd gone on the morning's sick call for bloody feet. They'd caught up with the regiment.

As the line shifted to the left, more men joined the desperate fight. They rushed the Rebels and then retreated as the other side counterattacked. More hand-to-hand fighting ensued.

Lawrence was concerned as he watched Captain Joe Fitch limp to the rear. A nasty wound in his thigh made it difficult for him to walk. Captain Keene was also down, a wound in his side. Billings was dead, and only God knew what had happened to Morrill, and his Company B. Four of his ten commanders were out of action.

He hoped Colonel Vincent was right about the importance of their little hill. He didn't want his men dying in vain.

Company L had done their part. They'd laid down heavy fire on the slant in the enemy's line. For a moment, the smoke had lifted. The Yankees' color stood alone. They climbed up the boulder. Then with all their might, they charged toward the flag. Yankees rushed to the defense of their colors.

Robert had used his pistol to shoot down a Yankee private, and then he beat off another with his sword. He urged the left flank forward. Three of his men fell to the ground. Then the regiment once again retreated. He had no choice. He ordered his men to fall back. They went down the ledge to the position where they'd started.

Elisha slumped against a tree and slid to the ground. "You all right?"

"I'm dizzy."

Hatcher was a few feet away, staring blankly at Robert. When his eyes rolled up, Robert could see only the whites of his eyes. Then Hatcher fell face first. Robert rushed over to him and rolled him over. No wounds, but he was out cold. Robert motioned for two men to carry Hatcher to the rear. As they disappeared into the woods, Robert searched the area to see what was left of the company. His heart sank. He saw only ten brave men still with him. Out of a company of thirty-eight, there were only eleven left.

I haven't forgotten you, the voice then said, coming from nowhere.

"Nor I you," Robert whispered.

A sharp pain shot through Robert's left leg. He cried out and fell to the ground.

"Bobby, you hit?"

Robert examined his leg. "No blood. Just a cramp." As he rubbed his leg, the pain started to ease.

"You okay?" Elisha asked.

"Yeah, it's better."

"What we gonna do? Neither one of us can walk."

"Speak for yourself," Robert said as he grabbed a tree and pulled himself to his feet. He put weight on the leg. It hurt like hell, but it supported him. "See, I'm fine."

"You liar."

Robert smiled.

"Damn you. If you can do it, so can I."

Robert reached a hand toward his friend, helped him to his feet, and then turned to face his remaining men.

"Listen up, fellows. I'm tired of climbing that damn ledge. I want to get out from in front of it. The regiment's left flank is vulnerable, so we're going to move there. Next time the regiment moves forward, I want you to hold your fire until we get right in the faces of those Yankees. Then we're going to blast them off that damn hill. Everybody understand?" With tired and weary faces, they all shook their heads in agreement.

With so few of them left, Robert wasn't sure what they could do, but they were going to give it their best try. There was another reason he wanted another chance to get up on the hill. He had some unfinished business he wanted to take care of.

The Rebels had disappeared back into the trees. Lawrence wondered if it was finally over. Had the Rebels decided to give up trying to drive off his regiment?

Puffs of smoke from the valley and the whistling of bullets through the trees answered his question. It wasn't over yet. "Sir, my company, is out of ammunition," Lieutenant Lewis from Company A reported. *His company?* It sounded strange to Lawrence. Company A was Charles Billings' company, but no longer. When Billings went down, the weight of command had fallen on young Lewis.

"Mine too, sir," said Captain Bill Fogler, commanding Company D.

Lawrence didn't know what to say or do. Vincent's words, "Hold at all costs!" told him what he couldn't do; he couldn't retreat.

"Colonel, come here quick!" Sam Miller yelled from down the slope toward the big boulder. Lawrence hurried down with Fogler following him.

"Sir, it's Private Buck. I'm afraid it's bad," Sam said.

Lawrence quietly knelt next to George and saw a large gaping hole in the man's chest that made a wheezing sound with each labored breath. A steady stream of deep red blood flowed from the wound.

Leaning over, Lawrence watched as George's eyes widen and his pale lips started to move. Lawrence spoke first.

"I'm sorry."

"Tell my mother I didn't die a coward," George whispered.

Lawrence felt a tear well up in his eye as he softly replied, "I will. I promise. And I will tell her you died a sergeant.

George Buck, for your faithful service and noble courage on the field of Gettysburg, I promote you to sergeant." Lawrence almost choked on his own words.

George smiled, and then he died. Lawrence let the single tear roll down his cheek with a heavy heart as he bowed his head and said a brief prayer; he then pushed one hand on his knee and stood.

"Sam, have the drummer boys take George to the rear."

"Yes, sir. Colonel, Ruel was hit too," Sam said. "He took one in the shoulder. He should be all right."

Lawrence was happy to see Tom standing right behind Sam. You fine, little brother?"

Tom nodded that he was.

"Sir, I need orders," Fogler said.

"I know you do, Captain. I know," Lawrence said, looking toward the woods. His eyes caught movement, and it is evident that the Rebels were getting ready for another attack.

He wondered what he would do. His men were out of ammunition. To stay and fight would be suicide. He couldn't; he wouldn't order a retreat. There was only one option. He knew his men weren't going to understand it, but maybe it was simply crazy enough to catch the Rebels by surprise.

"Captain Fogler, return to your company and get them ready to charge."

"Sir?"

"You have your orders. Get going."

"Yes, sir."

He would do a left wheel of the regiment, and, yes, crazy or not, they would fix their last instrument of death, their bayonets, and charge the Rebels.

Lawrence rushed the twenty yards back to the top of the hill where he found Captain Clark.

"Have the men fix bayonets."

"Sir?"

"You heard me right. We're going to charge. I'm going to order a left wheel of the regiment. Make sure the right flank remains tight with the Eighty-third."

"Yes, sir."

As Lawrence headed for the center of the line, he started to have second thoughts. Maybe there was a better plan, a more realistic option.

"Colonel." Lieutenant Holman Melcher ran up to him. "Colonel, Captain Keene is down. I'm in command of Company F. Sir; we left some men out in front of our line. I want permission to move my men forward so that we can pull them back to safety."

With those words, all of Lawrence's doubts left him. He couldn't help but admire the young man's bravery.

"Permission granted," Lawrence said, smiling, "as long as you don't mind if the rest of the regiment comes along."

"Sir?"

"I'm going to order a charge. Get your men ready."

"Yes, sir." The young lieutenant eased out a grin as he hurried away.

Lawrence turned to his left. It took him a moment before he spotted Captain Ellis Spear.

Lawrence knew that he needed to pass the orders on to him before they charged.

A yell then came from his left. Lawrence thought his heart would stop. Melcher wasn't waiting for orders. He was moving Company F forward.

Oh, God. If Ellis doesn't see the colors moving forward . . . He didn't finish the thought. He couldn't. If Ellis didn't advance, the regiment would split in two. It would be a mistake the Rebels would indeed exploit. They would be overrun. It would be a rout. The enemy would storm up the hill right into the rear of the brigade. Little Round Top would surely fall, and maybe the entire battle lost. It would be his fault.

He looked for Ellis, but the smoke blocked his view. Lawrence held his breath. A moment later, Ellis stepped out into the open, waving his sword and urging his men forward. With his next breath, Lawrence's confidence returned. He then made a quick step to the middle of the right flank. "Bayonet!" he cried out. A yell rolled up and down the right flank, along with the clanking of metal as the men fixed their bayonets to the ends of their rifles. With his sword held high in the air, Lawrence cried, "Charge!" And God help us all.

Through the trees, Robert could see something was terribly wrong. To his right, men were running to the rear. Some threw down their weapons: pop, pop, pop. There was gunfire coming from the rear of the right flank.

Flashes of blue streaked through the trees. He didn't want to believe it, but it was true: the Yankees were charging.

Relief swept over Lawrence. The Rebels were running. Gunfire from the left caught him by surprise. At first, he thought maybe they were counterattacking when suddenly it dawned on him that it must be Company B.

He caught his foot on a rock and stumbled. Quickly regaining his balance, he ducked under a tree branch and dodged another. He jumped over a small boulder and then righted himself; thirty yards ahead, a Rebel officer was staring at Lawrence. In return, Lawrence fixed his gaze on the officer's eyes. The tired, weary brown eyes had a strange, almost haunting look. Lawrence was surprised and alarmed when the man didn't turn away.

With tension in his chest, Lawrence didn't blink as the man brought up his pistol and held it with shaky hands and arms.

Lawrence had too much momentum. He couldn't stop. He couldn't turn away. His eyes fixed on the pistol. He could see the man pull the trigger. They were only ten yards apart. There was no way the Rebel could miss him. His only thought was of Fannie. He whispered a soft "Goodbye." The pistol fired. The flame shot toward him, but Lawrence didn't feel any pain, and he was still on his feet. The hand of God must have been upon me, Lawrence thought. The Rebel had somehow missed.

Robert brought up his sword. It was his last and only hope. The two blades clashed. He tried a thrusting move. The demon countered it and thrust his sword at him. Robert felt the warm steel press against his neck. He closed his eyes. It was over. It was time for him to join his sisters and brother. He smiled. "You didn't win," he said, his lips barely moving. "I'm not dying a coward."

As Robert waited for the next move, he was surprised when the demon didn't do anything. The sword didn't move. It just remained pressed against his neck. He forced his eyes open. Above him, a Union officer just stood as if he were waiting for something.

When Robert handed over his sword, the officer, a colonel, took it from him.

"I'll take the pistol too," Lawrence said firmly.

Robert turned it over, adding, "I'm your prisoner, sir."

Lawrence checked the pistol. Three bullets were left. It might come in handy. As he looked ahead, he saw his men moving on without him. He needed to catch up with them, but he couldn't let his prisoner go.

The sergeant major was nearby. "Sam, I need your help."

"Yes, sir."

"Take charge of my prisoner."

"Sir, I don't have any ammunition."

"Here, take his sword. Lieutenant—"

"Wicker, sir. Robert Wicker."

"Very well, Lieutenant Wicker, I leave you in the custody of Sergeant Major Miller. He will protect you from harm."

"Thank you, Colonel."

Lawrence rushed away, racing after the rest of the right flank of the regiment as it moved further ahead. They'd already cleared the front of the Eighty-third Pennsylvania and were starting to move in front of the New Yorkers.

All along the line, the Rebels' reactions were the same. They were running or surrendering without a fight. He heard some shouts about going all the way to Richmond. Lawrence ran faster. He had to get them reorganized just in case the Rebels were able to mount a counterattack.

"Sergeant Major, could I have a drink from your canteen?" Robert asked.

"It'd be my pleasure, sir."

Sam handed it over, and Robert took a couple of sips.

"None of my men have any water. Would you mind if I shared the rest of it with them?"

Sam nodded. When Robert turned, he saw that Elisha was nearby, lying on the ground. Kneeling next to him, he asked, "Are you wounded?"

"No," Elisha whispered, his lips barely moving.

Robert lifted Elisha's head and handed him the canteen. Elisha took a long drink.

"You feel any better?"

Elisha made a slight nod to indicate yes. Gently supporting his right arm, Robert helped Elisha back to his feet.

"Bobby, we could try and make a run for it."

"Can you run?"

"Well, no. You?"

Robert laughed. "I don't think so. I'm too tired even to try."

"Time to go, Lieutenant," Sam said, pointing the way to the Union rear.

Hearing a thud from behind, Robert turned to see George Henderson lying on the ground and his older brother Joe standing over him. Robert noticed the red smear on the front of George's coat, but his wound didn't seem too serious.

"Here, George . . . take my hand," Joe said. George reached up to his younger brother.

"Joe, you seen Charlie?" Robert asked.

Joe pointed back toward the big hill. Robert knew that at least some of the men had gotten away.

Joe and George hobbled over to Robert. He passed the canteen to them, and they drank the rest of Sam's water. Robert then gave the canteen back to Sam.

"Thank you for your kindness."

"You're welcome, sir."

The four men then joined the gray parade of prisoners. Walking along, Robert wondered if the Yankees would let him write home. He hoped so. He knew his mother would be worried sick about him when she found out he was missing.

"Colonel Chamberlain, over here!"

Lawrence looked up and waved at Jim Rice. "I can't believe you did that," Jim said. "Bayonet charge. I just can't believe it."

"Didn't have any choice, Jim. Vincent told me to hold at all costs. My men ran out of ammunition. I couldn't think of anything else to do. By the way, my men are guarding the prisoners with empty muskets. Do you know where Vincent is? I need to get someone to take them off our hands."

"Lawrence, Vincent's down."

"Dead?"

"Not yet, but he isn't going to make it. I'm in command of the brigade. I'll get you some help. In the meantime, I need you to get your regiment back in line. There may be more Rebels out in those woods." Rice said, pointing to the slope of Big Round Top.

"I'll take care of it, Jim . . . I mean, sir," Lawrence saluted and then called out, "Captain Spear, Captain Clark! Report."

The two men hurried over to him.

"Let's get the men back in line. Colonel Rice is getting us some help with the prisoners."

"Colonel Vincent?" Ellis Spear asked. Lawrence shook his head.

Something didn't feel right. Lawrence knew he was forgetting something. Tom.

"Have either of you seen Tom?"

"He's up ahead, sir; he's fine," Ellis said.

Lawrence gave a big grin. "Okay then, let's get the boys rounded up."

Epilogue

After the war, William C. Oates was elected to Congress and later served as Governor of Alabama. He also served as a general in the Spanish-American War.

In 1905 he copyrighted a book, *The War Between the Union and the Confederacy.* It serves as his memoir and regimental history of the Fifteenth Alabama Volunteer regiment. Oates also included a roster and a brief history of each of the men who served under him.

Of Robert Wicker, Oates wrote:

> *Was 21 years old when enlisted. He was a fine soldier; served through Jackson's Valley campaign, and at Cold Harbor, June 27, 1862, was severely wounded . . . [He] was absent in consequence about two months, but returned, and was at the surrender of Harper's Ferry, in the battle of Sharpsburg, Maryland, and was thereafter present in every battle until captured at Gettysburg, and not exchanged during the war. He was promoted to second lieutenant in October 1862. He was as brave a man as any*

in that regiment. Colonel Chamberlain, of the Twentieth Maine regiment, said in his report of that battle that he in person captured Lieutenant Wicker; that latter stood his ground until he came on him, and that Wicker fired his pistol in his face, and then surrendered. The colonel said that his gallantry was such that he protected the lieutenant from violence.

After Gettysburg, J.J. Hatcher was elected captain and served with Company L until the surrender at Appomattox.

The captured enlisted men from Company L ended the war at Fort Delaware prisoner of war camp. Robert Wicker, along with most of the Confederate officers captured after Gettysburg at the prison of war camp on Johnson's Island, Ohio.

After being released in June of 1865, he returned home to Perote. In 1867 he was a deputy sheriff in Bullock County.

On October 30, 1869, he married Clara A. Sellers, another of Oates' cousins. In 1870 Robert was teaching school in Perote.

With the birth of their first child, a daughter, they remembered Robert's sisters by naming the child Therpsie Martha Jane Wicker. On March 8, 1874, they had a son, Franklin Itasco.

On March 31, 1875, Clara died, and in July, fourteen-month-old Franklin also passed away. Robert left Therpsie with his Sellers' in-laws and joined his father's family, who moved to Texas.

On February 23, 1877, at the age of 39, Robert Horne Wicker died. He is buried next to his father in the Hope Cemetery in Henrietta, Texas.

Finn's Point National Cemetery is on the banks of the Delaware River. It is the final resting place for Confederate soldiers who died while being held at Fort Delaware. There you will find the graves of Bill Sellers, Elisha Sellers, and Joe Henderson.

The Yankees

For his actions at Gettysburg, Strong Vincent was promoted to brigadier general. He died on July 7, 1863, from his wounds.

John Chamberlain returned to Bangor Theological Seminary and completed his studies, graduating in 1864. He returned to the war serving as the chaplain of the Eleventh Maine. After the war, he went into business in New York, working as an inspector for the Internal Revenue Service.

In 1866, he married Delia Jarvis. On August 11, 1867, at the age of twenty-nine, John died from tuberculosis, the same disease that killed his older brother Horace several years before. With his parents, brother Horace, and sister Sarah, John is buried in the family plot in the Oak Hill Cemetery in Brewer, Maine.

Tom Chamberlain distinguished himself as an officer, rising to the rank of lieutenant colonel. After the war, however, he lived a troubled and unsettled life. He moved to New York where he worked for John. Four years after John's death, Tom married his brother's widow, Delia. The couple returned to Maine, but Tom remained moody with periods of depression. On August 12, 1896, he also died of a lung ailment.

After Gettysburg, Joshua Lawrence Chamberlain took command of the First Brigade, First Division, Fifth Army

Corps. While leading a charge at Petersburg, he was critically wounded by a bullet passing through his body. Promoted to brigadier general by U.S. Grant for heroism, he surprisingly returned to duty in time to lead his brigade in the critical battle at Five Forks, which sealed the Confederacy's fate.

He was picked by Grant to accept the formal surrender of the Confederate infantry at Appomattox. As the Rebel troops marched by on their way to surrender their weapons, Chamberlain called his men to attention, saluting their former enemy, an action which stunned and pleased the Rebel troops.

Lawrence returned home to Maine to widespread praise and accolades. He went back to teaching at Bowdoin, but he didn't stay long. In September 1866, he was elected to his first of four one-year terms as governor by the state's history's largest margin.

In 1871 he returned to Bowdoin College to serve as the school's president. In his later years, he wrote and gave speeches about the war. He enjoyed his home just across the street from his beloved Bowdoin.

In 1893, Lawrence was awarded the Medal of Honor for his actions on Little Round Top. He died on February 24, 1914, from complications from his old war wound. He is buried in the Pine Grove Cemetery, Brunswick, next to the love of his life, Fannie.

About the Author

Thomas M. Eishen holds a bachelor's degree in secondary education, social studies, with an emphasis on United States history from Indiana University at Fort Wayne. Tom is a member of the Gettysburg Foundation, The American Battlefield Trust, and Sons of Union Veterans of the Civil War.

You can follow Thomas on Facebook and Instagram. His website, tommyeishen.com has an extensive collection of modern photographs of Gettysburg National Battlefield.